Praise for the Davis

“Seriously funny, wickedly entertaining. Davis gets me every time.”

– Janet Evanovich

“As impressive as the amount of sheer fun and humor involved are the details concerning casino security, counterfeiting, and cons. The author never fails to entertain with the amount of laughs, action, and intrigue she loads into this immensely fun series.”

– *Kings River Life Magazine*

“Fasten your seat belts: Davis Way, the superspy of Southern casino gambling, is back (after *Double Dip*) for her third wild caper.”

– *Publishers Weekly*

“It reads fast, gives you lots of sunny moments and if you are a part of the current social media movement, this will appeal to you even more. I know #ItDoesForMe.”

– *Mystery Sequels*

“Fast-paced, snarky action set in a compelling, southern glitz-and-glamour locale...Utterly un-put-down-able.”

– Molly Harper,
Author of the Award-Winning Nice Girls Series

“A smart, snappy writer who hits your funny bone!”

– Janet Evanovich

“Archer’s bright and silly humor makes this a pleasure to read. Fans of Janet Evanovich’s Stephanie Plum will absolutely adore Davis Way and her many mishaps.”

– *RT Book Reviews*

“Snappy, wise-cracking, and fast-paced.”

– *New York Journal of Books*

"Hilarious, action-packed, with a touch of home-sweet-home and a ton of glitz and glam. I'm booking my next vacation at the Bellissimo!"

– Susan M. Boyer,
USA Today Bestselling Author of *Lowcountry Bonfire*

"Funny & wonderful & human. It gets the Stephanie Plum seal of approval."

– Janet Evanovich

"Filled with humor and fresh, endearing characters. It's that rarest of books: a beautifully written page-turner. It's a winner!"

– Michael Lee West,
Author of *Gone with a Handsomer Man*

"Davis's smarts, her mad computer skills, and a plucky crew of fellow hostages drive a story full of humor and action, interspersed with moments of surprising emotional depth."

– *Publishers Weekly*

"Archer navigates a satisfyingly complex plot and injects plenty of humor as she goes....a winning hand for fans of Janet Evanovich."

– *Library Journal*

"Archer's writing had me laughing out loud...Not sure if Gretchen Archer researched this by hanging out in a casino or she did a lot of research online. No matter which way, she hit the nail on the head."

– *Fresh Fiction*

"In the quirky and eccentric world of Davis Way, I found laughter throughout this delightfully humorous tale. The exploits, the antics, the trial and tribulation of doing the right thing keeps this story fresh as scene after scene we are guaranteed a fun time with Davis and her friends. #LoveIt #BestOneYet."

– *Dru's Book Musings*

DOUBLE TROUBLE

The Davis Way Crime Caper Series
by Gretchen Archer

Novels

DOUBLE WHAMMY (#1)
DOUBLE DIP (#2)
DOUBLE STRIKE (#3)
DOUBLE MINT (#4)
DOUBLE KNOT (#5)
DOUBLE UP (#6)
DOUBLE DOG DARE (#7)
DOUBLE AGENT (#8)
DOUBLE TROUBLE (#9)

Bellissimo Casino Crime Caper Short Stories

DOUBLE JINX
DOUBLE DECK THE HALLS

DOUBLE TROUBLE

A DAVIS WAY CRIME CAPER

Gretchen Archer

HENERY PRESS

DOUBLE TROUBLE
A Davis Way Crime Caper
Part of the Henery Press Mystery Collection

First Edition | June 2020

Henery Press
www.henerypress.com

Cover design by The Creative Wrap LLC
Author photograph by Garrett Nudd

Trade Paperback ISBN-13: 978-1-63511-567-3
Digital epub ISBN-13: 978-1-63511-568-0
Kindle ISBN-13: 978-1-63511-569-7
Hardcover ISBN-13: 978-1-63511-570-3

Printed in the United States of America

For Worth, my best girl

ACKNOWLEDGMENTS

Thank you, Henery Press. If it weren't for you, I wouldn't be published. Thanks for the wonderful memories.

ONE

I took my eye off the ball.

I was looking one way when I should have been looking the other.

I didn't see Birdy James disappear with five million dollars because at the time, which was six o'clock in the morning, my eyes were closed. Still, I should have seen it coming. I was wallowing about it on the phone with my best friend, Fantasy. At six fifteen in the morning. (Best friend, coworker, and at the moment, very groggy life coach.)

"Go back to bed." She yawned. "Five hundred dollars isn't the end of the world."

"Five million, Fantasy. Five million dollars."

"It's the end of the world."

"Thanks," I said. "You're a big help."

"I'm asleep, Davis. I'm trying hard to wake up," she yawned again, "and until I do, here's my best advice: take a breath. When the sun comes up, we'll find Bird Woman, turn her upside down, I'll take one ankle, you take the other, we'll shake the money out of her, and everything will be fine. You'll see."

All I could see were dollar signs. Five million of them. Obscuring my view of everything else. I could barely see the go button on my coffeepot. "It's hard to believe Birdy James would steal five million dollars, if for no other reason, she's too old to spend it. She's what? Ninety? Ninety-five?"

"She's old as dirt," Fantasy said. "I'll give you that."

What I needed was for someone to give me five million dollars.

"Have you told Bradley?" she asked.

Bradley was my husband. "No."

"Have you told No Hair?"

No Hair, our boss, had a real name. (Jeremy Covey.) We called him No Hair because he was bald, bald, bald. "No."

"Have you told Mr. Sanders?" she asked.

Richard Sanders owned the Bellissimo Resort and Casino in Biloxi, Mississippi, where half of us lived and all of us worked. Which made him everyone's boss. "No. I haven't told Mr. Sanders," I said. "For one, it's six in the morning here, which means it's the middle of the night in Vegas. And for two, if I haven't told Bradley and I haven't told No Hair, why would I tell Mr. Sanders?"

"Because it's his five million dollars."

"Not exactly."

"Then whose money is it?" she asked.

"Not the Bellissimo's and certainly not Birdy's," I said. "Which is why I'm not waking Mr. Sanders to tell him. He'll want to know whose money it is, and I don't even know. Another reason I'm not telling him is I don't want Bradley or No Hair to hear it from Mr. Sanders before they hear it from me."

"Then tell them."

"No."

"So no one knows."

"I know. And now you know."

"Surely Baylor knows," she said.

"No," I said. "He'd tell everyone else."

"Maybe I should tell Baylor, let him tell everyone else, then we could all go back to sleep."

"Do not tell Baylor," I said. "Do not."

Baylor, just Baylor, like Snoopy was just Snoopy, was the third and final member of the Bellissimo Resort and Casino's covert casino security team. It was me, Fantasy, and Baylor. Baylor was young enough to be fearless (late twenties), built like a lumberjack (but without the beard) (or the flannel shirt), and a deadeye with firearms (bang bang). But he had no background in law enforcement to my six years as a police officer in my hometown of Pine Apple, Alabama, and Fantasy's seven years as a corrections officer at Harrison County Women's Detention Center, so Baylor deferred to us. We made sure of it. We made him do all our dirty work. Like stakeouts. We made him run all our errands. Like lunch. And we kept all kinds of secrets from him. Like then. "Besides," I said, "why would I tell Baylor before I told you?"

"Good point," she said. "But you have called the police, right?"

"Not yet."

"You need to call someone."

"I did call someone. I called you."

"I meant call someone else. Besides me."

"I will." I blindly batted in the cabinet above the coffeepot, then poured straight caffeine into a holly and ivy mug with a candy cane handle.

"And you're waiting on...?"

"Christmas."

"It's June," she said. "And if you're not going to tell anyone else until Christmas, stop worrying. Surely we can scare up five million dollars by Christmas."

"Legally?" I asked.

"Probably not."

Because without a doubt, we knew how to obtain money illegally. It was our job, it had been for years, to apprehend casino cheats, and they'd taught us well. Fantasy and I could probably pull off a roulette scam, a Baccarat heist, and card count enough blackjack to net five million dollars by that afternoon. Each. Blindfolded.

"Then we do this the old-fashioned way," she said.

"What way is that?" I asked. "Smash and grab?"

"We follow the money trail until it leads us to the five million, then put it back where it belongs before anyone knows it's missing. We'll start with the Bird Woman."

"Too late," I said. "She's gone."

"You said yourself she's a hundred years old," Fantasy said. "She couldn't have gone far."

"I didn't say she was a hundred. I said she was old."

"What do you have on old Bird Woman?"

"Not much." I poured more coffee. "A sister, Constance, and a nephew, Malcolm, in Bossier City, Louisiana."

"If I were Bird Woman and I made off with five million dollars in the middle of the night, I'd go straight to my sister's in Bossier City, and it's practically next door," Fantasy said. "I can pick you up in an hour—" she hesitated "—or four."

"It's not next door to us," I said. "Bossier City is next door to Shreveport. And Shreveport is a six-hour drive."

"We can make it in four," she said. "We'll be back by dinner."

"I can't."

"Why not?"

"Their names are Bexley and Quinn."

My name is Davis Way Cole. I'm thirtysomething, happily married, and the mother of Bexley and Quinn, toddler twin girls I couldn't run off and leave. Not only was I a single parent with my husband in Vegas, I was all but singlehandedly in charge of the Bellissimo, a 1.2 billion (*billion*) dollar gaming property, while everyone else—Bradley, President and CEO, along with No Hair, Director of Security, and Richard Sanders, the owner of the Bellissimo—attended the Global Gaming Expo. The last thing I said to Bradley before he left for Vegas the day before was, "Don't worry. I've got this. I can handle the girls and the casino for one little week. Nothing will happen." There I sat, not twenty-four hours later, having let a little old lady sneak past me with five million dollars. So far, all I'd done about it was whine to Fantasy and brew coffee.

"Okay," she said. "Tell me the story. The short version."

"There is no short version."

"The sun isn't up yet, Davis. Try. Be efficient with your words."

I took a deep breath. "There was a typo. Someone entered the wrong routing number on a five-million-dollar wire. A bank in Philly accidentally wired five million dollars to us that was meant for a real estate closing in Seattle."

"That's it?" she asked. "The whole story?"

"I was trying to be efficient with my words."

"I'll give you a little leeway," she said. "There has to be more, because Bird Woman wasn't even in the story. You have one more minute, then I'm going back to bed."

It took two more cups of coffee and thirty more minutes.

Fantasy did not go back to bed.

And I smelled T-R-O-U-B-L-E.

TWO

It started the day before when I was trying to say goodbye to my husband as he left for Vegas.

That's not true.

It started the year before with a hurricane. In mid-October of the previous year, Hurricane Kevin blew through the Bellissimo. Not necessarily the Gulf, or even the city of Biloxi, but all the way through the Bellissimo. We were closed for four months while the demolished lower levels of the resort were remodeled. We reopened on Valentine's Day, bigger and better, to great fanfare, lots of heart-shaped fireworks, and several new venues—a new bank, a new convention center, and a new employee childcare facility—along with, much to my dismay, new responsibilities for my elite security team.

I was far from happy with the new program.

Before, as lead spy on our spy team of three, when the Daily Incident Report hit my inbox, detailing anything and everything of interest that had occurred at the Bellissimo in the previous twenty-four hours, I read it.

That's not true.

I skimmed it. I skimmed the Daily Incident Report. The ten percent of it that needed my team's attention got it. The other ninety percent, I let slide. There were seventeen hundred guest rooms in the hotel, which roughly translated to thirty-four hundred hotel guests, mostly couples, on vacation. Every other day, one of those seventeen hundred couples was going to do what they were going to do in the hotel elevators. What were we supposed to do the day after the fact when their indiscretion showed up on my Incident Report? Track them down and tell them to get a room? (They had a room.) (In our hotel.) Explain indecent exposure? (Indecent exposure was self-explanatory.) Call their mothers? Their priest? Their marriage counselor? ("Hey. Whatever you're doing, it's working.")

No Hair said that by not following up on every single incident, too much was slipping through the cracks, and that my team needed to be more thorough. Regardless of how large or small the incident, it was my team's new responsibility to resolve it. Report back. Close every small case every single day.

I said following up on a guest complaint that the $1,800 Dolce & Gabbana stilettos she purchased at Heels, the shoe store on the Mezzanine, pinched her toes, was a waste of our time and talent, and I went on to say No Hair had ulterior motives. Like burying me so deep in paperwork I'd be too busy to miss my old job. Which he denied.

He was the boss; he won. When we returned from hurricane break, the Daily Incident Report was divided into thirds and delivered in three parts to Fantasy's, Baylor's, and my inbox. Our new job was to work independently to resolve every single solitary entry on our Incident Reports. The good news was, we no longer argued about who would do what. (Which had been half our workday.) (Arguing about who did what.) If it happened in the casino, it was Baylor's responsibility. His Incident Report might say a fresh new gambler, wearing a "Finally Twenty-One!" banner below her twenty-one-rhinestone birthday tiara, won $100,000 on a single lucky spin of a slot machine—a highly unusual event, and more than anything else, our team pursued highly unusual events—Baylor would pull the surveillance video, watch the birthday girl win, watch the payout, make sure she made it to her hotel room safely, then electronically tag her and track her through the rest of her casino vacation until she was safely out the door. With her windfall.

Casino incidents were the most interesting.

Fantasy followed up on what were usually the most boring, from every square inch of the resort outside of the fifty-thousand-square-foot casino. She tracked down slip-and-falls at the spa, horseplay at the pools, elevator indiscretions, and the week before, attack lobsters. Two teenage boys charged three dozen lobster dinners to their gambling parents' in-room-dining tab, then from the top of an indoor waterfall on the mezzanine level, just above the lobby, the boys dropped the lobsters, one by one, whole lobsters, on unsuspecting guests' heads below. The guests thought attack lobsters were jumping out of the waterfall. Fantasy, with three mischievous sons of her own, knew the teenage-boy drill, and let those boys have it. They probably wouldn't eat lobster again for the rest of their lives, much less drop one on anyone's head.

So, Baylor handled the casino, Fantasy handled the lobsters, and me? Internal departments. I followed up on unusual events involving, regarding, or concerning the forty-five hundred employees who worked within the various departments of the Bellissimo, like Marketing, Human Resources, Payroll, Casino Services, Catering, Groundskeeping, and every other department, all the way down to the smallest department in all of Bellissimoland—Lost and Found. Which was where the problem with the missing five million dollars started, or maybe where the problem with the missing five million dollars ended, but for sure, it was how the missing five-million-dollar problem landed in my lap. Because while I was only temporarily in charge of Bellissimoland for the week, I was permanently in charge of Bellissimo Lost and Found.

And I'd already been warned.

When we returned to work after hurricane break and the responsibility for our forty-five hundred employees was dropped in my lap, my boss, No Hair, laid down the law. He had nothing to say about Food and Beverage, Hotel Operations, Casino Services, or any other employee in any other department, but he had a lot to say about Birdy James in Lost and Found.

"Davis, do something about Lost and Found."

"Do what about it?"

"A luncheon, a nice plaque, a big cake that says, 'Happy Retirement, Old Bird!'"

I couldn't tell if he meant it or not.

"You could have little birds on the cake."

It sounded like he meant it.

"Give her a gold watch," he said.

"We don't give gold watches, No Hair." (Did we?)

He leaned far enough over his desk—which was bigger than he was, and that was saying something, because he was the size of three regular desks, which made his desk the size of a garage door—to look me in the eye. "Do something about Birdy James."

"Why?"

"Because she's reached the state of confusion," he said. "She's flipped her old lid. Complaints are coming in right and left that she's addled."

"She's what?"

"Addled," he said. "Bewildered. Befuddled. Birdbrained. She can't keep things straight."

"Keep what straight?" I asked. "Lost and Found fingernail polish? No Hair, don't be cruel."

He pushed two folders my way. One was pamphlet thin, the other catalog thick. "Take a look."

"I'm not in the mood for paperwork, No Hair. Just tell me."

"This," he tapped the thin folder, "has every Lost and Found complaint filed since the Bellissimo ribbon cutting."

"Okay."

"This," he tapped the fat folder, "has every Lost and Found complaint logged since we reopened after the storm."

"What's your point?"

(Sadly, I could see his fat-file point.)

"Old Bird has turned a corner, Davis. She's not—" I could see him searching for the right way to say it "—not all with us anymore." He tapped a temple. "In the brains department."

"No Hair," I said, "that is so mean."

"I'm not trying to be mean, Davis. In fact, I think it would be an act of kindness to let Old Bird go. She needs to be playing shuffleboard on the Lido Deck. Enjoying her life. She's worked hard, she's done a great job, and it's time for her to sail off into retirement sunset. It's business," he said. "It's taking care of business. I'm telling you to take care of Old Bird business."

"How?" I still didn't understand. "Force her into retirement? Shouldn't you be talking to Human Resources?"

"Human Resources is afraid of her."

"No Hair, she's as old as the hills, she can barely see, she can barely hear, she's not even five feet tall, and she couldn't weigh more than eighty pounds," I said. "She's everyone's favorite aunt. What's to be afraid of?"

"I'll tell you what Human Resources is afraid of, the same thing everyone else is afraid of, Davis, the Dewey Decimal System. Everyone in the building is afraid of Old Bird's Dewey Decimal System. Those who aren't afraid of her Dewey Decimal business are afraid of her chicken-scratch shorthand."

"Oh, good grief, No Hair." I might have rolled my eyes. "That's ridiculous. What's so scary about the Dewey Decimal System? And what do you mean by chicken-scratch shorthand?"

"How she writes. She draws instead of writes. Symbols and slashes and dots. It's an old system people used to write things down quickly before they had phones to poke notes into."

"Are we talking hieroglyphics from caveman days?" I asked. "Or scribbling from secretary days?"

"Scribbling from secretary days."

"Shorthand was before my time, No Hair." For that matter, secretaries were too. Professionals hired personal assistants and office managers. Not secretaries.

"That's my point, Davis. Shorthand was before everyone's time. Old Bird makes notes in shorthand no one can read, then catalogs Lost and Found items in that dungeon of hers with long numbers no one can decipher, and bottom line, no one but Old Bird can find anything."

"Anything, what? Lost and Found is full of hairbrushes and cheap sunglasses. There's nothing to find. When has there ever been anything of value turned in to Lost and Found that wasn't claimed immediately? I'll tell you when, No Hair, never. That's when. So what exactly is it Birdy James is doing to offend you? Her job?"

He sighed. He tugged the stiff collar of his shirt. "Housekeeping, Davis. It's just housekeeping."

"What about Housekeeping?" (Another department very recently assigned to me.)

"Not Housekeeping the department," he said, "but housekeeping in general. No one wants to be the person who forces retirement on Old Bird, but someone has to." He tapped the thick file. "Yes, she's a sweet little old lady, Davis, I'll give you that, especially the old part. But that doesn't change the fact that it's time for her to go. In addition to the shorthand scribbling and the Dewey Decimal System nonsense, most of the time, Old Bird's asleep at her desk. When she wakes up, she thinks it's nineteen fifty-two. Her hours are ridiculous. She won't use a computer. She won't move offices. No one can get in Lost and Found when she's not there, and she's sabotaged every attempt to install surveillance in or around Lost and Found."

All true. Birdy James took long naps at her desk, was often mistaken about what century it was, refused to give up the keypad combination to the Lost and Found door out of fear someone would disturb an orphan sock lost in 2001, and all in all, was terrifically old school. But she was also really good at her job. The last time I'd visited Lost and Found, more than a year earlier, I was looking for a ten-carat diamond choker the owner's wife, Bianca Sanders, said slipped from her neck. (Since when do Harry Winston diamonds slip? Don't they have deadbolts?) I suggested, considering Bianca couldn't keep up with what day of the week it was, much less her own jewelry, she file an insurance claim and replace it. She suggested I find her choker, or she'd replace me. (A threat she made good on.) I went straight to Birdy James and asked if, by any chance, someone had turned in a ten-carat diamond choker. First, Birdy said no, then she said, "It's February."

(It was.)

"Nineteen seventy-nine."

(I let that slide.)

"If Mrs. Sanders went out, she wore a coat."

Bianca Sanders had gone out. The day before, she'd flown to New York City for lunch at Elio's on the Upper East Side. Which was probably where she lost the choker.

"She should check her coat."

Birdy was right. I found the necklace ten minutes later hooked on the silk lining interior of the $65,000 sable jacket Bianca had worn to lunch. My point? Birdy James had an eerie knack for resolving lost and found problems. And she was a Bellissimo institution. Everyone loved her. So—and it was my final word on the subject—I told No Hair if he wanted Birdy James gone, he had to fire her himself, because in the big scheme of things, that Birdy worked odd hours (napping through most of them), and was very comfortable in her cave of a basement office next door to Maintenance (my responsibility, all mine) across the hall from Waste Management (also under my jurisdiction, yay), and didn't want anyone who didn't know her particular twist on the Dewey Decimal System having access to Lost and Found (which was everyone), and that she didn't want "Big Brother" cameras watching her (see *1984* by George Orwell) (and half the time, Birdy thought it *was* 1984), and insisted her IBM Wheelwriter Lexmark typewriter was all she needed, because she'd "made it through the eighties without a computator and she could make it through the nineties without one too," hardly mattered. She was good at her job, and as risks went, Lost and Found—again, full of cell phone chargers and abandoned cardigan sweaters—scored a big fat zero. I said leave well enough alone. And by well enough, I meant Birdy.

No Hair stared at me, long and hard. Eventually, his stern look melted. All the way to patronizing sympathy. "I understand your job has changed in ways you didn't necessarily want or expect."

I studied a framed photograph on the wall, just over his left shoulder, as he took the Oath of Allegiance at the Mississippi Bureau of Investigation, where he worked for fifteen years before Mr. Sanders hired him as personal security. The picture was at least thirty years old, and even then, No Hair had no hair.

"I'm sorry about all that, Davis."

I studied a framed photograph on the wall, just over his right shoulder, of Mrs. No Hair, Grace, who had lots of hair.

"But you still have a job to do," he said.

Those were the only two pictures in No Hair's office.

Then he told me to drag Birdy into the twenty-first century, or else.

"Or else what?"

"Or else something's going to happen, Davis. Something's going to happen Old Bird can't handle, or mishandles, or panhandles, and when it does, it will be on you."

That was months ago. And as usual, No Hair was right. Which, at six o'clock in the morning—by then it was six thirty—on the phone with Fantasy, was almost the worst of it.

(Not counting the missing five million dollars.)

(Which was also the worst of it.)

THREE

The five million dollars showed up on my Incident Report the day before it officially went missing. It was Saturday morning. My daughters were just waking up and my husband was in his home office on the phone with his personal assistant, Colleen, going over everything one last time before he left for Vegas. For casino executives, the annual Global Gaming Expo was work. But it was play too. And fine dining and sleeping late. It was being a casino patron for a change, and it was comradery. I wanted him to go. He wanted to go. I didn't volunteer to take the Bellissimo helm while he was away—that would be the old me—but he'd asked me to keep an eye on things. And he'd asked nicely. At the time, I thought, what could go wrong? It was just a few days. I knew he was nervous about leaving me in charge, even though he wouldn't say it, and I was nervous about being left in charge, even though I wasn't about to say it. I no longer felt completely connected to my job, such as it was, and Bradley knew that, which was one of the main reasons he asked me to oversee operations in his absence. So I'd reconnect.

It was eight thirty on Saturday morning, and I was ready for nine when he'd leave. The sooner he left, the sooner he'd return. I killed time waiting for him to get off the phone on my phone. Might as well check my email. I accidently clicked open my Daily Incident Report, just to get it over with, when all I really did was get it going. First, Casino Credit showed a wire receipt of five million dollars.

I'd been standing in my living room at the veranda doors

facing the city of Biloxi. I dropped into the closest chair. Five million dollars was highly unusual. To my knowledge, that large an amount of money had never been wired to the Bellissimo. High rollers, defined as gamblers who had more money than sense, regularly wired money to the casino, more often than not, paying off markers, defined as money they'd borrowed from the casino. At outrageous interest rates. Sometimes, instead of wiring money after their casino trips to pay us back, they wired in funds beforehand to avoid borrowing money from us. (At outrageous interest rates.) But never astronomical amounts like five million dollars. I saw the same ginormous amount of money in the next column too, under Casino Credit transfers. *Transfer to Bellissimo Vault: $5,000,000.* Under comments, Casino Credit's notes read *12:15 a.m., large dark blue Bellissimo duffel bag requisitioned from Love containing $5,000,000 in cash, weight, 23.5 pounds*, which, had I read under different circumstances, I would have found interesting. (That five million dollars weighed twenty-three and a half pounds.) (Minus the negligible weight of the duffel bag.) (Our dog, a Goldendoodle, Candy, weighed thirty pounds. Candy was heavier than five million dollars?) But under present circumstances, I didn't care how much the money weighed. I was too distracted by the fact that Casino Credit received the hefty five-million-dollar wire, then for some reason cashed it, acquired a duffel bag large enough to hold it, stuffed the money in the bag, then transferred it to the main casino vault. A good place for five million dollars, under lock and key with armed guards in front of it, but from the very beginning of the story, against every standard operating procedure under the roof, first and foremost, we didn't accept that much money. From anyone. For any reason. To wire $100,000 to the Bellissimo took a hundred thousand signatures.

What in the world were we doing with $5,000,000?

I scrolled to Vault receipts.

No five million dollars.

I dropped my phone.

I stopped breathing.

Maybe it was the other way around.

I stopped breathing.

Then I dropped my phone.

I picked it up and looked again. Under receipts, Vault still didn't show five million dollars in a large dark blue Bellissimo duffel bag from Love. (Love, the tennis shop on the mezzanine. Cute skirts.) If Casino Credit sent the money to Vault, why wasn't it on Vault's receipt list?

I checked the time. By then it was 8:40. I had twenty minutes and Bradley was still on the phone with Colleen. I traded my phone for my laptop in my home office, just behind my kitchen, thinking maybe I'd missed something in small-screen translation. If so—scroll, scroll, scroll—I was missing it on the big screen too.

It had to be a paperwork error.

An Incident Report omission on Vault's part.

Because five million dollars couldn't disappear into thin air between Casino Credit and Vault. (Could it?)

I checked the time again—8:48. I'd get to the bottom of it as soon as I got Bradley out the door, but in the process of minimizing the screen, I made the grave mistake of flipping to the next and final page of my Incident Report. It was the page I barely bothered with, the page that hardly ever had anything interesting on it, the page that never raised even one of my eyebrows. It was the page of old-school typed then digitally scanned entries from Birdy James in Lost and Found. For the previous twenty-four hours, Birdy had logged eight miscellaneous electronic cords, seven cell phones, a six-tiered wedding cake, five miscellaneous articles of clothing, four key fobs, three baby stingrays (apparently caught in the Gulf and left swimming in a hotel bathtub, immediately handed off to Marine

Mammal Studies in next-door Gulfport, Mississippi), two sports bras, and one large dark blue Bellissimo duffel bag from Love. Beside the duffel-bag-from-Love entry, Birdy had scribbled notes. Or maybe drawn notes—I turned my head sideways, then the other sideways—two ducks riding in a school bus? With dots above the school bus? Or maybe those were raisins?

It was shorthand.

What No Hair said. Shorthand.

Birdy made notes beside her duffel bag entry in shorthand.

Notes I couldn't read.

Because I didn't read shorthand.

Was the blue Bellissimo duffel bag from Love on Birdy's Incident Report the same blue Bellissimo duffel bag on Casino Credit's Incident Report?

No way.

Could there have been two dark blue Bellissimo duffel bags wandering the halls the night before? Was the one in Lost and Found empty? Or full? And if full, full of *what*? Surely not money. Who would drop off five million dollars in Lost and Found? I checked the time, 8:50. I still had ten minutes before Bradley left for Vegas and Birdy James was still at her desk. I picked up the phone.

"Birdy? It's Davis. Mr. Cole's wife."

"Good morning, Davis, Mr. Cole's wife. How in the wide world are you?"

I might have woken her up.

Birdy worked Wednesday through Sunday, from six in the morning, when the Zest for Life minibus dropped her off, until noon, when the Zest for Life minibus picked her up to take her home. (Zest for Life was a senior living complex on Rue Magnolia Street. Birdy moved there when she turned sixty-five. Which was a million years ago.) Her workdays weren't that odd, with Mondays and Tuesdays being the days of the week casinos caught their breaths, but her hours were. And why half the staff at the Bellissimo called her Early Birdy. Her incredible age was why the other half called her Old Bird. (Except Fantasy. Who mostly called her Bird Woman.) Birdy came to the Bellissimo after retiring from her first career overseeing every library in the Harrison County School System, bringing her Dewey Decimal System with her, so she was old even when she started her second career in Bellissimo Lost and Found. There we were, decades later, and she was ancient. She was a widow, a strong believer in astrology, she had a black cat named Mortimer, and from what I understood, several other black cats named Mortimer preceded her present black cat named Mortimer, which had very little to do with anything else, so back to Birdy, who never knew what year it was, and who wore a really bad gray helmet of a wig, but who was cheery. Always cheery.

"I'm well, Birdy. How are you?"

"Fine and dandy."

I wondered if the report was wrong. (Actually, that was the exact moment I began wondering where the money was. Had it been in the dark blue Bellissimo duffel on Birdy's Incident Report, I wouldn't be calling her about it. She'd have already called me about it.) (Surely, she'd have already called me about it.)

"What can I do you for, Davis, Mr. Cole's wife?"

No sense of urgency whatsoever. (Which was the exact moment I realized Birdy might not know what was in the dark blue Bellissimo duffel bag on her own report.) "Birdy." I steadied my voice. "I'm looking at the Incident Report you filed this morning."

"What a shame," she said.

So she knew.

And she was right.

Losing five million dollars was a shame. A big shame. Five million shames.

"I found the girl who left it," Birdy said. "She's a Sagittarius.

You know what that means."

I did not know what that meant, but at the time, assuming she was talking about the person the money belonged to, I breathed a sigh of relief. Sagittarius, Pisces, Vegan, or Presbyterian, I didn't care. I needed to say goodbye to my husband before he left for Vegas. Not track down the gazillionaire who accidentally wired in five million dollars that bounced around the resort in a duffel bag all night.

"She doesn't want it back," Birdy said.

Wait a minute. "Who doesn't want what back, Birdy?"

"The bride. She doesn't want the cake back," Birdy said. "It's a beauty too. Buttercream frosting. She called off the wedding and doesn't want the cake back."

"I'm calling about the money, Birdy." Forget the cake. "I need to talk to you about the money."

"There is no money. I didn't charge anyone."

"For what?"

"The cake," she said. "I sliced the top three layers. I wrapped the slices in cellophane and sent them to the employee dining room. I didn't charge anyone for the slices. It wasn't my cake to charge for. I wouldn't even know how much to charge."

"Birdy." I took a deep breath. "On your Incident Report, you listed a blue bag."

"Yes," Birdy said. "It was left at my door during the night. It was waiting on me when I clocked in. The cake was already in my office."

I didn't care about the cake. "You've written a note beside the bag entry. What does it say?" (Something I cared about very much.)

"Well, I don't know. I'd need to see it."

"Would you mind looking?"

"You'll need to give me a minute to find my Xerox."

"By Xerox, do you mean copy?" I asked.

"Copy of what?" she asked.

"Your Incident Report, Birdy."

"I have the Xerox," she said, "somewhere."

I rolled my eyes. I checked the time. "Could you please find it?"

"I'll try," she said. "It's been a very busy morning. What am I looking for?"

"Your Incident Report, Birdy."

"From what day?"

I closed my eyes. I shook my head. "Friday, Birdy."

"Friday!" She said it as if it was the first she'd heard of it. "Here it is!"

Thank. Goodness.

"Could you read your notes to me, Birdy?"

"About the cake?"

"The bag, Birdy. The blue bag. The bag you said was left at your door during the night. The blue bag that was waiting on you. Did you look inside?"

"Yes."

"What was in it?"

"Money," she said. "Lots of money. More money than I've ever seen in my life."

I might have fallen out of my chair had my husband, his arms full of daughters, with Candy, tail wagging, circling his legs, not chosen that moment to fill my office door. I looked up from my desk and held up a finger, as in, *give me just a minute.* He raised an eyebrow, reading the frustrated look on my face. I let it slide to a smile, as in, *this is nothing*. I whispered, "I'll be right there."

I waited until he was out of earshot. If he knew I was in the middle of a five-million-dollar blue-bag snafu, he wouldn't leave until the problems, all five million of them, were resolved. Chances were it was nothing but a clerical error. The vault guards who picked up the five-million-dollar bag from Casino Credit weren't given clear instructions. They didn't know what was in it, didn't know what to do with it, and thinking it was just a blue bag, left it in the hallway outside of Lost and Found.

1. They were idiots.
2. The entire incident was a huge breach of protocol.
3. Monumental breach of protocol.
4. Casino Credit and Vault heads were going to roll.
5. I couldn't read shorthand.

I spoke slowly. "Birdy, what do your notes say?"

"Well, hold on," she said. "I need my glasses."

I shook my head.

"I left them by the cake," she said. "Hold on again."

I could hear her slower-than-molasses footsteps on the concrete floor of Lost and Found echoing through the phone.

"Davis, do you have a freezer?"

Did I have a freezer? Didn't every refrigerator in the world have a freezer? Was she about to ask me to put a five-million-dollar blue bag in my freezer? Because that was an old people thing—hide the money in the freezer. "Yes, Birdy, I have a freezer. But—"

"I'm going to cut you a big wedge of this cake," she said. "Enough for your whole family. If you don't have space in your Frigidaire, you could put it in your freezer."

The cake? We were still talking about the cake? Before I could begin to get her back on track, Bradley yelled, "Gotta run, Davis."

"I'm on my way," I yelled back.

"To get the cake?" Birdy asked.

"No, Birdy—"

Then Bradley yelled, "Our car is downstairs. Everyone's waiting on me."

I yelled back, "I'll be right there!"

"Could you bring a Tupperware cake carrier with you?" Birdy asked.

"Birdy," I said into the phone. And I said it firmly. "I'm not on my way to Lost and Found to pick up cake. Nor do I want to talk about the cake. Ever again. We're not talking about the cake. We need to talk about the blue bag full of money you found. I have a very important question for you. Are you ready?"

"Fire away."

"Where is it now?"

"The cake?"

I dropped my phone a second time. I threw my hands in the air. I turned a circle. Or forty. I picked up the phone again. "I'm talking about the money, Birdy, the money. Not the cake. Not one more word about the cake."

"You got it, Davis, except for this last word. If you're not coming right now, how about I put your wedge in my freezer?"

From my foyer, I heard, "DAVIS!" (my husband) and "MAMA!" (my daughter Bexley) and "ARP, ARP, ARP!" (my dog, Candy).

I lowered my phone to my side and yelled all the way through the house at my family. "I'll be there in a minute!" (He was flying to Vegas in a Bellissimo jet. It wasn't like the plane would take off without him.) Then, back on the phone, "Birdy?"

"Yes."

"About the money."

"What money?"

"The money in the blue bag, Birdy. The blue bag you found at your door."

"What about it?"

"Do you still have it?"

"Yes."

Whew.

"Is the money still in it?"

From the foyer, "DAVIS!"

"Well, I don't know," she said. "I'd have to look."

I was far past frustrated. "Birdy, where is the blue bag?"

"It's in 516.035."

I smacked my own forehead. She was speaking Dewey Decimal. "Has anyone claimed it?"

From the foyer, and sounding just a teeny bit more irritated, Bradley yelled again. "Davis! Have the girls had breakfast?"

"No!" I yelled back. They'd just woken up. They hadn't had time for breakfast.

"No, what, Davis?" Birdy asked.

"I was speaking to my husband."

"Such a nice young man."

Yes. He was. Nice, handsome, an excellent husband, and a wonderful father, all of which we could discuss any other time. "Let's back up, Birdy," I said. "Has anyone claimed the money? Has anyone walked in your door and said they've lost five million dollars?"

"No."

"Has anyone called about it?"

"Yes," she said.

"Who?" I asked.

"You."

I rolled my eyes. "Where is it now?"

"The blue bag?"

I might lose my mind. Right then and there, I might just lose my mind. "Yes, Birdy. The blue bag. Where is it?"

"In 516.035," she said.

"Birdy." I measured my words. "Where is 516.035?"

Like pulling senior citizen teeth.

"At the end of row five. It's the only cage I have large enough for the cake."

I vowed to never eat cake again. For the rest of my life. No cake. Ever again. Not one bite. Just say no to cake. "Stay right where you are, Birdy. Don't move a muscle. I'm sending someone to pick it up."

"How many someones?"

From the front door, Bradley yelled, “Davis, the girls are hungry. They want me to take them downstairs for pancakes and I don’t have time.”

Clearly, I didn’t either. I yelled back, “Can you call Room Service and have them deliver it here? Please?” Because that would buy me two more minutes. Then, to Birdy, I said, “How many someones what, Birdy?”

“How many someones are coming to pick it up?”

“Does it matter?” I asked.

“They’ll want cake.”

Someone save me from Birdy James.

I told her it wasn’t important. What was important was that they locked it in the vault, but I didn’t know how many guards would pick it up, probably two (maybe twenty), and at that point, I really couldn’t wait to get off the phone.

I flew to the front door.

“Is everything okay?”

I pasted on a fake, fake, fake smile. “Fine,” I said. “Everything’s fine.”

“You’re sure?”

“I’m sure.”

“Because if it’s not, tell me now, before I leave.”

“Everything’s under control.”

Everything was not under control.

He told me breakfast was on the way for all three of us, then he tipped my chin up and looked me in the eye. “Sorry I snapped at you.”

“It’s okay. Sorry I was on the phone.”

“What was that about?”

“Cake.”

“Cake?”

“I’m kidding.” I was not kidding. “Nothing I can’t handle.”

“You’re sure?”

I nodded. I wondered if I should tell him.

"You've got this, Davis."

I nodded. I wondered if I should tell him.

"It's going to be a fun week," he said.

I wasn't so sure. I wondered if I should tell him.

"I'm sorry I'm missing it."

"Me too." Then I wondered, for the very last time, if I should tell him.

He tipped my chin up. "You've got this?"

And that was when I said, "I've got this. Don't worry. I promise I can handle the girls and the casino for one little week. Nothing will happen."

He kissed my forehead, elicited promises of being good girls for Mom from Bex and Quinn, gave Candy one last head rub, said, "Viva Las Vegas!" then took off.

I should have told him.

I sent the girls, the two blondes and the furry one, to the kitchen table to wait for breakfast while I stepped into my home office to put the five-million-dollar problem behind me. I took a deep breath, then dialed the Bellissimo operator and had her connect me to the vault.

"Vault," a man said.

"This is Davis Way Cole."

"Good morning, Mrs. Cole."

No time for niceties. "How many guards do you have?"

"On payroll?"

I closed my eyes and shook my head. "At this very minute."

"Three," the man said.

"Send two to Lost and Found immediately for a pickup."

"And do what with the pickup?" he asked.

My doorbell rang. My dog barked her head off and ran for the door. My daughters flew after the dog.

"Straight to the vault," I told the man on the phone. Then I repeated it. "Straight to the vault until you hear back from me."

"Will do."

"And call me back the minute you have it locked up."

"Yes, ma'am."

He did. My phone rang eleven minutes later, it was Vault man, who said, and I quote, "All locked up, Mrs. Cole," just as I finished cutting pancakes into perfect triangles and sat down to eat with my daughters, almost too relieved to be hungry.

I was glad I hadn't told Bradley.

I was proud of myself for handling it.

It almost felt like the good old days.

After breakfast, I sent the girls to their room to change out of their pajamas and into their swimsuits—it was already a million degrees out—while I called Casino Credit with my very last five-million-dollar blue-bag chore before I changed out of my pajamas and into my swimsuit for a fun Saturday morning with my daughters. Tying up what I felt sure would be the last loose thread of my Incident Report, I would track down the cashier who'd received, then for some reason cashed, the five-million-dollar wire, only to be told she, Megan Shaw, wouldn't be back at work until two in the afternoon on Monday. I spoke to her supervisor, Gray Donaldson, a woman I'd known for years, and a woman I liked and trusted. Gray was married to a commercial scuba diver, Troy, who built and repaired bridges. She was captain of the Bellissimo's ax-throwing team, whatever that was, other than what it sounded like. And they had a retro travel trailer they hooked to the back of Gray's Durango and dragged to New Orleans for overnighters when the Saints played at the Superdome. Obviously, they had no children, because who could fit children into a teeny travel trailer? Instead, they had Schnauzers. Who were also Saints fans.

"Hi, Gray. It's Davis."

She said, "Oh, boy, I know what you're calling about." Gray was well aware of the errant wire. She explained the routing number hitch. She said her employee Megan Shaw cashed the wire to keep it off Casino Credit's books—understandable, from an accounting perspective, although not nearly a good enough reason to cash a five-million-dollar wire, but water under the bridge at that point—then went on to tell me the plan was to leave the cash in the vault until Monday afternoon when it would be wired to the title company it was supposed to go to in the first place, Nelson Title, in Seattle, Washington, at five Central, three Pacific.

"I still don't understand why she cashed it in the first place," I said. "Has she ever done anything like this before?"

"She's only worked for me since we reopened after the storm, Davis."

Flag.

Red flag.

"Where did she come from?" I asked.

"She was a cage cashier."

"For how long?"

"Several years."

"If she was a cage cashier for several years, she certainly should have known better than to cash that large a wire."

"I didn't say she was one of our cage cashiers," Gray said. "She was a cage cashier for Harrah's."

That was two flags.

Two red flags.

"Harrah's down the street?" I asked.

"Harrah's Las Vegas," she answered.

I backed it down to one and a half flags.

One and a half red flags.

Harrah's Vegas knew how to train cashiers.

"Did you fire her?" I asked.

"I wrote her up and sent her home for the weekend, but I didn't fire her on the spot. I didn't want to wake you in the middle of the night."

Gray was right. With that colossal a breach of protocol, firing Megan Shaw would be on me.

I hated firing people.

The only thing I hated more than firing people was being fired.

Honestly, it was easier to shoot people than to fire them.

"Not only that," Gray went on, "I need her signature to send the money to Seattle on Monday."

Well...I'd forged a few signatures in my day.

But only when I had to.

"I will say this, though," Gray said. "She was profusely apologetic and borderline mortified. A nervous wreck too. She said it was late, she was tired, and on her way out the door after a long day when the wire hit and she didn't realize the funds weren't meant for us until she was halfway through the transaction, then went on to tell me wire-cashing large amounts, regardless of who the money was from or who it was intended for, was common practice at Harrah's Vegas."

"She said what?"

Gray told me again.

"If that were true," I said, "all money laundering in the world would go through Harrah's Vegas."

After the longest, Gray said, "Oh, boy."

Oh, boy was right. The handling of monies that didn't belong to you followed a rule so rudimentary it didn't even need to be in place: don't take money that isn't yours. "There's nothing we can do about it now," I said, "and the money's in the vault. No harm, no foul, just gross negligence on Megan's part." I went on to tell Gray I'd personally accompany the cash transfer from Vault to Casino Credit on Monday and stay until we received a confirmation from Seattle that they'd received the money.

Then I'd take care of firing Megan.

I was already dreading it.

And I'd never met the girl in my life.

Gray said she'd see me then, at which point, there was

nothing left to say. We let it go. With the exception of the cash temporarily waylaid in Lost and Found, a five-million-dollar mistake I'd already corrected, I didn't think about it one more time until my phone rang Sunday morning, at what felt like the middle of the night Saturday night, when Zest for Life called Bellissimo Security sounding the Birdy James alarm.

I looked at the time first—six o'clock a.m.—then batted for the ringing phone and answered with something along the lines of, "What?"

"Mrs. Cole, this is Damon in Security. I just got an unusual call I thought I should pass along."

Zest for Life Senior Living called Bellissimo Security. Was Birdy James at work? (No.) Did we know where Birdy James was? (No.) She hadn't shown up for her five-forty-five minibus ride to the Bellissimo. The door to her Senior Living unit was wide open. Her apartment had been tossed, her bed hadn't been slept in, and her cat, Mortimer, was missing too. Birdy hadn't told anyone she was going anywhere, and she hadn't checked herself out.

Bellissimo Security had no idea, so they called me.

I only half listened—that's not true; I only one-tenth listened—until I heard Zest for Life and Birdy James, at which point, I sat straight up in bed, because Birdy-Lost-and-Found-blue-bag-five-million-dollars woke me up. I hung up on Damon in Security and immediately called—that's not true; it took five minutes for the switchboard to patch me through—Vault.

"This is Davis Way Cole. Mr. Cole's wife."

"Good morning, Mrs. Cole."

So far, there'd been nothing good about it. And six o'clock could hardly be considered morning.

"I need you to pull your log from yesterday and see if you picked up from Lost and Found."

"That'll take a minute."

By then I was out of bed.

"Can you give me a timeframe?" the vault man asked.

"Nine-ish."

"Morning or night?"

"Morning."

"Yes," he said. "We picked up from Lost and Found."

Whew. I found the money. Again.

"I had some," the man said.

I sat down on the bed. "Some what?" I asked.

"Cake," he said. "Wedding cake. Buttercream frosting."

Then I fell on the bed. "Wait," I said. "Read me the log. The entry. Exactly what it says."

"Under received, it says, 'Wedding cake, three tiers, to be locked in the vault until Mrs. Cole calls.' Is this you calling about the wedding cake, Mrs. Cole?"

I hung up.

I called Fantasy.

I told her the whole ugly story.

By the time I finished, it was six thirty. In the morning. Birdy James was missing and so was the five million dollars.

FOUR

Fantasy said, "There are all kinds of things wrong with this story."

"Without a doubt."

"The vault shows it received the cake, but no money," she said. "What does Birdy's transfer paperwork say? What do her notes say?"

"Her transfer paperwork says cake," I said. "It says Birdy transferred cake to the vault. And I can't read the note. She wrote it in Birdyhand."

"In what?" she asked.

"Shorthand."

"Did I hear you right?"

"You heard me right."

"Is her shorthand like her Dewey Decimal System? She made it up and she's the only one who can read it?"

"Does it matter?"

"It does," she said. "If it's normal shorthand and not Bird Woman shorthand, we could find someone to read it."

"Fantasy, I have no idea if it's normal or abnormal shorthand."

She processed for a long minute, then asked, "Are you sure you told her to send the money to the vault? Is there any way she could have misunderstood you?"

"Let's say she misunderstood every word out of my mouth."

"Okay."

"Still," I said, "common sense would dictate five million

dollars doesn't belong in a Lost and Found cage. Especially five million dollars that aren't even ours."

"But she doesn't really use common sense, Davis. Bird Woman uses the Dewey Decimal System."

"Which has nothing to do with anything."

"It probably has something to do with Bird Woman sending cake to the vault. Did she really send cake to the vault?"

"She sent cake."

"What flavor?" Fantasy asked. "Under the buttercream frosting?"

"Are you kidding me? Could we please get past the cake?"

"Davis, the power has gone to your head."

"What power?" I asked. "What head?"

"You've been in charge of the Bellissimo for less than twenty-four hours and listen to yourself. You're a wild woman. I asked a simple cake question."

"Fantasy." I spoke slowly. And ominously. "A little old lady and five million dollars are missing."

I let it sit there.

"Davis, remind me never to wake you up at six in the morning on your day off with a five-million-dollar problem."

"You didn't wake me up at six in the morning on my day off with a five-million-dollar problem," I said. "I woke *you* up at six in the morning on *your* day off with a five-million-dollar problem."

She let it sit there.

I finally said, "Strawberry. Strawberry cake."

"That's better," she said. "Now, who's looking for the money?"

"Me," I said. "And now you."

"No, I meant whose money is it?"

"Someone who banks in Philly buying property in Seattle," I said. "That's all I know."

"We've had the money since Friday?"

"Friday at midnight on the dot."

"Why didn't the Casino Credit cashier refuse the wire? Or wire it right back when she received it? I thought we wired money twenty-four-seven."

"I don't know if there's any such thing as refusing a wire. I think it just shows up. And we do wire money in and out twenty-four-seven," I said. "Clearly banks do too, because it arrived at midnight from a bank in Philly. But apparently title companies in Seattle don't. They only receive wire transfers during regular business hours. Someone has to physically be there to accept the wire. Title companies don't let that much money float around all weekend. Now the money is missing, and we have to find it in time to wire it to Seattle."

"Did you see that movie *Bird on a Wire*?"

"Maybe," I said. "Why?"

"Birdy. Wire. This is reminding me of that."

"Could we stay on the subject?"

"There you go again," she said. "When?"

"When what?" I asked.

"When are we supposed to wire the money back?"

"Before the real estate closing in Seattle," I said.

"When is that?"

"Three o'clock tomorrow afternoon."

"Our time or theirs?"

"Theirs."

"That gives us until five o'clock our time to scare up Bird Woman, and no doubt she's at her sister's in Shreveport," she said. "Road trip, Davis, find a babysitter."

"The sister doesn't live in Shreveport. She lives in Bossier City."

"Shreveport and Bossier City are the same thing," she said. "They're like Dallas and Fort Worth. One runs into the other. Which doesn't even matter. Get a sitter. We're hitting the road."

We did love a good road trip. And it had been a while.

Months on end of nothing but paperwork. No real roll-up-our-sleeves-and-work work. Honestly, my job had been so boring for so long, I was beginning to worry. Although, I wasn't sure, as acting Director of the Bellissimo, taking off on a Fast and Furious cash recovery job with the acting Property Manager was a good idea. I would need to run it by the acting head of Casino Operations.

I dialed. "Baylor," I said, "get up."

Baylor lived four floors below our twenty-ninth-floor Bellissimo President's Residence in a Bellissimo condo.

"It's six in the morning, Davis. I didn't leave the casino until four. I'm not getting up."

That was how it went with Baylor, and had been going, since we returned from hurricane break. He had the bigger job, the full-time job, he had the best assignment, and he took full advantage of it. "It's six forty-five in the morning, Baylor, and might I remind you, *I'm* in charge this week."

"Sure you are."

I didn't have time to go there. "This is a courtesy call, Baylor," I said. To let him know Fantasy and I were hitting the road for the day. Maybe into the night. Until we found Birdy James and five million dollars, I didn't say. "You should thank me for calling."

"Thanks, but no thanks, Davis. I'm hanging up."

"Wait—"

He interrupted with, "Yes."

"Yes, what?" I asked.

"Yes, whatever," he said. "Whatever it is, I vote yes."

He hung up.

On the Director of the Bellissimo.

Make that acting Director.

Who needed to act fast.

I dialed again. That time I called Baylor's much better half, July, Bex and Quinn's nanny, who happened to be on the other side of the bed. (Baylor and July were trying hard to get married. Their first attempt was rudely interrupted by Hurricane Kevin. Then Baylor missed their second wedding, what was to have been a holiday wedding, because of a blizzard in Kansas City. He'd attended a Casino Cage Operations conference at the JACK Cincinnati Casino, and afterward, boarded the plane to get married in Biloxi, only to be rerouted to Houston, then to Amarillo, then to Denver, where he was stuck at the airport for the next three days, including his and July's second wedding day. Their third crack at holy matrimony was just weeks away, and the weather, so far, was cooperating. There wasn't a hurricane, snowstorm, flashflood, tornado, mudslide, or artic cyclone in sight. We were in the middle of an unusual heat wave, but I'd never heard of a heat wave postponing a wedding. Third time could be the charm for them.)

"July, it's me."

Baylor must have heard me. Or maybe he just knew I'd call July next. "No," I heard him say. "Whatever it is, I vote no."

"Ignore him," I said.

"Are the girls okay?" she asked through sleep.

"They're fine."

"Are you okay?"

"I'm fine. But something's come up. Is there any chance you could keep Bex and Quinn today? Maybe into the afternoon?" She hesitated, which I knew meant no, so I let her off the hook. "It's okay, July. I understand. It's Sunday."

"It's not that," she said, "it's my bridesmaids. I'm meeting them in New Orleans this afternoon for their final fitting. The bridal salon is opening just for us because today was the only day I could go."

Those poor bridesmaids already had Hawaiian Aloha bridesmaid dresses, red velvet Christmas bridesmaid dresses, and now, baby-blue strapless sundresses. They were dedicated. And most likely, broke. From buying all the dresses.

I said, “Go back to sleep and don’t think another thing about it,” then hung up before she talked herself into canceling her afternoon with her bridesmaids, which I knew she’d do. I immediately dialed my sister, Meredith.

“Help.”

“Call me back when the sun is up, Davis.”

“Meredith, could you keep Bex and Quinn this afternoon?”

“Are you bringing them to me?”

Meredith lived in our hometown of Pine Apple, Alabama, a block from our parents, two hours from Biloxi, and in the opposite direction of Shreveport and/or Bossier City, Louisiana. “I can’t bring them to you, Meredith. I need you to come here.”

“You want me to get out of bed and drive two hours to babysit Bex and Quinn? Where’s Bradley?”

“He’s in Vegas.”

“Where’s July?”

“She’s with her bridesmaids.”

“At seven o’clock in the morning?”

I looked at the clock. Somehow it was seven.

“Davis, I can’t,” Meredith said. “Good luck. I’m going back to sleep.”

Then my sister, my only sibling, hung up on me, just in time for my phone to ring in my hand. At the decidedly unholy hour of seven in the morning, which, given that I’d already woken up four people with phone calls, was probably just karma paying me back.

It wasn’t.

It was Security. A large white envelope with my name pasted on the front in cutout mismatched magazine letters had been delivered to the front desk. Two Safety Officers were on their way upstairs with it. No one wanted to open it for fear of anthrax.

Big Security and Safety Officer babies.

It was just an envelope.

Big chickens.

I dialed Baylor again. "Baylor, get up here. I need you to open an envelope."

"No," he said. "Call Security."

"They're the ones who called me."

"Work it out." Then he hung up on me. Again. I dialed back and his phone went straight to voicemail. I couldn't leave Bex and Quinn alone to ride the elevator to Baylor's condo and beat on the door, and I wouldn't wake them and take them with me. Before I could decide exactly what to do, Security was beating on my front door. To deliver the envelope.

FIVE

Security at the Bellissimo was made up of two and a half components.

First, there was Surveillance, the eye in the sky, thirty-four hundred eyes, to be exact, scanning and recording every blink, every blank stare, and every Baccarat table. There were blind spots—in and around the residences, the upper-echelon executive offices, accounting offices that processed sensitive player information, and locations where nothing ever happened, like long boring employee-only passageways. Other than those few exceptions, Surveillance watched everything, even (and this is terrifying) (or maybe just creepy) the treatment rooms at the Bellissimo spa. Because of lawsuits. It wasn't like Surveillance could see anything; the lights were dim and the clients under wraps. But it was one of the reasons I never went to the Bellissimo spa. The other reason was the spa made me sleepy: the cricket music, the comfy beds, the warm blankets. A fifty-minute massage was a three-hour ordeal for me when I tacked on the two-hour nap after, and I didn't have time to nap my life away.

Where was I?

Security.

There was Surveillance, and there were boots on the ground, Guest Safety Specialists, 180 men and women who patrolled the casino and property twenty-four-seven wearing blue blazers and carrying two-way radios, handcuffs, and small canisters of police-strength pepper gel. Everyone in both departments was highly trained to spot cheating, suspicious behavior, and drunks. (The drunks were easy to spot.) Together, Surveillance and Safety protected the casino's patrons and assets. Then there was my team. (We were the half component.) We worked behind the scenes. Given that gaming involved such large amounts of money, and the temptation was there for casino guests and staff alike to steal, someone had to keep a closer eye than even Surveillance and Safety could.

That was us.

And I only worked part-time.

Make that quarter-time.

After Hurricane Kevin, I returned to the Bellissimo with a quarter-time job. What was a full-time-plus gun-slinging workweek when I was hired years earlier had rudely evolved to a quarter-time gun-free workweek. I couldn't say if I was happy about it or not, because I tried my very hardest not to think about it. And when I couldn't help but think about it, I forced myself to move on.

Moving on.

Ninety percent of my quarter-time job was from home and was digital—background checks, cyber security, and answering questions like these: why was the day shift VIP concierge, who mostly opened doors for high rollers checking in and out of the hotel, suddenly driving a white-on-white Mercedes-Benz A-Class sedan instead of his usual beat-up 2009 Honda Civic? (He'd helped a high rolling blackjack player hustle his girlfriend out of his hotel suite when his wife showed up unexpectedly.) (And got a new car for his troubles.) (Which, the high rolling blackjack player said, was way cheaper than a divorce.) Mostly, and certainly lately, right up until then, actually, things had been running like clockwork at the Bellissimo since our reopening, and Monday through Thursday from ten until two, while Bex and Quinn were with Nanny July at tumbling class or aqua-tots swim lessons, I didn't have much to do. Lately, my job had been so boring, I spent more than half my work hours playing Words Without Friends. Or gossiping with Fantasy over lunch salads. Or holding the phone while my mother droned on and on about my father's cat, my sister's daughter, or the latest comings and goings in my hometown of Pine Apple—population four hundred and fifty-four, one red light, zero Starbucks—where no one ever came. Or went. And that's what I did while I waited on Fantasy, who was at least willing to open the suspicious envelope with me, I called my mother. Bradley was in Vegas, July couldn't help, Meredith wouldn't help, and that left my mother.

She answered with, "Why are you calling me on the telephone so early in the morning, Davis? You barely caught me. I was about to tease my hair. I can't tease my hair and hold the telephone at the same time."

Why was my mother teasing her hair at the absolute crack of dawn? Because it was Sunday. Sunday School and Worship Service. I'd forgotten.

"I need your help, Mother."

"With what?" she asked. "Do you need a recipe?"

Not once, not ever, had I called my mother for a recipe. She must have had me mixed up with someone else, because I barely cooked. We lived above fourteen restaurants. Not only that, I wasn't friends with my new post-hurricane remodeled stove, an induction cooktop, whatever in the world that was. (It induced nothing. Certainly not bacon to fry. Or broccoli to steam. Or banana pudding to bubble around the edges.) I couldn't boil water on my new stove, much less cook. I was, however, friends with my Instapot. Six-Minute Instapot Mashed Potatoes were Bex and Quinn's favorite. I was friends with my microwave, and to a certain extent, my oven. And I was great friends with my toaster, because we went through the Pop-Tarts at House of Cole. Still, though, I wasn't calling my mother at the break of day for a recipe.

"I need your help with Bex and Quinn."

"Are my granddaughters okay? What have you done?"

My mother blamed me for Bex and Quinn's eighteen-month molars. As if their teeth were my fault.

"I need a babysitter fast. Can you come?"

"Is this your way of telling me your marriage is in trouble?"

I pulled the phone from my head. I closed my eyes. I pinched the bridge of my nose. I took a deep breath. I went back to the phone. "Bradley's traveling, Mother."

"Well, what's wrong with January?"

"Do you mean July?"

"January, February, July," she said, "I can't keep up."

"July is fine," I said, "and busy trying to get married."

"She needs to put her money where her mouth is," Mother said. "This trying to get married business. Who tries to get married? No one. They just get married. It took me two days to marry your father after he proposed."

Oh, good grief.

"And I'd say her being busy has nothing to do with trying to get married and everything to do with that germy daycare where she works," Mother said.

Apparently, she could keep up. "Who told you July worked at a daycare, Mother?"

"I have my sources. Never you mind who told me. And I'll have you know I'm not a bit happy about it. Now your nanny's loyalties are divided between my precious granddaughters and sickly stranger children. Did you think about that before you let her haul off and get another job? Of all the bad choices you've made, Davis, and you've made some whoppers, this might be the worst."

"It wasn't my choice, Mother. July is a grown woman who makes her own choices. Bex and Quinn are almost three years old. They'll go to preschool soon. And where does that leave July?"

"Helping you with your new baby, Davis," she said, "that's where it leaves her. Have you looked in the mirror lately? You're not getting any younger. If you intend to give your husband a son, something that despite my best efforts, I was unable to do for my own husband, you'd better hop to it. And in the meantime, your nanny had better not be taking my granddaughters with her to that filthy daycare."

"It's a childcare center, Mother, and it's spotlessly clean. Not a daycare. July is the director of our new spotlessly clean employee childcare center and Bex and Quinn's nanny. When she's not keeping Bex and Quinn in our home—" I leaned hard on the *in our home* part "—she works a few hours a week in an office at Play, our new employee childcare center. Not at a daycare."

"Don't split hairs with me, Davis. I'll see what I can do about coming tomorrow, but for today, you need to call your girl."

"I tried," I said. "She can't."

Silence.

More silence.

"Davis. Way. Cole."

Uh-oh.

"Are you telling me you called your nanny before you called me?"

"You just suggested I call her, Mother, and now you're offended that I called her? Which is it? And would it ever occur to you that I didn't call you first because I didn't want to bother you?"

"Well, you are bothering me, Davis. Being second fiddle with my own granddaughters bothers me. I already have to share them with Bradley's mother, and she has that nervous eye tic, and she's always clearing her throat, as if there's something she wants to say and can't get it out, and now you're telling me I'm playing third fiddle to your nanny?"

I pressed the tips of three fingers on the raging headache hammering between my eyes. My mother had been in somewhat of a bad mood since the day I was born, but that morning, lucky me, I'd managed to catch her in an extraordinarily bad mood. "Mother, I wouldn't dare call Bradley's mother. If for no other reason, she lives in Texas. And the only reason I called July before I called you is because she only lives an elevator away. But she can't help. It's Sunday. Between keeping Bex and Quinn a few hours a week—" I leaned hard on the *few hours* part "—and her new job at Play, Sunday is July's only day off."

"I know what day of the week it is, Davis. It's the Lord's Day. I'm leading Ladies' Sunrise Devotionals for Him this morning. And I need to tease my hair. Do you mind telling me what this is really about? If my granddaughters are okay and your marriage isn't in shambles, I'd appreciate it if we could have this conversation later."

"I really need your help, Mother."

"Why?" she asked. "Are you sick?"

"I'm fine. It's work. Something's come up and it's urgent." One little old lady and five million dollars of urgent. "I need to work."

"Take the girls with you, Davis. What do you think I did with you and your sister when I had to go to the market? You went with me."

"I can't take the girls to Louisiana."

"Louisiana? What do you mean by Louisiana?"

(How many things could Louisiana possibly mean?) "The next state over, Mother."

"When?" she asked.

"Now."

"What do you mean by now?"

(How many things could now possibly mean?) "Right now, Mother. This minute. As soon as you can get here."

She took a deep breath.

I braced myself.

"Davis, I'm sure you think I sit around twiddling my thumbs all day, and I'll have you know I don't. I'm very busy. Your father and his cat need my attention all day every day. We have the Tomato Festival coming up and I can't leave my tomatoes. They're blooming. Next, they'll bud. Then they'll produce. It's not like I can run off and leave them. They need to be watered, they need to be fed, and they need to be weeded."

I let her think about it a minute.

She thought about it a minute.

"Don't do this to me, Davis," she finally said. "Don't send me on a guilty trip because you and Bradley have such big and important jobs you can't even raise your own children. You know when you and your sister were little girls, I left you—"

"—every first Wednesday of the month for your Daughters of the American Revolution luncheon and that was it." I finished the sentence for her.

"I don't understand young couples having babies right and left, then going right back to their big jobs without a thought of who's going to care for the babies."

Who was sending whom on a guilty trip?

"The only thing I can do is have your father, who also has a big job, you might remember, load my tomatoes, and I'll bring them with me. I'll tend to them on your porches," she said. "It's not like I can just run off and leave them. If I have to drop everything this minute to help *you*, I'll have to bring my tomatoes with me."

I had a sudden vision of my mother driving down I-65 in her Chevrolet Impala with her garden, her whole garden, half an acre, in the backseat. Corn stalks, snap peas, bell peppers, and a scarecrow wearing Liberty overalls. "Mother, there's no reason in the world to bring your tomatoes."

"I'll decide what's best for my tomatoes, thank you."

"I'm not asking you to move in," I said. "Just help me for a few days."

"A few days could make all the difference in the world between a good and bad crop, Davis. If I run off and leave them, who is it you expect to take care of them? The Tomato Fairy? I'm only willing to go to all this trouble because I love my granddaughters. I don't want them to end up in a filthy daycare with child bullies while you work. And with this kind of trauma—"

"Mother, are you suggesting I'm traumatizing you because I need your help, or are you suggesting I'm traumatizing my own children because I work a few hours a week?" I leaned hard on the *few hours* part.

"I was talking about my tomatoes, Davis. The trauma to my tomatoes."

My head dropped on a sigh. I threw a hand in the air. Why in the world she'd drag tomatoes across a state line for a day or two was beyond me, but I knew better than to argue with her, especially about tomatoes, and I should have known better than to call her. Mother didn't like her schedule interrupted, she didn't like surprises, and she didn't like the phone. She was somewhat warmer in person. And by somewhat warmer, I meant two degrees above freezing.

"After all the trouble it will be to bring my tomatoes—"

It passed through my brain that Birdy James could keep the five million.

It was only money.

"—I don't want to hear a word, not one word, about my tomato crop this year," Mother said. "If you slice into a tomato and even start to tell me it's pale or mealy, I will tan your hide. And I'll probably need to bring backup. I can't tend to my granddaughters and my tomatoes all by myself. When would I rest?"

"When can you come?"

"Let me speak to your father. You know this means he'll

have to miss Worship Service."

I was pretty sure he wouldn't mind.

She lectured me for ten more minutes, mostly about the daycare business at the Bellissimo being very bad business, mark her words, then hung up.

That went well.

And I wanted a tomato sandwich.

By then, the sun, my daughters, and my dog were up. Just in time for a box of donuts to bust through the front door, Fantasy attached. I barely saw her, too busy wondering why my mother's tomato plants were blooming in June. All my life, by June, she was shoving ripe tomatoes down our throats at every meal. Sliced tomatoes with breakfast, tomato salads and tomato soup for lunch, and tomato casseroles for dinner. Tomato relish, tomato chutney, stuffed tomatoes, pickled tomatoes, and tomato sauce on everything. Tomatoes, tomatoes, tomatoes.

From across the living room, Fantasy raised an eyebrow.

"Tomatoes," I said. "I was thinking about tomatoes."

She rolled her eyes. "Where is it?"

I pointed to my dining room table.

For a good long minute, we stared at it.

"There's no anthrax in that envelope," she said.

"Then open it," I said.

"I'm here to lend moral support from afar while you open it, Davis."

We stared at it over strawberry-frosted donuts. We used kitchen gadgets—chopsticks, salad tongs, and steak knives—to push it around. After another cup of coffee, we were just about to rip off the Band-Aid and open it when Bex and Quinn finished their breakfast donuts in the kitchen. By the time I dressed them in their bedroom, then pushed the play button on the television remote for Disney's *Frozen* in the living room—they were allowed to watch *Frozen* once a day, and only once, otherwise they'd watch it on a loop—the envelope had been on the dining room table for almost an hour.

"This is old school," Fantasy said. "These cutout letters."

"Old school as in old people." I took a hard look at my name made up of nine different fonts, eight different sizes, and three different colors. "An old person did this. Anyone else would type and print it."

"An old person as in Old Bird Woman," Fantasy agreed. "Or Old Bird Woman's sister. I told you, Davis. Bird Woman ran off with the money."

"And with five million dollars in her purse, she'd take the time to cut out my name in magazine letters and what? Confess?"

"We won't know until you open it."

From the living room, Bex sang "Let it Go" at the top of her lungs. Quinn tap danced on the coffee table in pink cowgirl boots. Candy howled at the moon.

"Look at it this way," Fantasy said. "If we're right, and it's from Bird Woman, there's no anthrax. Where would she get anthrax?"

"We should open it," I said.

"Go ahead."

"Let's open it outside."

"Let's put on gloves and masks just in case."

We pilfered through my dresser drawers and left my bedroom with scarves over our heads and covering our mouths and noses, sunglasses protecting our eyes, and mismatched fuzzy gloves on our hands.

Fantasy said, "You look ridiculous."

I said, "So do you."

I peeked in on Bex, Quinn, and Candy, still busy with Anna, Elsa, and Olaf, then we stepped out the kitchen door to one of my three sunny porches.

"Go ahead," Fantasy said from behind her scarf.

By then, I'd had it with the envelope, wondering what was

in the envelope, and trying to talk someone—anyone—into opening the envelope, so I did it. I ripped it open. Not easy to do wearing fuzzy gloves. Fantasy and I read the note from two feet away. We stepped closer to read it from one foot away. Then, coming out from behind our scarves, sunglasses, and fuzzy gloves, we read the note from an inch away.

I've got your old lady.
I'll sell her to you for $5,000,000.
I'll be in touch.
Elvis

We fell into porch chairs, exhausted from our efforts.

Fantasy picked up the magazine-letter note and fanned herself with it.

"Did you come in through the lobby?" I asked.

"I did."

"And?"

"A hundred," she said. "At least."

"At seven in the morning?"

She checked the time on her phone. "Davis, it's nine."

How had that happened?

I grabbed the magazine-letter note from her and fanned myself with it. "Tell me. Just tell me."

"There were tall Elvises." She took a deep breath. "There were short Elvises. There were black, white, blue, and I counted ten Asian Elvises without even trying. There were women Elvises, children Elvises, and I kid you not, dog Elvises, all checking into the hotel. Worse than that? Most of our employees are wearing Elvis costumes. Almost every employee I saw was in some manner of Elvis disguise. The only way to tell the Elvis employees from the Elvis guests is the employees are wearing nametags. And that, Davis, was just the lobby."

"Wouldn't the plural of Elvis be Elvii?" I asked. "Like the

plural of radius is radii?"

"His name wasn't Elvius."

"I think the plural is Elvii."

"Does it even halfway matter?" she asked. "Our problem is, of all the Elvises, or Elviis, one of them has Birdy James."

"And wants five million dollars for her. Five million dollars we don't have."

"And the convention doesn't even officially start until tomorrow," she said. "It's—" she checked the time again "—nine fifteen in the morning the day before the convention starts and we probably have a thousand guests and two thousand employees who look like Elvis in the building right now. And that's not counting the Elvises on the street. The people behind the counter and everyone in line at Krispy Kreme were dressed as Elvis." She leaned in. "Davis. The donut special today is Elvis. The donuts have chocolate Elvis hair."

It was the Bellissimo's first Elvis convention, and the entire Southeastern United States was excited about it. Twelve hundred Elvis lookalikes were descending on us and staying five nights. Elvis fan clubs from as far away as Michigan, Missouri, and the Mojave Desert who couldn't book rooms at the Elvised-out Bellissimo were celebrating the King of Rock and Roll at every other casino up and down Beach Boulevard, spilling over to chain motels and Airbnbs around the city, and, bottom line, Biloxi had Elvis Fever. The Bellissimo lobby had been transformed to a Graceland vignette. The VIP lounge was serving bite-sized peanut butter, banana, and bacon grilled sandwiches. What was formerly a poker room in the casino was currently the Love Me Tender Chapel, with more than fifty weddings scheduled, officiated by five different ordained Elvii. Rumors were rampant that before the week was out, Elvis's only child and heir to his vast estate, Lisa Marie Presley, would make an appearance. Included in the week's festivities at our resort alone were impersonator performances, lookalike competitions, a Bellissimo-sponsored Run With the King 5K, a King of Cadillacs car show on the Mezzanine, a Hound Dog parade through the grounds, live concerts by the Jail House Rockers from California and the Blue Suede Shoes from New York, a seated luncheon book signing with the top ten Elvis biographers, Elvis-themed menus in all fourteen Bellissimo restaurants, and probably the biggest event of them all, on Friday night, the top twenty-five scores in the week-long Elvis slot tournament would be cast as extras for the remake of *Double Trouble*, an old Elvis movie.

When I first heard about the convention, months earlier, I didn't think a thing about it other than it sounded like fun. (Who doesn't love Elvis?) For the most part, Bellissimo conventions ran themselves, very rarely hitting our team's radar. Or radii. But given present circumstances, with thousands of guests and most of our employees all trying to look like one person, how in the world would we pick out the one who had Birdy James? And where were we supposed to get five million dollars? Even if we found the five million already missing, we had to wire it to Seattle, not buy back an old lady. I could only find a single sliver of light in the five-million-dollar-Birdy-Elvii darkness. "At least we don't have to go to Louisiana." As soon as I said it, I stood.

"Where are you going?" Fantasy asked.

"To call my mother. If we're not going to Birdy James's sister's house in Louisiana, I don't need my mother."

"You called your mother?"

"Fantasy, you were the one who told me to get a sitter. We were going on a road trip. But if an Elvis has Birdy James, then she didn't necessarily steal the five million dollars, and this is internal. The person we're looking for is here. Under our roof. Surely, between you, me, Baylor, and July, we can handle Bex and Quinn." Two seconds later, I was back in my porch chair with my phone speed dialing my father, because by then, I remembered, my mother would have been praising the Lord.

"Daddy."

"Punkin'," my rock, my hero, my parent who not only loved me, but also liked me, said.

"Stop doing whatever it is Mother has you doing to the tomatoes," I said. "I don't need her help after all."

"I'm assuming that's good news," he said. "False alarm?"

"Not really," I said, "but it doesn't look like I'll need to travel. Sorry for the trouble. Put the tomatoes back in the ground."

"I'm not sure I'm following. Your mother's tomatoes weren't in the ground. They were in ten-gallon paint buckets. I loaded them on the truck for her—" he hesitated "—almost an hour and a half ago."

Then I was the one not following. "Wait, Daddy. Where's Mother?"

"On her way to you. She was out the door fifteen minutes after you called. She had me call her prayer circle and tell them she was under the weather. She should be there soon."

Fantasy leaned in, her face a huge question mark. I shrugged, my face a huge I-have-no-idea mark.

"Daddy, I'm so confused. Mother lied to her prayer circle?"

"Technically, she had me lie."

"What's going on with her tomatoes? Since when did she grow them in paint buckets? And since when does she drive a truck? Has mother ever driven a truck? Full of tomatoes?"

"Since blight," he said. "Do you know what blight is?"

"No." I halfway knew it killed tomatoes and I didn't want to know the other half. "But keep going."

"Your mother lost her entire crop of tomatoes to blight. She took it hard. You can't believe the mood she's been in."

Oh, I believed it.

"Honey, when she settled down after your call, she thought about it, then started packing. Rather than an inconvenience, she realized it was an opportunity."

"For her tomatoes?"

"She had to start her crop over from seedlings, Davis. She's desperately worked them night and day so they'll bear fruit before the Tomato Festival. We're looking at a week of rain while you're looking at ninety-five-plus degrees of sun every day. You may have saved her tomatoes and her Best in Show winning streak."

I slumped in my porch chair.

Thanks a lot for the guilty trip, Mother.

Who was doing whom the favor here?

Across the table, over the magazine letter note from Elvis, Fantasy gave up. "Don't tell me," she mumbled. "Get me out of bed in the middle of the night, make me bring breakfast, make me open an anthrax letter, and don't tell me."

I waved her off. Six o'clock wasn't the middle of the night, I hadn't made her bring breakfast, and she hadn't been much help opening the anthrax letter.

"Watch out," my father said, "they should be there any minute."

I'd have asked if by they, he meant Mother and the tomatoes, but had to say goodbye quickly, because just then, Bexley, Quinn, and Candy raced through the kitchen and out to the porch. "There's an old lady man wearing jewelry pajamas here, Mama," Bex, who was Communication Director for Quinn and Candy, said.

"A what, honey?" I asked. "Is it Nana?"

Quinn leaned over to whisper in her sister's ear. Bex nodded, then said, "Is Nana coming?"

"We hope not," Fantasy said.

I smacked her arm.

"It isn't Nana. It's an old lady man wearing jewelry pajamas," Bex said.

"Your nana is an old lady man," Fantasy said. "Not sure about the jewelry pajamas."

I smacked her arm again.

"Did you let the old lady man wearing jewelry pajamas in, Bex?"

Quinn cupped her hand over Bexley's ear. Bexley nodded, then said, "No. Stranger Danger. We don't know the old lady man wearing jewelry pajamas."

Quinn whispered in her sister's ear again. Bex nodded, then announced, "Candy didn't bark." Which was proof, to my daughters at least, that whoever or whatever was at our front door wasn't a threat. I assumed whoever or whatever at our front door couldn't possibly be much of a threat, because Security, who screens all traffic to my home, allowed the person up. They usually called first, but it had been a very unusual morning.

I stood. "Let's go see."

Fantasy stood.

"Do you want to see too?" I asked.

"An old lady man wearing jewelry pajamas? You bet."

We paraded to the front door, where we found the oldest human on God's Green Earth, and Bex was right; at first glance, it was impossible to tell if it were an old man or an old woman. Over what looked like a woman's faded flannel nightgown, circa 1820, he/she wore a man's heavily embellished blue silk cape, circa Elvis. On he/she/Elvis's feet, blue suede slippers with young Elvis's likeness. He/she/Elvis was shorter than me (and I'm not tall), and so old, he/she/Elvis looked mummified. The vintage gold souvenir Elvis sunglasses covering half of his/her/Elvis's face slipped down an inch to reveal concrete gray eyes darting everywhere, looking for a place to land. I matched them up with the concrete gray wig helmet he/she/Elvis had on the top of his/her/Elvis's head, and that's when I knew. "Birdy!" I would have yanked her arm and dragged her inside quickly, but she was so frail, I was afraid I'd come away from it with a Bird arm in my hand.

Fantasy had no qualms about it. She grabbed Birdy by her Elvis cape. "Get in this house, Bird Woman."

"I lost my glasses," Birdy said. "Someone please help me find my glasses. I can't see."

Bex and Quinn—no flies on them—jumped clear of the old lady man wearing jewelry pajamas who couldn't see, lest they, so close to the ground, were stepped on. Then Candy darted past all of us to bark at the elevator, which meant she could hear it; our private elevator was on the move again. Someone else was on their way up to invade my otherwise peaceful life. Fantasy stepped in front of Birdy, hiding her, from whoever was behind the parting elevator doors. And that was when my ex-ex-mother-in-law, Bea Crawford, stepped out of the elevator, then I wanted to hide behind Birdy, who was hiding behind Fantasy.

Bea Crawford, all of Bea Crawford, wearing nude leggings, as in tights the color of skin, under a black tank top featuring fighting cats, so at first glance, Bea looked naked under the fighting cats, dropped into a wide-legged nude-leggings squat, threw her arms out, then yelled at the top of her lungs, "It's your Banana Nana Bea Bea!"

My daughters, who, bless their baby hearts, knew no better, who only associated Bea Crawford with sweet slow country life in Pine Apple, ran in for hugs.

Until my mother stepped out of the elevator.

Then they ran for their nana.

Next, four bellmen, pushing two double-wide flatbed rolling carts, the kind of double-wide flatbed rolling carts that could hold small swimming pools, ten racks of wood, and hybrid cars, struggled out.

The elevator doors closed behind them.

Before I could shove my ex-ex-mother-in-law back on it.

I surveyed the carts, stuffed with white plastic buckets. The buckets were filled with dark soil. Above the soil, and peeking just above the rims of the buckets, were two-inch tomato plants.

The gray helmet of a wig poked out from behind Fantasy. Birdy leaned north, her nose in the air, sniffing like a geriatric hamster. "Are those tomato plants?" Her blank eyes roamed the crystal chandelier centered in the recessed vestibule ceiling, ten feet above everyone's head, fifteen feet above the tomatoes.

I answered her. "Unfortunately, yes. Those are tomato plants."

Birdy leaned farther north to blindly address the tomato-plant guardians. "Did somebody get the blight?"

"We got the blight alright." Bea shifted her considerable weight. "Our butts got blighted all the way to Biloxi."

Why was Bea Crawford there?

I slowly shifted my gaze to my mother. I narrowed my eyes. "Mother?"

"I can't drive a truck, Davis," she said, by way of explanation, as to why she'd drag my ex-ex-mother-in-law with her. "My feet don't reach the pedals."

Birdy leaned out from behind Fantasy again. "I haven't driven a car since nineteen and thirty-four."

"Boy—" my ex-ex-mother-in-law beamed, taking in the Bellissimo, my home, and my children "—it's good to be back! I'm here and so is Elvis! Elvis is in the house!" Then, in her nude leggings, slinging a very generous hip out, she snarled her upper lip and howled, "*I'm a hunka hunka hunka hunka burnt love.*"

Bex sang, "*Hunka, hunka, hunka.*"

Quinn danced.

Candy barked.

I cried.

"Say." How Bea started almost every sentence. "Guess who we ran into?"

I watched my mother's hand slide behind Bea's arm. I knew that move. She was pinching the soft flesh of the back and just inside Bea's upper arm.

"Oww, Caroline." Bea smacked Mother's hand away.

"Guess," Bea said. "Just guess who we saw."

Beside me, Fantasy was discreetly slashing a finger across her throat, as in, *shut up, Bea.*

I side-eyed her.

Her hand slowly dropped to her side. She smiled. Innocently.

"Miss Hoity-Toity herself," Bea announced.

I turned to Fantasy.

"Bianca is here?"

"She is?" Fantasy was wide-eyed and full of wonderment.

"You knew and didn't tell me?"

Worse than that, if Fantasy knew, it meant my husband knew. And my boss, No Hair. And Baylor, that punk. Everyone knew Bianca Casimiro Sanders, the owner's wife, who lived in the Penthouse above me, who'd fired me from half of my part-time job, who I hadn't spoken to since just after Hurricane Kevin, was back in residence after an eight-month absence.

And no one had bothered to tell me.

I had to hear it from my ex-ex-mother-in-law.

Who shouldn't have even been there.

SIX

Before everyone and everything settled, a dark spattered trail of Alabama soil led from the elevator, through the vestibule, into my foyer, then down the main hall, where it split and branched off in three different directions. First, the dirt trail led down the guest hall to the balcony between the guest bedroom suites, then through my living room to the veranda, and finally, down the main hall and through the kitchen to the kitchen porch, the same kitchen porch that still had a magazine letter note on the same kitchen porch table. The whole time, the thermometer continued to climb. It was a humid ninety-six degrees out. And it wasn't even noon.

Bea Crawford, who shouldn't have even been there, under any circumstances, was busy issuing tomato orders to the bellmen like they were her personal field slaves. Point this bucket that way. Get that bucket out of the shade. Line them up better. One ten-gallon bucket, one marked with a tiny red B, which meant it was Bea's, as opposed to my mother's B-less buckets, was missing—find it. "It's a Cherokee Purple Heirloom," Bea said.

"What is, ma'am?"

"The missing bucket." Bea was cracking whips. "My tomato bucket, dummy."

"Ma'am, they all look the same to me."

And to me. Every dirt bucket had a two-inch green stalk sprouting furry leaves. "Bea," I said. "You're being rude. Apologize."

"I'm not a bit sorry, Davis, because he's being dumb."

Bea was sweating with such force, the fighting cats on her tank top were surely drowning. I glared at her while speaking to the bellman. "Excuse her. She's had too much sun."

"I'll tell you who better be getting too much sun, and that's my Cherokee Purple Heirlooms, that's who." She tipped her head back. "Here sunny-sun-sun! Come get Bea's heirlooms!"

When the tomatoes were finally, finally where she wanted them, Bea, fists buried in generous hips, said to one of the bellmen, "You boys are going to need to rig us up a irrigator."

"I'm sorry?" Sweat rolled down his sharp nose and dripped onto his bellman's uniform.

"Water?" Bea said. "You ever heard of water? These tomatoes need water."

Her mouth was open to explain water to the bellmen when I interrupted. "That's enough." I turned to the sweaty bellman. "Thank you for your help. We'll take it from here."

Bea turned to me. "Since when do you know how to rig up a irrigator?"

I totally and completely and thoroughly ignored her.

Meanwhile, inside, Bexley, not yet three-year-old Bexley, had been busy vacuuming. Helping Mama. Quinn was mopping. Also helping Mama. The problem was, Bex's Fisher-Price Light-up Learning Vacuum wasn't vacuuming. It was spreading and smashing. And the ten-gallon plastic bucket full of dirt and a tiny tomato plant, clearly marked with a red B, into which the girls emptied an entire bottle of shampoo and a gallon of almond milk for Quinn to slosh her Melissa & Doug Let's Play House! mop around in wasn't mopping. It was slopping and slinging. The girls had gone through the foyer, down the hall, and into the living room spreading, smashing, slopping, and slinging soapy milky mud. In the time it took to place the tomato buckets on the porches, Bex and Quinn had managed to coat at least half of our ten-thousand-square-foot home in mud.

Candy, a toy broom in her mouth, happily playing along, was clearing every flat surface with the straw end of the broom and scraping every wall in the house with the broom handle, her tail wagging wildly as she tracked muddy pawprints everywhere.

I couldn't begin to describe the chaos.

"*Fantasy*!"

Everyone above me and everyone below me, all the way to the casino, twenty-eight floors down, and all the Elvii all over the building, surely heard me.

Fantasy's head popped up from behind the dining room table. "What, Davis? What?" Then she took a look. "Oh, dear Lord."

"Did I ask you to watch the girls?" I demanded. "Did I?"

"Yes, Davis, you did. But you also asked me to get information out of Bird Woman. I can't do both, so I asked your mother to watch the girls."

Birdy James, from deep in a dining room wingback chair, waved. "Are you talking to me, Davis?"

"Bird Woman's hearing aid fell out of her head," Fantasy said. "Now she can't see or hear. I'm looking for her damn hearing aid."

"Ugly word jar!" Mud-covered Bex pointed and yelled. "Fantasy, you said ugly words! Put a quarter in the ugly word jar!"

"I'm going to empty out the ugly word jar, Bexley," Fantasy said, "because your mother needs the money. She's lost five million dollars."

Fantasy was right. Not about me losing five million dollars, but about five million dollars being lost. Hearing aids, tomatoes, mud, my insufferable ex-ex-mother-in-law, who shouldn't have even been there, not to mention Bianca Sanders making a surprise appearance aside, I still had a five-million-dollar problem, the thought of which stopped me in my tracks. I just stopped. I did the 4-7-8: I inhaled for four seconds, held it for seven, then let it go for eight. I did it three times. Lest I kill someone. When I'd calmed down enough, I eased the toy cleaning equipment away from Bex and Quinn and asked if they'd like to watch *Frozen* again.

They did. They very much wanted to watch *Frozen* for an unheard of second time in one day.

"I won't tell Daddy," Bex said.

Quinn nodded.

"I'll tell Daddy," I said. "We don't keep secrets from Daddy."

Fantasy laughed. Slapped-her-leg laughed. Doubled over laughed.

I didn't appreciate it a bit.

I called Housekeeping and asked for a cleanup crew. A very large cleanup crew. Wet/dry vacs, industrial carpet and upholstery shampooers, the works. Immediately.

My mother, who was supposed to be watching my children, appeared, wearing an apron over her summer-weight double-knit jogging suit. She'd set up camp in my kitchen. She was cooking—when the going got tough, my mother got cooking—by way of watching Bex and Quinn. To her, feeding them was watching them. She surveyed. "Davis, you've let your children run hog wild again. I'm trying to prepare them a balanced meal, and you've let them tear up the house."

My jaw was slack. My head shook slowly of its own accord.

"Where's your sweet tea?" Mother demanded. "Do you not have a pitcher of sweet tea? Bea's about to fall out. I've made us a nice platter of liverwurst and pickle-loaf sandwiches with boiled beets and sliced persimmons," Mother said, "and we need something to drink besides soda pop. Soda pop gives Bea gas."

Fantasy said, "Since when do you eat liverwurst, Davis?"

Mother answered. "I brought groceries with me, Fantasy. Davis never has a bite of nutritious food in this house. She feeds my granddaughters garbage. Pure garbage. It's a wonder they don't starve to death."

From the wingback chair, Birdy yelled, "Did someone say liverwurst?"

Bexley asked, "What's a worse sandwich?" She tugged at the hem of my t-shirt. "Do we like worse sandwiches, Mama? Worse than what?"

I didn't say a word to any of them. I gathered my daughters, Candy trailing behind, stopped by their room for clean clothes, then marched everything and everyone to my room. I locked the door. I bathed the girls, put them in the middle of my bed, then turned on the television. I cued *Frozen*. I hit play. Candy, who was next in line for a bath, hopped on my bed before I could stop her. She settled her muddy self between the girls. She thumped her muddy tail on my pillow.

I closed my eyes and shook my head.

Quinn leaned over to whisper in Bex's ear.

"Mama, we're hungry." Candy's muddy tail pounded my pillow. "Candy's hungry too."

I gave up.

I sent a text message to Fantasy. *I'm going to need a minute.*

"Scoot over, Candy." I climbed into bed with my daughters and my muddy dog, at noon, on a Sunday, a Sunday I was in charge of the Bellissimo Resort and Casino and a Sunday five million dollars were missing, a Sunday thousands of Elvii were invading the twenty-eight floors below me, leaving a half-deaf half-blind centenarian wearing a nightgown who might or might not know something about the missing money, an irritated and sleep-deprived best friend and partner, my mother, who I had nothing to say about just then, and my loud-mouth, plus-sized, orange-haired ex-ex-mother-in-law, who shouldn't have even been there at all, much less wearing nude leggings, to fend for themselves.

I reached for the phone.

"What do we want for lunch, girls?"

I ordered a large cheese pizza and four banana splits.

And that was after breakfast donuts.

And those were after pancakes the day before when it all started.

I said, "Let's not tell Daddy. We don't want his feelings hurt because he's missing all the fun."

I tried to close my eyes, but couldn't stop staring at the ceiling, trying to stare through it to the Penthouse. I wondered if Bianca Sanders could feel me below her with the same intensity I could feel her above me.

* * *

The girls and I didn't leave my bedroom until they'd watched *Frozen* for a record-breaking third time, I'd bathed Candy twice, changed the linens on my bed, and Housekeeping, along with Maintenance, had cleared most of the mud from my home. There were still traces, and the carpet in my living room was scheduled to be replaced the next morning—living above a resort had its perks—but for the most part, I was mud-free by late afternoon. I wasn't Mother free, or Bea Crawford free, or Birdy James free, but mostly mud-free.

When I finally braved the world outside my bedroom, because Bex and Quinn were bored and Candy was tired of being bathed, Fantasy had gone home to salvage a few hours of her day off with her husband and three sons. She'd left me a note: *I couldn't get a thing out of Bird Woman. For one, she can't stay awake. She fell asleep mid-sentence several times. When she was awake, she couldn't hear me over the cleanup equipment and Bea. What is Bea doing here? Does she ever shut up? Back to Bird Woman, because I've had about enough of Bea, I showed her the Birdyhand business she drew on her Incident Report and she couldn't decipher it because she couldn't see it. She thinks she has a spare pair of glasses in her Lost and Found desk. Think you could sneak down there for them tonight when things settle down? Sorry about your carpet. And Bea. And I'm really sorry I didn't tell you Bianca was back in town. In my defense, I didn't know about it until Baylor texted last night, and I fully intended to tell you first thing this morning, but between the money and your mother and the mud, and good grief, all the Elvises, I couldn't find the right time. It'll be okay, Davis, I've got your back. Good luck tonight. Talk tomorrow.*

Elvii, Fantasy. The correct word for more than one Elvis was Elvii. And she could have found the right time. How long would it have taken to say, "By the way, Davis, gird your loins, Bianca is back."

I turned the corner to my living room slowly.

My carpet was the color of wastewater.

I found my mother trying to incinerate herself frying pork chops in a cast-iron skillet over a roaring fire in the RumbleStone firepit on the veranda—by then the mercury had climbed just past the one-hundred-degree mark—and the only thing Mother had to say about it, shouting at me through the veranda door, the tomato buckets pushed back into a semi-circle behind her, far from the inferno, was, "Your stove isn't worth taking out back and shooting, Davis."

My mother and I were so, so different. If I were going to shoot the stove, I'd shoot it where it stood.

Bea Crawford, who shouldn't have even been there, at all, was on my kitchen porch watering tomato plants, the porch, the porch furniture, the sky, the glass doors, and every thirty seconds, herself. She turned the garden hose on herself. She yelled at me through glass. "I hope you know it's hotter than hell out here, Davis."

As if I could do something about the heat.

Birdy James was mouth-wide-open snoring in one of my

dining room wingback chairs that had been relocated to the living room. She was still wearing her flannel nightgown under the heaviest winter blanket I owned, her gray wig askew, and her frail hands on top of the blanket were clasped in open-casket mode.

It ran through my mind that I could quickly pack a bag for myself, Bex, Quinn, and Candy (who travels light), call Transportation, tell them it was an emergency, because it sure felt like an emergency, then fly to Vegas for the comfort, the sheer comfort, of my husband. He'd know what to do. But I stopped myself. I stayed put. I needed to figure out what to do. My husband trusted me to know what to do. He was counting on me to know what to do. I was counting on myself to know what to do. He could have very easily done what everyone expected him to do and left Baylor in charge while he was away, but he hadn't. And I didn't want to let myself, or him, down. So I woke Birdy as gently as I could. I made her a cup of the strongest ginger tea I thought she could swallow. I turned on *Frozen* for the unheard of fourth time in a single day, and after parking Bex, Quinn, and Candy in front of the television, I led Birdy to Bradley's home office, settled her in, then, through two more cups of ginger tea, dragged the following information out of her:

She had no idea who left the blue bag full of money at the Lost and Found door during the wee hours of Saturday. She couldn't lift it, so she solved the problem in 516.035. (Who? What? Where?) Class 500, she explained, was the Birdy Decimal System denotation for Lost and Found suitcases. Division 10, she explained, was Lost and Found black suitcases. Section 6 meant Lost and Found black spinner suitcases. The subclass decimal designation of .035 meant that there were thirty-five black spinner suitcases in Lost and Found inventory, and the one she chose to transfer the blue bag to had been there the longest. I asked how long. She said she'd have to check her log, but at least since Roosevelt was in office. (Why did I ask?) She rolled 516.035 to the hall just outside the open door of Lost and Found to the blue bag of money. She emptied it. (Seven articles of ladies clothing, two pairs of ladies' shoes, size nine, a large makeup bag, and a set of Clairol hot rollers.) (Maybe the suitcase had been there since Roosevelt was in office.) Then she rigged a pulley by knotting one leg of a pair of men's trousers from 340.988 to the straps of the blue bag and knotting the other leg to the base of her rolling desk chair, then sitting in the chair and inching forward, she managed to lob the blue bag into the black spinner suitcase. She zipped the spinner closed, extended the handle, then rolled both black spinner suitcases to 516.035. (Both?) "Both, Birdy?" I asked. "What do you mean by both?" Then she asked me what *I* meant by both. So I asked, "Did it take two suitcases to hold the money?" Then she asked what I meant by two suitcases. On a very heavy sigh, I said, "Keep going." All I'd really learned was that at some point the money was in a blue bag and the blue bag was in a black suitcase somewhere in Lost and Found. "What'd you do next?" Next, she said she rehomed the former contents of 516.035, including the Clairol hot rollers, to a Bellissimo shopping bag and recategorized it to 842.116. (I didn't ask.) (But I did wonder how in the world she remembered Dewey Decimal details when she had no idea who was President.)

When we spoke Saturday morning, Birdy clearly heard me say, "Call Room Service." And she was right; I said it. But it was meant for Bradley about pancakes for Bex and Quinn, not for Birdy about five million dollars. She called Room Service, then sent 516.035 with a girl Elvis. Room Service Girl Elvis had spiky gold hair and was wearing a skin-tight gold lamé jumpsuit under a gold lamé cape. Birdy told Gold Lamé Elvis the whole story, all five million details. She asked Gold Lamé Elvis to deliver the suitcase straight to the boss's wife. (It would have been a good time to mention to Birdy that Gold Lamé Elvis, in fact, did *not* deliver the suitcase straight to the boss's wife, but I didn't want to confuse her lest she go off on a wedding cake tangent.) (I wasn't about to bring up the subject of the wedding cake, because Birdy was confused enough already.)

Fifteen minutes after she sent the spinner suitcase with Gold Lamé Elvis, when the vault guards showed up, both dressed as Elvis in black slacks and white jackets over black silk shirts, Birdy told them the whole story, the whole five-million-dollar story, including the blue bag part, the 516.035 black spinner suitcase part, and the Gold Lamé Elvis part, then sent them on their merry way with three tiers of wedding cake—there it was—to be, as she misunderstood it, locked in the vault.

Minutes later, her shift over, and as Birdy was preparing to leave for the day, another Elvis walked in Birdy's Lost and Found door asking if anyone had turned in his black spinner suitcase containing only one item: his award-winning Elvis belt. His most beloved possession. His wife, Mrs. Elvis, described the belt: made of shirt-weight leather, visible tailor's chalk marks (hers) on the flip side, wide strips of Velcro on both ends, embellished, in an original pattern designed by hers truly, with silver studs and blue rhinestones attached with shoe glue. She showed Birdy pictures. Birdy admired the photographs, then told them she'd had five million dollars turned in (adding five million dollars' worth of blue-bag, black-spinner-suitcase 516.035, Gold-Lamé-and-Black-Suit-Elvii fun facts), three baby stingrays, and the cake! The wedding cake! But no Elvis belt.

Birdy clocked out, gathered her lunchbox and red plaid Aladdin thermos, rode the elevator to the lobby, then made her way to Valet East, where the Zest for Life minibus was waiting. After passing him a generous slab of wedding cake, Birdy told her sweet minibus driver, Robbie, who was like a great grandson to her, the story of her odd day. The blue bag waiting on her that morning. The five million dollars in the blue bag. The 516.035 black spinner suitcase she moved hot rollers out of and money into. Gold Lamé Elvis. Black Suited Elvii. The baby stingrays.

Mr. and Mrs. Elvis and the missing silver-studded belt. And the cake! The wedding cake!

At seven that evening, she changed into her nightgown, ordered two glasses of warm milk from the Zest for Life cafeteria—one for herself and one for her cat Mortimer—then waited for the warm milk to be delivered to her Senior Living door. It was, a little later than usual—and by guess who? Elvis! Beautiful Elvis! That one a deep brunette wearing skimpy red silk undergarments, maybe swimwear, beneath the most beautiful red silk Elvis cape Birdy had ever seen. And red high heels. Beautiful red high heels. She would have invited Bikini Elvis in and told her the story of her Elvis-wedding-cake-five-million-dollar day, but she wasn't dressed. And it was time for her show. Which was just before her bedtime. So she tipped Bikini Elvis twenty cents, a dime for her warm milk and another dime for Mortimer's, then at seven thirty, she sat down in her easy chair to watch *Wheel of Fortune*, sipping her good-to-the-last-drop milk. The very next thing she knew, it was morning, and she woke up in Lost and Found at the Bellissimo. She was very concerned about the state Lost and Found was in. Everything upturned. Everything out of place. As if a tornado had run through. Cages were open, bags and suitcases had been emptied, their contents strewn, and the slices of wedding cake she'd hidden in her desk for her coffee breaks were gone. She wasn't wearing her bathrobe, or her slippers, so she borrowed from items that had made their way to Lost and Found since her last shift: an Elvis cape and Elvis slippers. Birdy was overly concerned about returning the items as soon as possible.

She straightened Lost and Found as best she could (probably destroying any evidence left behind), coded herself out, locked the door behind her, then ran straight into a Bellissimo Safety Officer, another gorgeous girl Elvis. That particular gorgeous girl Elvis was a dusty blonde, hair cut in a long bob, wearing a white silk Elvis miniskirt beneath a white silk fringed jacket. The fringe went almost to her knees. Birdy, not knowing where to go or who to ask for help, thought of me and my vested interest in the wedding cake (I wasn't the least bit, much less vestedly, interested in the wedding cake), and asked Fringe Elvis if she'd mind allowing her access to my elevator. Fringe Elvis complied. No, Birdy didn't catch Safety Officer Fringe Elvis's name. Yes, she told Fringe Elvis everything. Every detail. The blue bag, the five million dollars, the black spinner 516.035 suitcase, Gold Lamé Elvis, vault guard suited Elvii, the stingrays, Mr. and Mrs. Elvis and their missing silver-studded belt, Red Bikini Elvis delivering warm Zest for Life cafeteria milk, Pat Sajak, Mortimer, waking in upended Lost and Found, and the cake! The wedding cake!

I showed her the magazine letter note delivered to my door that morning. I gently explained it indicated she'd been abducted from Zest for Life. I asked if she remembered anything. Anything at all. She remembered bits and pieces—riding in a black car, riding in a Bellissimo freight elevator, lying down on a bed of Lost and Found articles of clothing she made for herself from 827.168. And that was all she could remember. Then she asked how it happened. I explained her warm milk had most likely been spiked. She asked why someone would do that. I gave her the obvious answer she should have reached on her own: the person behind the note, her abduction, and the spiked milk needed Birdy to enter Lost and Found. She asked why. I told her because the person, who was obviously looking for something, couldn't get in the door without her. She asked what they were looking for. I told her they were probably looking for the five million dollars. She asked how anyone could have possibly known about the five million dollars. I didn't even halfway bother answering. She asked if that person had made the big Lost and Found mess. I said probably. She studied the note at length, then asked if that person had seen her in her nightgown. "I assume so, Birdy." She asked about Mortimer.

Had anyone checked on Mortimer? Did that person also sedate and abduct Mortimer? I told her I felt certain Mortimer was safe and sound at Zest for Life, then promised her I'd call.

I passed her a magnifying glass and a copy of the Incident Report she'd filed Saturday morning. I asked her to translate the shorthand for me. She couldn't. The magnifying glass made her Birdynotes too big. She needed her glasses.

I took a deep breath and asked if she thought it was possible that Gold Lamé, Red Bikini, and Fringe Elvis were all the same woman. Birdy said no, because one had gold hair, one had dark hair, and one had dusty blonde hair. I asked if, hair color aside, the three women had any other similar physical characteristics: age, height, weight, eye color, scars, tattoos, voice, mannerisms. She said no, not that she noticed, and besides, she said, the three Elvii couldn't be the same woman because she didn't think it was possible for one woman to work for Room Service *and* Security at the Bellissimo, and at the same time, work for Cafeteria Delivery at Zest for Life.

I, on the other hand, thought it was entirely possible. All the way to probable. And I thought her name was Megan Shaw. Miss Casino Credit Cashier Harrah's-Vegas-Does-It-All-The-Time Megan Shaw. Who knew about the money first. It seemed obvious to me Megan had stolen, then lost or misplaced the five million, and spent the rest of the night trying to find it.

I was hoarse from raising my voice for so long, because not only could Birdy not see without her glasses, she couldn't hear without her hearing aid, but before I let her go, I managed to choke out, "Is that all, Birdy? Is there anything else? Do you want to tell me anything else at all?"

"Well, one more thing."

I leaned in.

"I need to ask you something, Davis."

I nodded. Go ahead.

And that was when, in all seriousness, she asked if Elvis

was performing at the Bellissimo. She, her sister, Constance, and her nephew, Malcolm, had seen him two years earlier in 1975 at the Hilton Hotel in Las Vegas. If Elvis was at the Bellissimo, did I have tickets? He was, like her, a Capricorn. Did I, by any chance, have an extra ticket? Was there the slightest chance I had two tickets? Because she knew for a fact her nephew would love to see The King again too. If I didn't have two tickets, could she buy two tickets?

I told her I'd check.

By the time I'd finished with Birdy, it was far too late in the day to make a mad dash for my husband—clearly, I should have left the minute it crossed my mind—but I wasn't opposed to Plan B, in which I gathered my daughters and my dog and locked myself in my bedroom again until he came home at the end of the week. It was too much. I'd been the acting Director of the Bellissimo for a day. One little day. It had nothing to do with believing in myself or my ability to do my job. It had everything to do with the fact that Birdy James had told everyone who'd listen about the money, almost all of them Elvii, plus Mrs. Elvii, and even Robbie, her Zest for Life minibus driver. All said, I had a small village of people who knew about the money, and if even one or two of those people told anyone else, the number of people who knew five million dollars was rolling around the property in a black spinner suitcase was the size of a small city. I was on the verge of a sudden onset panic attack when a tap on the office door brought me back around.

It could be a break in my five-million-dollar case.

Someone with news of the money.

It wasn't.

The door cracked open and my mother peeked in, without money news, but with dinner news. "Davis, I have some nice, thick, fried pork chops, potatoes and gravy, sliced cantaloupe, fried okra, a pan of biscuits, and a chocolate cobbler with vanilla ice cream. Come on and eat."

Bea Crawford, who shouldn't have even been there, squeezed her head in above Mother's. All I could really see was her bulbous red nose and her thin white lips. "Say, Davis. Can you call somebody at your beauty parlor downstairs and have them come up here after dinner and give me a good feet rub? With Mentholatum?"

To my mother, I said, "That sounds wonderful. Thank you."

To Bea Crawford, I said, "No."

* * *

At dinner, Birdy squinted across the table at Bea Crawford. "Now, who are you?"

Bea stopped gnawing on a pork chop bone long enough to pull it from her mouth and aim it at me. "She married my son." Pork chop bone back where it belonged, she spoke over, under, and around it, "Twice."

"Oh, that's nice." Birdy turned to me. "So, this is your sweet husband's mother?"

"No," I said. "No, no, and no."

Quinn whispered in Bex's ear. Bex nodded, then announced, "Banana Nana Bea Bea is Uncle Eddie's mommy."

"Bex? Quinn?" I held my mortification in check. "Eddie is not your uncle."

"Who is Eddie?" Birdy asked.

"Oh, that's a long story," Mother said. "You want more gravy, Birdy?"

Bea shot her free hand in the air, the one not attached to the pork chop bone, flagging down the gravy.

"Then who is this large woman?" Birdy asked me. "And why is she here?"

Good question.

* * *

After dinner, and after I tucked my girls in for the night, I went straight to my office. I made good on my promise to Birdy and called Zest for Life to check on her cat.

"Zesty good evening! How may I zestily help you?"

I didn't know how to return the greeting.

"My name is Davis Way Cole," I said. "I'm with the Bellissimo Resort and Casino. I'm calling about our employee, a resident there, Birdy James, who is on vacation. She asked me to check on her cat. Mortimer."

"Oh."

All zestiness gone.

"Mortimer." She said it with even less zest. "So sad."

I braced myself.

"They say he'll be fine. Eventually."

Then it was my turn. "Oh?"

"He's at PawPaw's," the Zest woman said.

"Excuse me?"

"The pet hospital?"

I'd never heard of it. "What happened to him?"

"He got drunk, fell off the top of Birdy's refrigerator, and broke his nose."

Were we still talking about a cat?

"He landed on his nose," she explained.

Obviously.

"That's how it broke," she added.

You don't say.

"Do you know how we can get in touch with Birdy?" she asked. "They want to know how the cat got so drunk and they want her to pick him up tomorrow."

I told her I'd take care of it.

"The bill is fourteen hundred dollars."

"How much?" Surely, I misunderstood her.

"Fourteen hundred dollars."

"For what?" I asked. "Did the cat have a nose transplant?"

"I don't know for sure," Zesty said. "I think most of the charges were for the IVs they gave him to sober him up, but those didn't really work, because for one thing, they said whatever Birdy let him drink was stronger than their IVs, and would probably be in his system for at least another week, and worse than that, he had an allergic reaction to the IVs and wouldn't stop chasing his tail, so they gave him allergy medicine for the allergic reaction and the allergy medicine made him sneeze, which I thought was weird, because allergy medicine is supposed to make you *not* sneeze, so they had to give him a different allergy medicine, which made him sneeze even more, and they think he's all the way around allergic to allergy medicine, because last I heard he was still drunk and still sneezing, but he can't really sneeze with his nose broken, and to beat it all, turns out Mortimer is a girl. Past that, you'll have to talk to PawPaw's."

That was way more than enough information, and again, I told her I'd take care of it.

Then I took care of Megan Marie Shaw.

I was on my computer until midnight.

Megan Shaw never worked for Harrah's Vegas in any capacity, much less accounting. There was no record of Megan Marie Shaw having ever lived or worked in Las Vegas. I couldn't find any evidence to suggest Megan Marie Shaw ever set foot in Las Vegas.

Megan was twenty-four years old, the single mother of a one-year-old little boy, Oliver, and other than her baby, she only had one other living relative, her mother, Louise Juliette Shaw. Louise lived at The Clare Estate on Knollwood Drive in Mobile, Alabama, sixty miles and one state line east of Biloxi. She'd lived there seven years. The Clare Estate was a memory care facility.

I turned away from the screen and gave myself a minute.

When I could face Megan Shaw's life again, I hacked into Louise Juliette Shaw's patient records at Clare Estate and found

Megan listed as Louise's Guardian. Louise's condition was categorized as "very severely declined dementia." Her room and board at Clare Estate was $5,500. A month. And that was before additional charges for medical and therapy procedures that Medicaid and insurance, of which there was very little, didn't cover.

Megan lived around the corner from Clare Estate in an efficiency apartment with a one-year-old and a two-hour round-trip commute to her new Bellissimo job. Her rent was $499 a month for nine hundred square feet of living space in a thirty-three-year-old apartment complex. She drove a 2007 GMC Yukon with 260,000 miles on it. For the past six years, since graduating from W. P. Davidson High School, Megan had been a bank teller at BB&T, Branch Banking & Trust, on Hillcrest Road, where she'd apparently learned to misdirect money.

I searched for and studied Megan's Bellissimo Human Resource file. She was a pretty girl: fresh-faced, innocent, with a shy smile that didn't match her hollow eyes. Her entry-level salary was twenty dollars an hour.

Not nearly enough.

With a very heavy heart, I switched to surveillance and tracked Megan through her last day at work. I pulled video from Friday when she clocked in and checked her baby boy into Play, then zipped through the video feed aimed at the Casino Credit door for the rest of Megan's shift until midnight. She walked out of Casino Credit with her purse on her left arm and a big blue Bellissimo duffel bag from Love on her right.

I watched her walk the long hall from Casino Credit, past Accounting, past Audit, past Compliance, past Gaming, past the Director of Slot Operation's office, past the Director of Table Game's office, through the casino and up one floor to the executive offices, where she coded herself into the door of Special Events.

That woke me up.

How did Megan Shaw have access to the Special Events office? And what business did she have in Special Events, which was nothing more than a dressing room?

Megan cracked the door, took a deep breath, then looked up.

For guidance?

For inspiration?

In celebration?

I couldn't see her facial features, but I could see the slump of her shoulders, her defeated posture from behind, but that didn't mean a thing. Given what I'd learned about Megan's life had totally defeated me. I could only imagine what it felt like to live it.

She hiked the heavy duffel bag from Love on her shoulder, then pushed through the door where I lost her. There was no surveillance inside. Seven minutes later, Megan exited Special Events with a different bag, what might have been a backpack: smaller, still blue, but a different bag. Which meant Megan had hidden the money in Special Events or dropped it off for an accomplice to pick up. Either way, it looked like Megan wasn't acting alone. And I didn't like the implications of who she was acting with at all.

At ALL.

I followed her down the hall, into the elevator, then picked her up again stepping into the Bellissimo lobby where she was swallowed by late-night Elvii. I painstakingly followed her as she took the most indirect path she could to the basement and stepped into the dark hall that led to Lost and Found, where I lost her for good. Searching high and low, I couldn't find another trace of Megan Shaw in our system. She'd disappeared. It was as if Megan Shaw left the hall that led to Lost and Found by magic carpet, wearing an invisibility cloak, or she hadn't left at all. I set up system-wide alerts asking various Bellissimo identification programs to notify me immediately should she reappear and blasted out a Security BOLO—be on the lookout. Then I shut down my computer because I just couldn't take anymore. The end of my road looked clear: I'd have to arrest and help prosecute a young woman upon whom two other humans were completely and helplessly dependent. But first, I'd have to find her.

I flipped off lights on my way through the house, checked on sleeping Bex, Quinn, and Candy, then walked the guest hall like I was walking the green mile. I tiptoed in and sat on the edge of my mother's bed.

"What is it, honey?"

She wore a bonnet of pink sponge rollers.

"Can you help me find something for Birdy to wear?"

SEVEN

It wasn't that my daughter Quinn couldn't talk, it was that she wouldn't talk. She let her sister do the talking for her. Quinn was more than happy to supply Bex with whispered ideas from behind her little cupped hand, like let's climb the kitchen cabinets and make chocolate milk, and Bex was more than happy to take Quinn's ideas and run with them. (Like, let's climb the kitchen cabinets and make chocolate cupcakes.) We knew Quinn was vocal—we could hear her whispering to her sister and to Candy—and we knew her vocabulary was as large, if not larger, than Bex's, because for one, she did so much listening, and for another, she'd aced every cognitive and comprehension test every pediatric speech pathologist could give her.

Speech processing and auditory conditions were ruled out early; Quinn did not have dysarthria, disfluency, or an expressive language disorder. But still, she'd stopped speaking aloud. Even to me and Bradley. At the midway point between their first and second birthdays, Quinn turned the talking over to Bexley. Before, she'd repeated everything Bex said, never initiating speech, but she would repeat it. After, she kept quiet. The best the many specialists could do was, "It must be a twin thing." Quinn was adorable, happy, healthy, a good girl, she understood every word we said to her, and she was completely expressive in every single other way except verbally. So Monday morning, at eight o'clock Central, which was nine tiny hours from three o'clock Pacific, with five million dollars still missing and Casino Credit Cashier Megan Shaw completely in the wind, I called for a ride to Quinn's standing, weekly, speech-language therapy appointment.

My daughters were worth more to me than five million dollars.

My daughters were worth more to me than my quarter-time job.

My husband would call when he woke in Vegas to hear how Quinn's session went.

(My motivation for stopping everything for Quinn's speech-language appointment.)

(In no particular order.)

My cell phone rang in my purse as soon as we stepped into the elevator. A chill ran through me—surely it wasn't Bradley calling already—but dissipated quickly, because for one, it was so hot out, the only way to stay chilled would be to climb into a freezer, and for two, it wasn't Bradley at all. It was Fantasy.

"Well?" Her hello.

"Nope." My hello. "Big fat nothing."

Bex and Quinn, on either side of me, jumped (and jumped, and jumped), trying to catch that fleeting feeling of elevator weightlessness.

"How early did you get up?" she asked.

"Too early."

"When did you go to bed last night?"

"I'm not sure I did."

"So you and Bird Woman were in Lost and Found all night?"

"Not so much."

"Were her glasses in her desk? Did she read her Birdynote? What did it say?"

"I don't know, Fantasy. No one knows. We may never

know."

"What does that mean? Her desk was gone?"

"I have no idea if her desk is there or not," I said. "Things didn't go exactly as planned."

"When do things ever go as planned?"

She made a good point.

"I thought the plan was to sneak Bird Woman to Lost and Found for her spare eyeglasses so she could read her own Birdyhand business," she said. "What happened?"

I tucked my phone between my ear and shoulder and held two little girl hands as we exited one elevator to somewhere between twenty and ninety Elvii at eight o'clock in the morning, only to take two steps forward and call another elevator. "That was the plan," I said, "but I had to find a portable sewing machine first."

"Portable as opposed to what?" she asked. "Mounted? What did you need with a portable sewing machine?"

New elevator, more jumping from Bex and Quinn.

"I had to come up with something for Birdy to wear," I said. "I couldn't parade her through the Bellissimo in her nightgown. She's half my mother's size, she's one one-hundredth Bea's size, and my clothes are five decades too young for her. There's an Elvii out there looking for her, and I couldn't risk anyone recognizing her."

That's when I remembered I had to push a button on the elevator panel or I'd risk my daughters jumping in a motionless elevator all day. I pushed the button. The elevator whirred to life.

Jump, jump, jump.

"And just where was it you found a moveable sewing machine in the middle of the night?" Fantasy asked.

"Portable. And in the theater costume room."

"And what did you do with your portable sewing machine?" she asked. "Ported it, I assume."

"I didn't do a thing with it. My mother sewed Birdy an Elvis suit from a pair of white leggings I had to buy from Bea—"

"Wait a minute," she interrupted. "Bea charged you for leggings? She should pay you to burn them. If there was ever a human who doesn't need to be seen in public, or in private, for that matter, wearing leggings, it's Bea Crawford. I can't believe they even make leggings in Bea's size. And if she wears the flesh-colored leggings again, I'm going to have her arrested for indecent exposure. Just how much did Bea charge you for a pair of her two-dollar leggings?"

"Fifty dollars. She claimed they were her fancy dress-up leggings."

The second set of elevator doors opened. I asked Fantasy to hold a minute while the girls and I stepped out of the private lobby and through the private entrance to a hot June morning and a waiting car. My driver, Crisp, and I smiled hello. Bex and Quinn ran to him, held out a chubby hand each, then antsily waited as he carefully checked his pants pockets, then his hat, then under his shoes, then his shadow, then the pockets of his blazer, where he finally found two shiny quarters. He placed one on each outstretched hand and was rewarded with little girl curtsies.

We climbed in.

(I could drive. But for security reasons after Bex and Quinn were born, Crisp did all my driving.) (Plus, I didn't have a car.) (Which was another reason Crisp drove us around.)

Crisp caught Quinn's eye in the rearview mirror. "Is Miss Q ready to talk Dr. Tyler's ears off?"

Always good for Monday morning giggles.

I buckled my little gigglers into their booster seats, then it was back to the phone, where Fantasy had been holding for the entire find-the-quarters routine. "Where was I?"

"Bea's fancy leggings."

Right. "Mother made the entire Elvis jumpsuit for Birdy

from one leg of Bea's fifty-dollar leggings," I said. "Then she hot-glued costume jewelry to it and dyed Birdy's wig Elvis black."

"Where'd she find black dye in the middle of the night?"

"She busted a Sharpie."

"Did anyone at your house sleep last night?"

"Bea and Birdy."

"Figures," she said. "So your mother sewed Bird Woman a new Elvis suit, then you took her to Lost and Found. How'd it go?"

"It didn't."

"What?"

"By the time Mother finished sewing, I couldn't wake Birdy."

"Why didn't you go alone?" she asked. "Come to think of it, in the first place?"

"What do you mean?"

"I mean," she said, "why didn't you go to Lost and Found without Bird Woman and get her glasses?"

"Because I couldn't get in the door," I said. "Birdy's the only person with the keypad combination to unlock the door."

"I keep forgetting that."

"It's certainly why she was abducted. Someone wanted in and she's the only way."

Crisp tried to act like he wasn't listening.

I knew for a fact he'd heard worse.

"What do we think the someone who wanted in was looking for?" she asked. "The money?"

"I'm assuming," I said, "but I don't think they found it."

"If that's the case, we need to shoot our way in and get this over with."

"We might as well tell Baylor first," I said, "because someone from Waste Management or Maintenance will hear us and report it. Then we'll have Baylor hounding us."

"He's already hounding us," she said. "We're scheduled to

work the Elvis slot tournament this afternoon. Dressed as Elvises."

"Elvii, Fantasy."

"Elvii sounds stupid, Davis. Stop saying it. My point is, where are our Elvis costumes?"

"Didn't you pick them up?"

"From where?" she asked.

"From wherever you ordered them."

"I didn't order them. I thought you were ordering them."

Problem One Thousand. No Elvis costumes.

"Let's do this," she said. "Shoot our way into Lost and Found, find the money, wire it to San Francisco, then go get Elvis suits. That's what we need to do."

"Seattle." We were at a red light. "We need to wire the money to Seattle." Which was when I noticed what I needed to do was switch Bex and Quinn's shoes. They'd traded shoes after I dressed them. A trick they loved to pull on me. They were wearing red gingham sundresses with red butterfly sandals, with Bex wearing two left sandals and Quinn two right.

"And I don't know for sure the money's in Lost and Found, Fantasy. I said there's a possibility it could be there." I had a lap full of butterfly sandal possibilities. "Like a fifty-fifty chance."

"If it's not there, where is it?"

"Long gone with the Casino Credit cashier."

"Do we have a lead on her?"

"Not so much," I said.

"So we're nowhere."

I was nowhere. With the butterfly sandals. Between talking to Fantasy and trying to switch the girls' shoes in the backseat of a moving car, I wound up with Bex wearing two right sandals and Quinn wearing two left. Which they thought was hilarious. "Not exactly nowhere." It wasn't the time or place to explain Megan Shaw's impossible life, or what I'd painstakingly dragged out of Birdy before pork chops. Then I painstakingly got the correct sandals on the correct feet of the correct child. "The truth is, Fantasy, the money could be anywhere. Reading between the Birdylines, it sounds like the money chain of custody was broken at some point. I feel certain Birdy knows something useful, but I can't get it out of her. We have one last chance with the Birdynote she scribbled on her Incident Report, and if we can't get her to decipher it this morning, we'll have no choice but to bust into Lost and Found."

"This is the worst," Fantasy said. "The absolute worst. If we could slow down enough to break into her Zest apartment, which would surely be easier than breaking into Lost and Found, we could get her glasses. Then she could read her Birdynote and stop running into the walls. If we could find her hearing aid, we could stick it in her ear. Then we could stop screaming at her. We have to find an easier way to communicate with Bird Woman. When I tried to talk to her yesterday, I didn't get the feeling it was registering with her that we'd lost five million dollars. Or that she'd mishandled five million dollars. For some reason, she kept talking about cake. Every question I asked, I got a wedding cake answer. Bottom line, Davis, Bird Woman isn't worried about the five million dollars. She's worried about cake, her cat, and her glasses."

"We have glasses," I said.

"You just said you didn't go to Lost and Found."

"But I did go to Walmart."

"In the middle of the night?"

"Yes."

"How'd you get there?"

"Bellissimo limo."

"What'd you buy?"

"Five-hundred-dollar hearing aids and reading glasses in every strength I could find."

"Okay," she said. "Now we're getting somewhere. What'd the note say?"

"I have no idea. I couldn't wake her up. I fed her ginger tea earlier to wake her up and when the caffeine from it wore off, she crashed. Or maybe she was tired from all the excitement. I tried again fifteen minutes ago and got nowhere. She can't hear me calling her name because the five-hundred-dollar hearing aids are still charging, and I've shaken her to the point of rattling her bones. She sleeps like Rip Van Winkle."

"So we're nowhere."

"Not nowhere," I said. "I found her cat."

"Does the cat happen to know where the money is?"

"Pick it up on your way into work and we'll ask it."

"Pick it up? Where is it?"

"At PawPaw's."

"Who's?"

"It's a cat hospital on Iberville Drive. Swing by and pick it up on your way in."

"You want me to pick up a cat?" she asked. "We have no money, no leads, no Elvis suits, and I have to pick up a *cat*?"

By then, we were pulling into a parking space at Pediatric Speech-Language Pathology on Courthouse Boulevard. "We have leads," I said. "I'll tell you all about them after Quinn's appointment."

"Give me the headlines," she said.

"I will," I said. "After you pick up the cat."

"And do what with it? Take it to your house?"

"What am I supposed to do with a cat?" I asked. "I already have a dog."

"So do what with the cat?"

"First, make sure it looks like a cat."

"As opposed to a what?"

I had no idea what the hungover cat with a broken nose might look like. "I'll tell you what," I said, "take him to our office. I'll meet you there."

"Our office-office?"

"Would you rather try to work at my house?"

"Oh, hell, no."

I didn't think so. "I'll drop off the girls to stay with Mother until July picks them up and check on Birdy while I'm there. Hopefully I can catch her awake so she can decipher her scribbling and/or give me the keypad combination to Lost and Found, then I'll meet you in the office-office."

"What time?" she asked.

"Ten. Ish."

"Sounds good," she said. "One last question. What's going on with the tomatoes?"

"I'm about to kill one of the tomato farmers with my bare hands."

I said it just as I stepped up to the receptionist's desk.

The receptionist stopped typing, her fingers frozen over her keyboard.

I told Fantasy I'd see her soon and hung up.

I smiled at the receptionist.

Who tried to smile back.

Fifty minutes later, Bexley on my lap, only-child snuggling the entire time, and after Dr. Tyler's apologetic smile—always the same, conveying sympathy, frustration, and a sliver of let's-not-give-up hope, which was his way of letting me know my daughter hadn't spoken a single word aloud during her session—it was nine o'clock in the morning Central, seven o'clock in the morning Pacific, and I was only certain about one thing: I should have listened to No Hair. I remembered his Lost and Found words of warning very clearly: "Something's going to happen Old Bird can't handle, and it will be on you."

I felt it on me.

I felt it.

Then I gathered my quiet Quinny in my arms and all I felt was her.

* * *

The temperature had climbed to ninety-six degrees by the time we returned to the Bellissimo. Opening the car door was like opening the oven. The sun, barely up in the sky, was boiling. The glare from it, bouncing indiscriminately from one object to the next, then back again, was blinding, and the heat was nothing compared to what I found when I checked the messages that had parked on my phone in one short hour.

From Bradley: *Give me a call after Quinn's appointment.*

From Bradley's Personal Assistant, Colleen: *Housekeeping needs in Lost and Found.* And *Need casino verification on a Dragon Links jackpot in High Stakes.* And *Vault requesting permission to dispose of molding cake.* And *VIP needs in Lost and Found.* And *Elvis Tribute Concert scheduled for tomorrow night (Blue Suede Shoes) oversold by 280 seats.* And *Casino Services needs in Lost and Found.* And *All parking garages at maximum capacity. What to do with incoming guest vehicles?* And *Smoke alarm malfunction on fifteenth floor of the hotel tower. Guests evacuated for systems check. Need authorization to credit all rooms.* And *Casino Operations needs in Lost and Found.* And *Rumors of kitchen walkout at Chops tonight if Wagyu beef not replaced after chocolate mint contamination of yesterday's shipment mistakenly delivered and temporarily stored in the chocolate mint ice cream freezer at Scoops.* And *Guest Services needs in Lost and Found.* And *Trouble reported with the ovens at Danish.*

Just what I needed. More trouble.

From Baylor: *Where are you?* And *Where are you?* And a third *Where are you?*

The elevator doors parted, and my home, such as it was, was in sight. "Who wants to watch *Frozen* with Nana?"

Everyone wanted to watch *Frozen* with Nana. Including me.

We stepped into a foyer full of living room furniture.

The mud carpet.

In all the pandemonium, I'd forgotten.

I struck out with Birdy, who was still asleep, and decided I'd wasted enough time waiting on her to wake up. I asked Bex and Quinn to be good girls for Nana, telling all three I'd see them in a few hours. I called out goodbye one last time, then opened and closed the front door as if I'd left. I slipped off my shoes, hugged walls, ducked behind doors, and sneaked all the way past Bex and Quinn's playroom, where *Frozen* was already on, past carpet people in the living room, through the kitchen and to my office without anyone knowing I was still there. My first real victory of the day. I opened my office door quietly, slipped in, then closed it even more quietly. I sat on the edge of my chair, my purse still on my arm, and logged on to my laptop. After checking the security alerts I'd set up on Casino Credit Cashier Megan Shaw—nothing, no hits—I opened the Bellissimo personnel database to quickly pull every bit of information about Birdy James and Lost and Found I could find. I'd make it the first stop on my way to the office to meet Fantasy.

For one, according to Colleen, everyone in the building needed in.

For two, if the five million dollars was still there, it wouldn't be there long.

I scanned the Birdy info on the screen for common password criteria: her birthday, her Zest for Life apartment unit number, the first four digits of her Social Security Number, the last four digits of her Social Security Number, the year she was born. (Not that it would be right on our records, since Birdy probably had no idea.) If nothing worked, I'd do it Fantasy's way; I'd shoot my way in. I was jotting the last numerical note, about to make my escape, when my phone rang. I'd made every move so stealthily, and all for naught, because my phone sounded like a fire drill. After all the trouble I'd gone to, I'd forgotten to mute my phone. My heart sank to the floor when I saw who it was. I took a deep breath. I answered. “Why didn’t you tell me Bianca was coming home, Bradley?”

EIGHT

Because he didn't think I'd want to know.

And he was right.

I didn't want to know.

He asked about Quinn's speech therapy. I answered truthfully. He asked about the Double Trouble convention. Again, I told the truth, adding I had no idea the convention was so large. He pointed out we knew months ago we'd be at full capacity. I told him the convention had spilled out of the Bellissimo and through the streets of Biloxi. It wasn't just us on an Elvis bender. It was all of Biloxi. Then I asked if he thought the plural of Elvis was Elvises or Elvii. He said he didn't know. I asked if he thought Elvii sounded stupid. He said he'd get back to me on that. Then he said he'd received a text message weather alert predicting record-breaking heat in Biloxi for the entire week. We marveled at the fact that it was cooler in Vegas than it was in Biloxi. By then, he needed to go. He was meeting No Hair and Mr. Sanders for breakfast at The Venetian's Bouchon Bistro. Then before we said our I-love-yous and goodbyes, he asked if anything else was going on. That was when I lied through my teeth. "Nothing."

When the truth was everything.

After assuring my husband all was well—no mention of wedding cake, millions of missing dollars, or new carpet in our living room—I had to talk myself down from the ledge our conversation left me on. I hadn't lied to him so much as I'd withheld information. (Wedding cake, millions of missing dollars, new carpet.) Much like he'd withheld information from me. (Bianca Sanders was back in town.) If it got right down to it, I'd say to him what he'd just said to me: I didn't think he'd want to know.

By the time I'd finished not telling him what I didn't think he'd want to know, it was ten o'clock. Eastern. I paused for just a second before I made my escape to do a little math. Ten in the morning Central was eight in the morning Pacific. Seattle was barely awake. At two that afternoon, Megan Shaw, single mother of one-year-old Oliver and guardian of ailing mother Louise, probably wouldn't clock in.

That gave me four hours.

Megan's supervisor, Gray Donaldson, wouldn't notice until two fifteen.

She'd stop what she was doing and try to locate Megan, who I had a feeling she wouldn't find. In fact, I had a feeling we'd seen the very last of Megan Shaw we'd ever see.

At two thirty, Gray Donaldson would take the five-million-dollar wheel.

That gave me four and a half hours.

Gray's first order of business would be to requisition the cash Megan sent to the vault Friday night so she could prepare the wire for transfer to the title company in Seattle at three Pacific. She'd call Vault and ask for the money. They'd say they didn't have it. She'd assure them they did. It would take Vault an hour to pore over their paperwork, then turn the vault upside down, before breaking the news to Gray they still didn't have the money.

That gave me five and a half hours.

Next, Gray Donaldson would scramble. She'd dodge Philly bank calls, because by then, Philly would have realized their five-million-dollar wire had misfired. Surely dodging phone calls would take an additional hour. I could dodge phone calls for days. Case in point, while I'd been hiding in my office, I'd dodged two from Baylor and three from July. Then I dodged Baylor's text messages. *ANSWER YOUR PHONE.* And *I need help with Clone and I need it right now.* And *Who just used my Bellissimo debit card to pay a $1400 bill at a cat hospital?*

The nerve of him. Clone was not my responsibility, not my employee, and not my problem. In fact, she was persona non grata to me, and I'd help with her exactly never.

What was I up to? Six hours? Six and a half hours?

I might have an additional half hour, which would give me seven, during which Gray Donaldson processed the cold hard truth—the money was gone—and worked up the nerve to tell me. I stared at my phone, knowing it wouldn't be long enough, but hopefully at least seven hours, before she called with, "Davis, we have a problem."

All I had to do was find the money in the next seven hours.

Piece of cake.

And I wasn't talking about moldy wedding cake.

I checked the time. Just after ten. I had just enough time to bust into Lost and Found before I hightailed it to the office to meet Fantasy. I stuffed the piece of paper I'd jotted Birdy numbers on in my pocket, stood to leave again, then sat back down hard. It was the moment I realized I'd never find the money in time. I'd spent so much time figuring out how much time I did and didn't have that I ran out of time altogether, because just then I heard the banging of pots and pans, and it wasn't my daughters playing kitchen. It was my mother on the other side of my office door. And she wasn't playing. She was dead serious. I was trapped in my office, unless I wanted to run into my mother and explain why I was still there, and running into Mother would mean food, because my mother was no doubt preparing lunch. At ten in the morning. She'd insist I eat. Food was her Love Language. To not eat what she lovingly prepared was the same as saying, "Sorry, Mother, I don't love you." The problem was, she insisted on showing her love all day every day.

Mother's life was a never-ending buffet, meals piling on top of each other, the cleanup from one ending ten minutes before the prep for the next began, which was part of the lifelong bond between Mother and Bea, because food was Bea Crawford's Love Language too. (But from a different perspective.) Bea loved nothing better than a buffet, and to be with my mother was to have a seat at her never-ending buffet.

I eyed my office window. I could raise it, climb out to the kitchen porch, which led to the balcony patio, then sneak through the front of the house and hopefully escape undetected.

It would work.

I'd had lots of practice as a teenager.

I gathered my things, turned for the window, then, like a nightmare, Bea Crawford appeared. The minute I devised an alternate escape route, it was blocked too, by, of all people, Bea, who shouldn't have even been there. That woman had been in my way my entire life. Mother was blocking one of my exits banging pots and pans and Bea was blocking the other tending tomatoes, wearing an ill-fitting pea-green sports bra over what she called farmer shorts and what I called an atrocity. A sin against nature. A tragedy. Bea wasn't a small woman. I only knew one person larger than Bea, and that was my boss, No Hair. So not only was Bea not a small woman, she wasn't a small human. She came that way. She was probably a twenty-five-pound newborn. I clearly remember the first time I saw my mother's second grade class picture when I was a little girl, flipping through old photo albums, landing on the black-and-white photo with somber children's faces near the top and a line of scuffed saddle shoes near the bottom, then asking Mother why there was a man in her second grade class. I could see the teacher, her cat-eye glasses covering half her face, holding a terrifying wooden paddle brandishing the words "Mrs. Hitt's 2nd Grade Class, Pine Apple Primary School," and standing next to her, shoulder to shoulder, what looked like an angry man child.

"That's Bea, Davis. You know Bea." Bea Crawford kept growing even after second grade. And growing. And growing. A few years earlier, she'd cleaned her act up and lost a ton of weight. More than a hundred pounds. (And discovered sports bras, bicycle shorts, and athletic tights, which eventually led to her discovery of leggings.) It was right around the time her four-decade-long marriage ended (to the relief of everyone, especially her husband), but after her initial burst of divorcée energy, Bea realized being single and skinny wasn't all it was cracked up to be. She turned to her lifelong friend Caroline Way (my mother) for comfort. Meatloaf, mac and cheese, and Mississippi Mud Pie comfort. Bea gained every ounce and more back in a tenth of the time it took to take it off. And that was when she fell in love with leggings. They grew with her. She declared herself done with men and done with zippers. At almost sixty years old, Bea was a perfect specimen of poor health and questionable hygiene, and she was on my kitchen porch, wearing what she called her farmer shorts, which were nothing more than sawed-off leggings. Cutoff denim jeans had the structure and stamina to do the job of shorts. The flimsy synthetic fabric of Bea's leggings did not. They had nothing to hold them down. They wouldn't stay in place. The thin hacked nylon rolled and climbed the girth of Bea's snow-white thunder thighs. I flattened myself against the wall beside the window, peeking, catching glimpses of her roaming past the patio widow in her pale pink chopped-off leggings with the rolling problems. When Bea wasn't dragging the tomato buckets, talking to the tomatoes, singing to the tomatoes, watering the tomatoes, watering herself, or marking miniscule tomato stalk growth on wooden paint sticks, she was desperately trying to manipulate her shorts, I suppose out of fear they'd roll all the way to her throat and strangle her. How my mother could even think about food with Bea on the other side of the French doors, wide-legged, stooped over, and digging for rolled-farmer-shorts gold, was beyond me. And if I intended to find five million dollars before three o'clock Pacific, I needed to find a way to sneak past them both.

I was studying the ceiling, thinking about cobwebs and crawlspace when it no longer mattered. My cover was blown. My office door burst open, Fantasy filled the space, then yelled over her shoulder, "Call off the dogs. I found her."

I heard Bea through the pane of glass that separated us. "Good." Then she tipped her head back and yelled, "I got a bone to pick with you, Davis."

My mother poked her head in my office. "Well, aren't you the quiet mouse today. I didn't even know you were back. Are you two about ready for lunch?"

I grabbed my phone, my purse, and my partner (by the ear), then flew out before Mother could feed me. "We can't."

"Why not?"

"Mother, we have to go to the office. Call me if you need me."

By then, Bea was sweating a puddle on my kitchen floor. "I could eat."

Fantasy froze in her tracks, trying to decide what Bea was wearing, or if Bea was wearing anything at all under her skimpy sports bra. I grabbed her by the other ear and we made a run for it, but stopped cold when we got to Birdy in the living room. Sleeping in her wingback chair. Beside her chair, a plastic crate. On top of the plastic crate, my dog. Inside the plastic crate, mortar fire.

I turned to Fantasy.

"It's the cat," she said.

"You were supposed to take the cat to our office."

She pointed. "Listen to it. How are we supposed to work, as loud as that cat is?"

"What's wrong with it?"

"It can't stop sneezing."

"That's not sneezing, Fantasy."

"Its nose is broken."

Curious Candy pawed at the crate. "Candy," I loud whispered. "Get down."

Candy would not get down. She was too interested in the lawnmower backfire noises coming from the crate. We stared at the dog on the cat crate for two more seconds, looked at each other, then flew.

Mother could handle it.

My mother, when it got right down to it, could handle anything.

We couldn't call the elevator fast enough.

"About the cat." Fantasy slumped against the elevator wall opposite the one I was slumped against, catching my breath. "The vet said if the cat comes back drunk again, they're calling Animal Services on Birdy."

"When we get to the office—" I was still trying to catch my breath "—let's stay."

"Forever," Fantasy said.

"But we need to try to bust into Lost and Found on our way to the office."

She patted the gun at her hip.

I pulled the Birdy note from my pocket and waved it at her.

"What's that?" she asked.

"A cheat sheet."

Neither worked.

When the elevator doors opened and we saw the long line of Elvii waiting at the Lost and Found door, we stayed put. "When does the next round of the slot tournament start?" I asked.

Fantasy checked her watch. "In forty-five minutes."

"We'll come back then."

"We're supposed to be working the next round of the slot tournament, Davis. Baylor will kill us."

"He'll get over it."

* * *

Our office was in the basement. The sub-basement, really. Two and a half levels below the sea, which made it two and a half levels below the casino, and it took three elevators to get there. Three elevators, a digital handprint, and a retina scan.

Our phones beeped on the same beat.

We didn't bother looking.

We knew exactly who it was.

She said, "One of us is going to have to answer."

"And say what?" I asked. "Hey, Baylor, we lost five million dollars? The minute he gets wind of our—" I searched for the right word "—predicament, he'll tell. He'll be on the phone with No Hair so fast, Mr. Sanders will have a fit, and Bradley will fly home and divorce me."

We turned the last corner. Our office door was in sight.

"Have you talked to him at all?" I asked.

"Bradley?"

"Baylor," I said.

"No. But I did shoot him a text to say I was at the dentist."

"We use the dentist excuse too much with him."

"That's what he said."

My phone buzzed in my pocket. Solo. So it probably wasn't Baylor for the four-hundredth time. It was a text message from my mother.

Great.

I stopped to read it. Fantasy stopped with me.

Bater is talling for you and cares neither a tabid bobby bare or a stunk in a gauge in your divvy doom.

"That dirty dog."

"Who?" Fantasy asked. "Which dirty dog? We know several dirty dogs."

"Baylor." I showed her my phone.

She zoomed in. "What does that even start to say?"

I read it to her. "Baylor is calling for you and there's either a rabid baby bear or a skunk in a cage in your living room."

She shook her head.

A photo dinged in. From my mother. Taken through the kitty carrier door.

I showed it to Fantasy.

"I know," she said. "I had to drive it around."

Its nose was crooked, leaning way left. Its face was swollen. Its mouth was wide open and its eyes looked like snake slits. With the fur on its face blown back, probably from the recoil of the revolutionary-war-cannon sneezing, it did look a little like a baby black bear. What passed through my mind wasn't that I had to share my home with a recuperating cat that sounded like fireworks exploding, in addition to my mother, Birdy James, my ex-ex-mother-in-law, who shouldn't have even been there, plus enough tomatoes to feed the world. What passed through my mind was how desperate Megan Shaw must have been to have done that to an innocent animal.

Poor cat.

I texted my mother back. *Mother, that's Birdy's cat. It needs some love. And it might be a good idea to put it in my bedroom and close the door so Bex and Quinn won't want to play with it. I don't think it feels well.*

She texted back: *I've had it with you two.*

Then Baylor texted: *I will crook it pish.*

The messages came in on top of each other and I may have mixed them up. Baylor was sick of us and my mother would cook pish for the cat.

Because all cats loved pish.

We finally made it to our office-office door. Which was just one of the reasons Fantasy and I worked so much from my home office, because it took forever and a day to get to our office-office. That, and because our office-office, much like everything else at the Bellissimo since the hurricane, wasn't quite what it used to be.

Fantasy showed the digital pad her eyeball.

I showed her my phone. "Baylor again."

Our office door clicked open just as she said, "If one of us doesn't call him back, he'll beat on your front door."

"My mother will answer."

"Or worse," she said, "Bea."

"No." We stepped in. "Way worse," I said. "Birdy might answer. Then we won't have to tell him something's up. He'll know."

"Birdy won't answer the door," Fantasy said as we stepped in. "She won't hear the doorbell."

That was when we heard the door. The groans and grinding gears of the office door behind us. Its lockdown feature had been engaged.

We made a U-turn and stared at it.

"Who locked the door?" She looked at me. "Did you lock the door?"

"No," I said. "Did you?"

"No."

We checked our phones. Neither of us had accidentally asked the door to lockdown, because it couldn't even happen accidentally. It took a ten-digit code. Had the door malfunctioned? I tried to open it. I couldn't. I showed it my retina. It didn't authorize me to leave. Fantasy, her hand not registering on the digital handprint screen, said, "What the—"

Our phones dinged on the same beat. It was Baylor. *You two stay put until I get there.*

"Who does he think he is?" she asked.

I took a right.

"When he gets here," she said, "we'll lock him up."

Over my shoulder, I said, "Then who'll work while we chase money?"

"Good point," she said. "And where are you going?"

"To Command Central."

"Why?"

"To reprogram the door. So we can get out before he gets in."

I had two degrees from the University of Alabama at Birmingham. One in Criminal Justice, the other in Computer Information Science. Both came in handy all the time. Like then, when I needed to hack through lockdown software.

"What do you want me to do while you open the door?" Fantasy asked.

"Clothes," I said while waking up my computer. "We need clothes and IDs."

"What kind of clothes?" she asked. "What kind of IDs?"

I ran through the list. "We know what happened in Casino Credit, so we'll skip it and hit the Vault first as Gaming auditors, so suits and Gaming IDs. Then we'll hit Room Service as Immigrations and Customs to see if we can track down Gold Lamé Elvis. So same suits, different IDs."

"Who is Gold Lamé Elvis?"

"We won't know until we get to Room Service."

"Why?" she asked. "This is Keystone Cops, Davis. Why are we doing this?"

"So we can find Megan Shaw and five million dollars."

"I thought the plan was to bust into Lost and Found."

"We can't bust into Lost and Found until the traffic dies down. Let's use the time between now and then wisely. We'll do flybys in the departments I think the money made stops in on our way to Lost and Found. By then, everyone will be at the slot tournament."

"Except not us," she said, "because we don't have Elvis costumes."

"We'll go in our suits," I said. "Find us follow-the-money-trail suits and they'll have to do."

"Okay," she said, "following-the-money-trail suits. Do you

want to follow the money as a blonde or a brunette?"

"See if you can find my chestnut brown ponytail wig," I said. "And anything but green contacts. I'm not in a green-eyed mood. I'm in a blue-eyed mood."

"Got it," she said. "Suits, IDs, ponytails, and blue contacts. I'll do my best. If you need me, I'll be in the closet."

* * *

Our office was comprised of three large rooms. First, and just inside the door I was attempting to open, the room we called our bullpen. It was our base of operation, our conference room, and often, our lunchroom. It had a kitchenette, a pedestal dining table with four leather chairs, two sofas, and a brand new 4D UHD HDR Smart TV, in front of which, Fantasy and I spent most of our office-office hours. On the sofas, actually, in front of the television, and for the most part, we watched the Hallmark Movies and Mysteries Channel.

Like I said, our new jobs were boring.

In addition to there being nothing interesting to do, because Baylor did everything interesting, we considered watching Hallmark mysteries continuing education. Research. On shrewd investigative procedure and clever apprehension techniques. We loved our Bravo time too, which we also considered research, because celebrities frequented the Bellissimo, and we needed to keep up. Baylor, who requisitioned our new office television (and swears he didn't) (actually, he didn't, but one thing Fantasy and I knew how to do, and we did it well, was stand our ground), and after a terrible chewing out from No Hair for requisitioning a new television when there was nothing wrong with the brand new guestroom television we had (except it was a preprogrammed Hospitality television, with restrictions I didn't want to spend a week of my life bypassing), told us to scoot over, because he had every right to watch the new television too. Since he'd apparently requisitioned it. While in a coma. The problem was Baylor watched sports. ESPN, and SOCCER, and BASKETBALL. Which forced me to reprogram our new television to permanently block all sports channels. What was he thinking? Watching pickleball tournaments when he was supposed to be working? And for all the trouble it was to hack our new television, I could have saved myself the time and trouble by hacking the Hospitality television in the first place.

To the right of the bullpen was Command Central, full of computers, video surveillance monitors, printers, and desks. The room was dark, cold, and it hummed. Command Central was where I generally did my best work. Like then, breaking through lockdown doors.

Our third room, and to the left of the bullpen, was our closet, our very large closet, where we used to get dressed. The problem was a car had blown up directly above our office-office when Hurricane Kevin paid us a visit the year before. It wasn't like the car blew up in our office-office, or even close, but being directly underneath, we'd suffered water damage. Basically, our office-office, specifically our closet-closet, died. We replaced the computers and surveillance monitors in Control Central first. Then we refurbished the bullpen. We had yet to completely restock our closet. We'd restocked our inventory of Bellissimo uniforms, which was a simple after-hours visit to Human Resources with a laundry bin, which we filled with Bellissimo uniforms, because we never knew what department we might need to sneak into. Since the resort reopened after hurricane break, among other tedious assignments, we'd paid a visit to Chops, the steakhouse in the casino, dressed as servers, to have a few words with a casino guest who pinged every Bellissimo Security radar as a very wanted and very deadbeat dad. (Wanted by the authorities, his many baby mamas, and his seven offspring.) (And he was only twenty-six years old.) Another time it was Payroll, dressed in green jumpsuits from Horticulture, so we could speak to the payroll clerk behind a row of potted plants we were there to mulch, who'd taken it upon herself to triple her own salary. And two weeks earlier, it was the Olympic-sized Bellissimo pool, dressed in Pool Server bikinis with matching sarongs, so we could have a chat with the passed-out sunburned frat boys who'd used fake IDs to play slot machines all night the night before. So while we had Bellissimo uniforms galore, and could sneak all over disguised as employees, we hadn't quite gotten around to replacing our mix-and-mingle-with-the-general-public-incognito wardrobes. It was one thing to pass ourselves off as entry-level employees, as quickly as entry-level employees came and went with a staff of forty-five hundred. It was quite another to work incognito. To disguise our true identities in street clothes. And we hadn't been in any big hurry to restock our incognito street clothes, because it was proving harder and harder to fool management. Since our reopening, we'd been recognized three times. Once with a cart full of empty luggage, trying to check into the hotel. (Because someone at the front desk was passing out unoccupied hotel room keycards to their buddies.) We weren't in front of the desk for a full minute before someone behind the desk said, "Aren't you the boss's wife?" And that forced us to go to greater and greater lengths to hide our true identities, an equally slippery slope, because neon purple tinted contact lenses and pink wigs attracted too much attention the other way. Management didn't recognize us so much as anyone they knew, but the crazier we looked, the more they recognized us as mental-hospital escapees. About the only thing we could successfully pass ourselves off as anymore were old lady slot-machine players. (Which was fun.) (But old lady makeup was hell to get on and even heller to get off.)

So the incentive to restock our undercover wardrobes hadn't really been there. And that day, for the first time in forever, we needed to work undercover. But we couldn't work undercover until I opened the lockdowned door, which was proving difficult, in spite of the fact that I'd written the program and installed the software myself. Yet there I sat, having trouble hacking through my own work.

"Davis!"

"What?" I yelled across the bullpen.

"Do we want designer chic or dead serious suits?"

"I don't care." Then I did care. "On second thought, dead serious."

"I don't know why I asked," she yelled across the bullpen. "We don't have either. We need to go shopping. Put that on our to-do list, Davis, we need to buy clothes. Maybe we need to forget going undercover and try Lost and Found again in what we're wearing. Follow the money trail backwards."

"If I can't get us out of here, how is it you think we're going to get in there? If the money's locked up in Lost and Found, it'll be safe until we can get in." I yelled. "Why do you want to switch gears? Why do you want to follow the money trail backwards?"

"Because we don't have suits."

"And you think we're going to find suits in Lost and Found?" Speaking of backwards, I changed directions. I was trying to hack through the lockdown door from the inside. It wasn't working. I rolled my chair to the next computer and logged on to try to hack through from the outside. "Isn't my gray pinstripe in there?"

"Davis, you caught that thing on fire."

She was right. Back in the day when our jobs were fun, Fantasy and I had been on assignment at Snifter, the private after-dinner jazz bar behind Catch, the seafood restaurant on the Mezzanine, keeping an eye on Snoop Dogg. (Rapper, actor, funny guy.) (Who's a Guinness World Record holder in the Largest Paradise Cocktail category.) Snoop Dogg and his entourage stopped by unannounced. No Hair asked Fantasy and me to keep an eye on him. Snoop and his friends ordered a round of Playing with Fire, which was nothing but flaming cognac, into which, one of Snoop's long thick braids landed, and I wound up playing in fire. My pinstripe suit didn't survive. And, useless trivia, Snoop's braids were extensions anyway.

"How about my white linen suit?"

"You sank that suit," she yelled.

She was right. We'd been on assignment in hot pursuit of a Walker, defined as a gambler who owed the casino big money, won big money, then walked off without paying the casino back. And that man should have been walking. Not driving. We chased him through all of Biloxi, into a subdivision, took a corner too hot, and wound up in a side-yard swimming pool. The Bellissimo limo we'd confiscated *and* my white linen suit drowned that night. (Lessons learned: limos don't take corners well and pools go behind houses. Not beside. Unless you want a limo floating in your side-yard pool.)

"Let's forget the suits and shoot into Lost and Found," she yelled.

"Last time," I yelled. "We can't shoot through a pack of Elvii."

"ELVISES!"

Just then, my phone rang.

So irritating.

I took one hand off one keyboard to dig my phone out of my pocket, pulling the list of Bird numbers with it, and when I saw who was calling, my heart stopped.

It was Gray Donaldson in Casino Credit. I glanced at the time. Gray was sounding the five-million-dollar alarm way off my timeline. Hours off my timeline.

"Okay, you win," Fantasy yelled. "I'm digging through our ID bucket. Did you say Mississippi Gaming Commission or American Gaming Association? Are we shutting them down or auditing them?"

The yelling was getting to me, but I yelled back anyway. "Hold on, Fantasy. I need to take a call."

I took the call.

"Davis?"

"Yes?" My heart was beating out of my chest.

"I'm sorry to bother you. I called Security, they sent me to Mr. Cole's office, and Mr. Cole's office told me to call you."

I took a deep breath in preparation for the news that was surely coming.

"What can I do for you, Gray?" I waited for her to say I could scare up five million dollars for her, but she didn't. She said she'd just received a call from The Clare Estate, a memory-care facility in Mobile, Alabama. They were worried about Megan Shaw, guardian of their resident Louise Juliette Shaw, who they hadn't seen since Friday afternoon. Was Megan at work? Was everything okay? Did Gray Donaldson know if Megan had changed her phone number? In all the years Megan's mother had been with them, Megan had missed only a handful of days visiting her mother in and around the time of the birth of her son the year before. They were worried. They contacted Megan's landlord, who hadn't seen or heard from Megan. The day before, Sunday, they'd called the police, who knew nothing about Megan's whereabouts, then every hospital between the Bellissimo and Megan's apartment complex in Mobile, where, thankfully, they didn't find Megan, and having exhausted every other possibility, they called the Bellissimo. Megan Shaw was missing. Did Gray Donaldson know where Megan Shaw was? Could she shed any light on what might have happened to Megan Shaw? Did anyone at the Bellissimo know anything about Megan Shaw? Should they file a missing person's report? Could someone at the Bellissimo help locate Megan Shaw? Then Gray Donaldson said to me, "I think I should call the police."

"No, Gray," I said. "Let me." I made sure she heard me. "Do not call the police. I will." I asked her not to touch Megan's desk, take her own work and clear out, lock the door behind her,

Biloxi Police Department detectives would be there shortly, then I hung up and tried to breathe.

4-7-8.

Inhale for four, hold for seven, exhale for eight.

When I was almost dizzy, I stopped. I resumed a normal breathing pattern. I tipped my head back to let Fantasy know that in addition to our Gaming and Immigration IDs, she needed to dig out our Biloxi Police Department detective badges, but couldn't answer her, "Why do we need our Biloxi PD IDs?" before Baylor stormed in. I hadn't heard the door open because I had yet to hear anything past Gray Donaldson's news that Megan Shaw was truly missing and had been missing since she cashed the five-million-dollar wire.

"Davis? Fantasy? What the hell is going on?"

I crept to the door of Control Central to see Fantasy had crept to the Closet door, both of us open-mouthed staring at Baylor, standing at the front door. On his left shoulder, the strap of a big blue Bellissimo duffel bag from Love. Under his right arm, upside down, chubby little arms flying, teeny little Nikes kicking, a baby boy.

Megan Shaw's baby boy. Oliver. Who made it through five shift changes at our employee childcare center before the day, graveyard, and swing shifts, who were well versed in Bellissimo parents' overtime, double-time, and all-the-time shifts, compared notes and came to the horrifying conclusion that the baby had been at Play since his mother dropped him off Friday afternoon. July got the call at six that morning. After exhausting every effort to locate Oliver's mother, and having been unable to reach me, she called Baylor.

I rushed for the baby before Baylor dropped him. The second I had him upright and in my arms, his little head tipped back, he grinned wide, then his whole little body fell forward to give me a big slobbery kiss, his little hands cupping both sides of my face. He smelled like sunshine. Fantasy wanted in on the baby action. She reached for him. "Come here!" He lunged for her. She wrapped him in her arms. "You're too cute, little guy."

I went for the duffel bag.

Inside, I found Megan Shaw's Casino Credit uniform.

I texted my mother. *Mother, could you do me a big favor?*

She texted back. *If cores.*

I think that was the moment I knew, just then, texting with my mother, that we'd never find Megan Shaw. We'd seen the last of her. Alive, anyway. Either Megan saw the five-million-dollar light at the end of her desolate life tunnel—her mother was too ill to know she'd deserted her, her son too young—and we'd never see or hear from her again, or someone set Megan Shaw up to take the fall for their five-million-dollar heist. If it were the latter, that someone would be difficult to find, because it would go all the way back to when Megan was a teller at Branch Banking & Trust in Mobile, Alabama. I didn't know Megan Shaw at all, but holding her baby, all goodness, light, and four of the cutest little teeth I'd ever seen in my life, I had a sneaking suspicion it was the latter.

NINE

In unanimous agreement (which hadn't happened in a long time) and given that (so, so, so sadly) no one was looking for Oliver Shaw, we decided that for the time being we wouldn't call Child Services. Who would take immediate custody of Oliver just after they locked the Play doors for good. I wasn't sure if there was a statute on the books covering "failure to realize a child was in your care for three straight days" or not. (There should be. We, especially July, were mortified, and maybe that was the underlying reason we didn't immediately call Child Services.) In the end, right or wrong, after almost seventy-two hours straight at Play, we agreed the baby was better off at my house being rocked by my mother than he would be in the system.

Or maybe we were hoping against hope that Baby Oliver's mother would show up for him, at which point, we might be forced to turn him over to Child Services, because his mother could very well be on her way to prison.

July raided Play for baby supplies—formula, diapers, and Speed Racer footie pajamas—while the rest of us settled Baby Oliver in at my house, which took dragging out and setting up a baby bed, video monitor, stroller, a Pack 'n Play, and other miscellaneous baby equipment from storage. We left the tired little guy sleeping peacefully with Bex, Quinn, Candy, Mother, Birdy, and Bea Crawford, who shouldn't have even been there, cooing over the baby bed. Had I been able to stay, I'd have been cooing over the baby bed too. Oliver Shaw was adorable.

Two heavy hearts and one sleepwalking hot head returned to the office-office, where inside the door Fantasy and I still couldn't open, we confessed all to Baylor. When we finished, he sat on the sofa opposite us blank-faced staring for so long I thought maybe we'd hypnotized him.

We hadn't.

When he finally stood to tower over us, he reminded me of a bull scuffing the ground before it charged.

Baylor was mad. And not just a little.

To get us back for (among many, many other things) being mad at him since the Bellissimo reopened on Valentine's Day, being lazy, which had him working the Elvis reception alone, the Elvis welcome breakfast alone, and the kickoff of the Double Trouble slot tournament alone, plus for not answering his texts or calls, plus for not trusting him enough to tell him that the Casino Credit cashier had run off with five million dollars, plus for wearing out the at-the-dentist excuse, when he knew good and well neither of us went to the dentist three times a week, plus for being the reason he'd had no sleep in two days, Baylor offered us a deal. He said he wouldn't call our bosses (including my husband) in Vegas that very minute and tell them everything if we agreed to work the Elvis banquet that night so he could have a few hours off. Which sent him off on another little he'd-only-had-four-hours-of-sleep-in-two-nights tangent, something we were already well aware of because he ended almost every sentence with it. When he finally got back on track, he told us he'd give us the afternoon to find Oliver's mother, but we had to agree to work the night shift. And that was only if we found the money by three Pacific. If we didn't find the money, he was telling anyway. Clearly, Baylor was getting his No Hair on. Huffing and puffing. Pointing fingers. Pacing. He sounded like a military recruiter: duty, justice, truth, honor, obligation, three squares a day.

We let him get it off his chest. We sat there and took it like the soldiers we were. I only yawned once to Fantasy's three times. And the reason we were falling asleep was because he wouldn't shut up. When he finally sputtered to a stop, like an engine dying, we opened our mouths to protest. He cut us off.

I held up a finger.

Tired of pacing, he sat. He barely nodded, granting me permission to speak, at the audacity of which, beside me, Fantasy made a single-syllable noise I easily interpreted: Baylor was digging his own grave. We would get him back. In a big way. We just weren't in a position to do it right then and there, mostly because we were down by five million dollars, there was a baby at my house, and we didn't have the energy, which gave Baylor the temporary advantage. That, and most of what he'd said was true.

He pivoted around. "What'd you say, Fantasy?"

"I said way to boss up, Baylor."

I cheered along. "We're proud of you."

He eyed us back and forth, questioning our sincerity.

(With good reason.)

"However." I cleared my throat. "I think you're missing the big picture. You're looking at this like it's a money problem, which it is," I said, "but our people problem is larger. One of our people, Baylor, her innocent baby, and her dying mother."

Fantasy weighed in. "Who do you think you are, Baylor, trying to make us work tonight when there's a poor old woman in an Alzheimer's hospital and a baby upstairs we need to take care of?"

With one finger, he stabbed the air. Repeatedly. And in the direction of my home. "There are enough women up there to take care of ten babies."

I couldn't argue with that. So I found something else to argue with. "If we work the Elvis banquet so you can sleep, Baylor, who solves the problem of the baby's missing mother? How are we supposed to work tonight, track down five million dollars, and find the baby's mother at the same time?"

"The baby's mother? The Casino Credit cashier?" He shot forward on the sofa. "She *is* the problem. Don't you see, Davis? It's as plain as day. You just told me, your words, she cashed the wire and ran off with the money."

"We're not working tonight," Fantasy said to no one in particular.

I said, to Baylor specifically, "I just told you she cashed the wire and lost the money, Baylor. Or someone stole the money from her. We don't know that she ran off with it. We know for a fact that somewhere along the way, the money made it to Lost and Found."

"Davis." He leaned in. "Get real. The Casino Credit cashier parked the money in Lost and Found until the coast was clear. Trust me," he said. "She's long gone and so is the money."

That would be a clever trick: cash the wire, stash in Lost and Found until it cooled off, saunter in Monday morning, ask Birdy James for the bag the money was in, and Birdy would have gladly handed it over. With wedding cake on top.

"Megan Shaw may very well be a thief," Fantasy said, "I'll give you that. And she might be a liar, because we know she never worked at Harrah's, but she wouldn't run off and leave her baby. Who does that?"

Baylor leaned all the way in and answered as if English weren't her native tongue. "How do you know that's really her baby and not someone else's baby?" he asked. "How do you know she's not faking us off with a stranger baby?"

"Baylor, what are you talking about?"

"I'm talking about a criminal mastermind, Davis." His bloodshot eyes were bugging a little. "She set this whole thing up. The baby at your house may very well be a fake baby."

"Baylor," Fantasy said, "there's no such thing as a fake baby. That's a very real baby. Have you lost your mind?"

"Where does her Alzheimer's mother fit into your fake baby

theory, Baylor?" I asked. "Did you not hear me say Megan Shaw was her Alzheimer's-riddled mother's guardian?" (Try saying that five times.) "If I'm hearing you right, you're suggesting Megan Shaw found a baby, oh, let's say on the street, substituted it for her own baby at Play, and ran off with the money. Are you adding a fake Alzheimer's patient to your sneaking suspicions? She's run off with five million dollars, her own baby, her own mother, and left subs in their places to throw us off?"

"It could happen," he said. "For all you know the three of them are in Tahiti with the five million dollars."

"Baylor?" I narrowed my eyes. "Have you been watching Hallmark mysteries?"

He shot off the sofa. "There's nothing else to watch!"

I really hoped he wasn't right, but having personally watched almost every Hallmark mystery filmed, I knew firsthand that crooks went to great lengths to cover up their crimes and make clean getaways. (Hallmark mysteries, and I'd worked in law enforcement my entire adult life.) I should check flight manifests on the very off chance Hallmark and Baylor were right. And just then, he-who-might-be-right stood. "I have work to do." He turned for the door. "And so do you."

Yes, I did. I'd missed four calls from Bradley's assistant, Colleen. Four calls and a text message. *Davis, I'm sorry to bother you, but we have a dessert problem. Something's wrong with the ovens at Danish. The convection part of the ovens has stopped working. If we don't get them repaired right away, the buffet and seven other restaurants Danish bakes for won't have desserts.*

I didn't have time to text Colleen back and point out that we were saving waistlines and teeth. I did text Maintenance: *Fix the ovens at Danish.*

They texted back. *No one speaks German, Mrs. Cole.*

What that had to do with broken ovens, I had no idea. *Find a translator*. I had way bigger problems than dessert. I had baby problems. I texted July. *Are you okay?*

She texted back. *I'm still shaking.*

July, I'm sorry I wasn't there for you.

Davis, we need tighter security at Play so this doesn't happen again.

Do you know how it happened in the first place?

She texted, *Five different staff members were responsible for him. It wasn't until one had him twice that the log was checked. And that wasn't until this morning. Have you found his mother?*

Not yet.

I texted my mother. *Is Birdy awake?*

Mother texted back. *Know. She wasp but fill sloop. Thin she waked UPS with staff trees. Put hers in whippoorwill tab with episode salt. She butter but now she's gnat awake.*

I'd begged my mother to stop using voice-to-text.

Begged her.

She wouldn't, because she had better things to do than poke on her phone, so I'd learned to interpret. At some point, Birdy was awake, but fell asleep again. She woke the second time with stiff knees. Mother put her in a whirlpool bath with some manner of bath salts, and afterward, knees better, she fell asleep again.

How is the baby? I asked.

Tootest bobby boy tether.

(Cutest baby boy ever.)

I took a moment to cover my face with both hands and groan.

Then I covered Megan Shaw with additional cyber alerts after checking my surveillance watches already in place (nothing), pinging her phone (more nothing), scouring traffic reports in and around Biloxi (even more nothing), then checking flight manifests near and far, I netted a whopping nothing again.

Where was Megan Shaw?

I tried to breathe.

"Do your fourteen-ten breath thing, Davis," Fantasy, beside me, said.

"It's four-eight-seven."

"Whatever it is, do it."

"I did it a little while ago." I looked at the time on the corner of the screen. "If I do it too soon after I just did it, I get dizzy."

"You know what you need, Davis? Brown paper bags."

I pulled surveillance up on two computers. "What I need is to know how many different ways there are to get to Lost and Found. That's what I need." (That, and Megan Shaw. And five million dollars. And Bea Crawford out of my home.)

"Davis, there are fifty ways to get to Lost and Found."

She was close. Maybe there weren't quite fifty, but there were easily ten.

"Why?" she asked.

"We need to watch surveillance video of every entry point to Lost and Found from Friday, midnight, until six in the morning Saturday, when Birdy found the bag of money. At least we'll know if Baylor's right and Megan Shaw turned in the money herself so she could steal it back."

"I thought you already did that."

"I didn't do it hard enough."

"It will take a week to look at every entry point. What we need is surveillance in Lost and Found. Or anywhere near it."

"Well, we don't have it. Which is why we're looking for entry points," I said. "The last locations we have surveillance before Lost and Found."

"We don't have time for that, Davis. We don't have time for any of this," she said. "You need to face facts. At this point, we're probably not going to find the money."

I sat back and slow blinked at her. Several times.

"We've already hit two walls," she said. "Bird Woman is

absolutely no help and the Casino Credit cashier is nowhere to be found. This is a wild goose chase."

I slow blinked more.

"We're doing nothing but spinning our wheels," the voice of reason in the seat next to me said, "and with every tick of the clock, the money's further out of our reach."

I was about to slow blink myself into a coma.

"What we need to do is take a step back," she said. "We didn't steal five million dollars. We didn't stuff it in a blue bag, we didn't put it in a suitcase, we didn't roll it around on a food cart, and we didn't feed Birdy James spiked milk or see her panties."

"Nightgown."

"Whatever," she said. "We didn't have anything to do with Megan Shaw disappearing either. We didn't park her baby at Play for three days. We're innocent. We need to slow down, because this is going in too many directions, and if you ask me, they're all the wrong way. We need to call Vegas. We'll get Bradley, No Hair, and Mr. Sanders on a conference call, spill our guts, beg for mercy, get their permission to requisition the five million from the vault, wire it to Seattle, and be done with it."

She sat back.

She crossed her arms.

I studied her. I tilted my head and studied her from a different perspective. "What's the real problem here, Fantasy?"

"We don't have decent suits."

I nodded. "Let's see the indecent suits."

* * *

We stared at each other in a full-length mirror.

Fantasy's suit was a leftover from The Prince Experience, a Prince Tribute concert we'd worked back in the day. Because we wanted to go to the concert. Fantasy's suit was purple silk. Shiny purple silk. Shiny reflective purple silk. It was Donna Karan, it was stylish, it was a great cut, but it was still shiny purple silk. The only suit I had left in the closet was worse. It was wool, for one thing. In addition, it was sunshine yellow with wide black stripes. It was Diane Von Furstenberg. It fit fabulously. It cost a fortune. But still, I looked like a bumblebee.

"How fast could we get Elvis suits?" I asked.

"In and out of Josette's?" she asked. "I'd say twenty minutes."

"If we call on the way, fifteen."

Fantasy, six feet tall and dark skinned, dressed head-to-toe in shiny purple silk, and I, barely five-foot-two and fair skinned in my bumblebee suit, said it on the same beat: "Let's go get Elvis costumes."

Our ensuing justification:

I said, "We're never going to pass ourselves off as Biloxi PD detectives dressed like this."

"We have to have Elvis costumes anyway," she said.

"And honestly, Fantasy, we're going to stand out more if we aren't dressed as Elvis than if we are."

"You're absolutely right," she said. "And it wouldn't be too much of a stretch to think detectives would want in on the Elvis action, would it?"

Oh, but it would.

Just not quite the stretch that Prince's Number One Fan Fantasy and Queen Bee Davis were.

We donned wigs, terrified anyone would even remotely recognize us before we could hide behind Elvis costumes. The problem was, we only had two wigs left. Her wig was old-lady silver. Mine was a shoe-polish black bun, lending even more credence to my yellowjacket getup. The only tinted contact lenses I could find were sienna, which sounded dark to me, but on my eyes, which were the color of cinnamon to begin with, the sienna produced more of a terrifying tangerine effect. Fantasy chose large square eyeglasses, at which point, with her silver wig, she looked like Retired Professor Prince. With Gaming Commission and Immigration IDs around our necks, Biloxi detective badges clipped to our waistbands, and pistols in shoulder holsters under our jackets, just in case, we set out for Elvis costumes, if for no other reason, because we looked positively bizarre.

We were quiet on the elevator ride.

We stepped out on the Mezzanine and ducked our heads.

Best to avoid eye contact with anyone. Especially orange-eyed me.

"Do we want to walk or drive?" Fantasy asked.

"Drive," I said. "It's a million degrees outside."

By that time, we were halfway down the Mezzanine steps. "I don't have my car keys."

I stopped. "Where are they?"

"In my purse."

"Where's your purse?"

"I left it in the office," she said. "Do we want to go all the way back to the office?"

"We have to."

We ran all the way back only to realize we were still locked out. I never finished hacking the door. Had Baylor not left it cracked when he'd stormed out, we'd still be locked in. I pulled my phone from my bee pocket and texted him. *Take the office door off lockdown.*

He texted back. *I'm at the dentist.*

What goes around comes around.

Cabs were nonexistent in Biloxi, so on our way back to the lobby, I tried Uber. The closest car was eighteen minutes away. Fantasy tried Lyft. The closest car was twenty-four minutes away. Obviously, the drivers were busy because of all the Elvii and the raging heat. I dug my phone out of my wasp pocket again. "I'll call Crisp."

After two seconds on the phone with Crisp, I grabbed Fantasy's elbow and dragged her into a stairwell. Because calling Crisp for a ride didn't turn out to be its usual five-second exchange.

"You're where?" I asked again.

"On the twenty-ninth floor, Mrs. Cole." He sounded out of breath. "At your residence."

"Why, Crisp? Did Bexley call and ask you to drive her to Disney again?"

"No, ma'am," he said. "Your mother-in-law called Mr. Cole's personal assistant and she called me."

"She's not my mother-in-law."

"My apologies," he panted.

"The woman who isn't my mother-in-law called you why?"

"To run an errand," he said. "An errand I've almost completed. If you'll give me time to change clothes and switch cars, I'll be happy to pick you up."

Fantasy made walking fingers.

I shook my head no. Josette's Costumes, on Howard Street, was a fifteen-minute walk and, considering the Elvii traffic, a ten-minute drive, but by then, it was a million and a half degrees out. And we looked like extraterrestrials. Which was beside the fact that Bea Crawford, who shouldn't have even been there in the first place, was once again bullying Bellissimo employees like she owned the place. My husband's personal assistant, Colleen, did not take orders from Bea, and my driver, Crisp, didn't run errands for her either.

"Change clothes and switch cars?" I asked. "I don't understand."

He hemmed. He hawed.

"Spit it out, Crisp. What's going on?"

"Mrs. Cole, everything's under control. Maybe not the carpet, but everything else."

"The carpet?" I asked. "What about the carpet?" Surely, he

wasn't talking about my living room carpet that had only been on the floor for three hours. By then, maybe four.

"It's my fault, Mrs. Cole," he said. "And I'll do what it takes to make it right, even if that means replacing the living room carpet."

He was talking about my living room carpet. And it had already been replaced.

"Start at the beginning, Crisp. I have very little time. I don't understand what's going on, and what it has to do with the woman who isn't my mother-in-law."

Bea Crawford, the woman who wasn't my mother-in-law, and who shouldn't have been there, had the nerve, the absolute nerve, to call my husband's personal assistant, identify herself as my mother-in-law, which would make her Colleen's boss's mother (and she was *not*), to order fertilizer.

The tomatoes.

Colleen explained to Bea that the Bellissimo didn't stock fertilizer, to which Bea reacted, Colleen said, violently. Bea threatened to report the Bellissimo to the Salvation Army, the Humane Society, and to every single one of Donald Trump's kids, in addition to leaving horrific reviews "over the line," if Colleen didn't produce fertilizer in a hurry. Colleen found an organic fertilizer, Black Kow, at Home Depot on Elizabeth Boulevard. Home Depot said the Bellissimo could have the Black Kow, their entire inventory, and at a steep discount, if we'd pick it up right away. For one thing, Black Kow wasn't a huge seller. The aroma, they said. It was aromatic, they warned. For another, it was sitting in the sun behind Home Depot, and they weren't entirely sure, under the extremely blistering circumstances, it wasn't combustible. Colleen sent Crisp to pick up the fragrant and possibly flammable organic fertilizer. Crisp said the smell was so strong he could only transport it in the trunk, for fear he wouldn't be able to get the odor out of the car's interior, and on the third delivery trip, lumbering through my home with one of the last bags of the nasty stuff, he'd tripped on a leg of sleeping Birdy's wingback chair on his way to the veranda. A ten-cubic-pound bag of what amounted to cow manure had burst open on my brand-new carpet. According to Crisp, he, my mother, and my mother-in-law (not), were all desperately trying to clean the spill, not having much luck, but rest assured, he took full responsibility. That being said, he couldn't drive me anywhere without changing uniforms and switching cars. And to be honest with me, Crisp said, he probably needed a shower. Quickly amended to definitely needed a shower. Black Kow, said Crisp, was pungent.

I could barely say goodbye.

I could barely lift my index finger to end the call.

I turned to Fantasy on the stairstep beside me. "Crisp can't drive us."

TEN

"Davis, when are you going to buy a car? Would you please buy a car? Who, in this day and age, doesn't own a car?"

Fantasy and I were on our way to Valet to do something we shouldn't have. After ignoring a baker's dozen text messages from Colleen in Bradley's office—six about Lost and Found, five about my ex-ex-mother-in-law, who shouldn't have even been there, another saying considering the scented circumstances at my home she'd been made aware of, she could possibly move us to a single hotel room with two double beds on the fourth floor, but Housekeeping couldn't have it ready for at least an hour, plus a bonus text message in all caps that dinged in as I was reading the last one, the final one about the inoperable ovens at Danish—I was on the phone with July explaining that there'd been a mishap at my home. I told her I was trying my hardest to locate Baby Oliver's mother (not exactly true, because securing Elvis costumes wouldn't necessarily help find Megan Shaw, but all the alerts and alarms I had set up could, so technically, I was working hard to find her), and I couldn't get home because I had an errand to run. If I didn't run the errand, I wouldn't be able to work the Double Trouble banquet that night. If I couldn't work the banquet, Baylor wouldn't be able to sleep. (Preying on her emotions.) I asked July if she could possibly pick up Bex, Quinn, Baby Oliver, and Candy, who was, according to my mother, *two interesting whiff the sneeze calf* (a sneezing cat, who, given the new fertilizer circumstances, I'd totally lost interest in) and keep everyone at her condo until she heard back from me. July said she'd do her best. She knew about the Black Kow accident because she'd stopped by my home a half hour earlier to check on Baby Oliver. Initially, she'd hustled Bex, Quinn, Baby Oliver, Candy, Birdy, and the sneezing cat to the cavernous master closet of my bedroom, because all the air outside my closet was unbreathable. She was running back and forth from the closet to the cleanup. She said the fumes were overwhelming. She'd called Maintenance. They'd delivered three industrial fans, which meant opening all the exterior doors: patio, balcony, and veranda. The fans weren't helping much because they might have been exchanging indoor Black Kow air for outdoor Black Kow air, as there was so much Black Kow on the patio, balcony, and veranda. She didn't know if the heat was bringing in the chemicals or the chemicals were bringing in the heat, but they couldn't close the doors because of the living room carpet. A crew was on the way to rip up and replace the carpet for the second time in a single day, everyone was wearing disposable face masks and goggles, but she felt certain everything would be okay soon.

"Initially?"

"What?" July was panting.

"You said initially."

"Initially, what, Davis?"

"You initially moved Bex, Quinn, the baby, Birdy, Candy, and the sneezing cat to my closet. Initially. Where are they now?"

She didn't answer.

"July? Did you check Bex, Quinn, and the baby into Play?"

Number One: I think we'd all had enough of Play. Especially Baby Oliver.

Number Two: Since the Bellissimo reopened after Hurricane Kevin with an employee childcare center—think Sesame Street—Bex and Quinn had been there exactly once. It was supposed to have been a quick stop by July's office so she could sign a requisition for an order of Fisher-Price Lift-the-Flap board books for the toddler library room. It turned into an all-day Play pass for Bex and Quinn. It took five hours and Bradley leaving a board meeting to coax the girls home. We hadn't tried Play again. Mostly because we didn't want our daughters moving out before they turned three. And, given what had just happened with Baby Oliver, there was a chance Bex and Quinn would be lost at Play until they were ten.

"It's okay if you did, July. Under the circumstances. Just tell me."

She still didn't answer.

"July?" I asked. "Are my children and Baby Oliver in the casino with Baylor?"

"They're *not* in the casino."

So they were at Baylor and July's condo and Baylor was babysitting.

He who carried a baby upside down.

He who, lately, wouldn't spit on me or Fantasy if we were on fire, but would stop everything and keep my children, a one-year-old, my dog, a sneezing cat, and even Birdy James at the crook of July's finger. The worst part of Baylor helping July, and by proxy helping me? There'd be no one—absolutely no one—in charge of the Bellissimo until Fantasy and I returned.

Fantasy tugged the waspy sleeve of my jacket. "Do you need to go home?"

I might have needed to go home. I most certainly didn't want to go home.

I covered the mouthpiece of my phone. "There and back in twenty minutes?"

"If that," she said.

I looked at my watch. Then, to July, I said, "Let me run this one quick errand. Quick, quick. I'll be back in twenty minutes. Thirty, tops. Call Housekeeping and requisition as many clean-air machines as they can get their hands on, and as soon as the carpet is replaced, set up the clean-air machines, get everyone home, and let them watch *Frozen*."

"I'm on it."

We hung up.

"Who has Bex, Quinn, and the baby?" Fantasy asked.

"Baylor."

"That dirty dog."

And that was when Fantasy and I did what we shouldn't have, which was march our alien-suited selves to the Valet window, flash our Gaming Commission badges, and tell the attendant at the Valet desk we'd lost our ticket.

"It's a black SUV," I said. (Because the roads were packed with black SUVs. Surely our parking garage was too.)

"What make?" the boy asked. "What model?"

"Mercedes," Fantasy said. "And brand spanking new. We just bought it. Be careful with it."

Ten minutes later, we were pulling out of the Bellissimo in a highjacked Mercedes GLS 550 SUV with 410 miles on it.

"This car is nice." Fantasy ran her free hand along the mahogany dash.

"It should be." I was sticker-shocked staring at the dealer flyer that had been removed from the car window and shoved into the glove compartment. "Someone just paid ninety-seven thousand dollars for it."

The light changed. Fantasy hit the gas and pulled onto Beach Boulevard traffic. "We're only borrowing it for twenty minutes. We'll put it right back where we found it."

Except we didn't.

The streets were laden with Elvii. They were gathered at every crosswalk, stuffed in every seat of every car on the road, and hawking Elvis t-shirts on every corner.

"Did we know this Elvis business would be this big a deal?" Fantasy honked at an Elvis standing in the middle of the road with a karaoke boombox on his shoulder. She lowered her window. "You're not in the ghetto, fool. You're in the middle of the road. Move."

"I knew we were booked solid with Elvis fans," I said. "I knew the slot tournament seats filled the day registration opened. But who could have possibly predicted the whole city would go Elvis crazy?" The Elvis in the road was still singing about the ghetto. If he didn't move soon, with Fantasy at the wheel, he'd be singing about the hospital. "Go the back way."

"What back way?" she asked. "There is no back way." She studied the screen on the dash. She poked it aimlessly, and among other things, like dim disco lights appearing at our feet, my seat started vibrating.

"What are you looking for?" I asked.

"Why doesn't this car have navigation?"

I reached to the screen and poked. "It does. It wasn't on."

The Mercedes' COMAND navigation system roared to life. It asked where we wanted to go. "Josette's Costumes on Howard Avenue," Fantasy told it.

The brilliant car had us around traffic, down one alley, and in front of Josette's in under two minutes.

Except it wasn't Josette's.

Josette's Costumes on Howard Avenue had, unbeknownst to us and COMAND, closed. What was a Biloxi institution before was a payroll advance store after. The sign in the window said, "COMMITTED TO SOLVING BILOXI'S CASH PROBLEMS."

We parked in front of formerly Josette's, currently We Got Your Money.

"Wonder how much cash they have in there," Fantasy said, "because we definitely have a cash problem. You think they have five million?"

I thought not.

The Mercedes also had air-conditioned seats. "I wonder whose car this is." Under the window sticker in the glove compartment, I found catalog-thick owner's manuals, and that was it.

"This car is amazing," she said. "We need two of these."

Then we needed lawyers.

Four Biloxi Police Department squad cars, lights blazing, sirens screaming, swarmed, blocking us on all sides. An unmarked car pulled up right behind the squad cars. We were charged with felony grand theft auto, felony impersonation of gaming officials, felony impersonation of government officials, felony impersonation of law enforcement officers, and carrying concealed.

(Weapons.)

Which the officers quickly confiscated.

Retired Professor Prince Fantasy pointed out to tangerine-eyed Bee Me that the police didn't charge us with looking like idiots when they easily could have.

* * *

My biggest disappointment, when unceremoniously tossed in the holding tank at Biloxi PD, was that Megan Shaw wasn't there too. In all my efforts to locate her, I hadn't checked booking reports in and around Biloxi. She could have been pulled over for speeding, searched, and held for questioning over the five million big ones, or even turned herself in. As chaotic as things were at PD headquarters—about like the Bellissimo lobby, but the mood, atmosphere, and décor much worse—she'd probably still be in holding.

She wasn't.

No Megan, but plenty of Elvii.

Our holding cellmates were all dressed as Elvis, except for one Priscilla Presley and one Ann-Margret. Both prostitutes. We didn't overreact. We'd been arrested before. Several times, in fact. We'd been in holding cells with prostitutes before. Several times on that score too. And like all the other times, it was only a matter of finding the right person within the department to explain our situation to. We didn't steal the car from the dealer. We innocently borrowed the car from our employer. The problem was everyone on the city's payroll was busy chasing random Elvii all over the city. We were stuck with baby intake officers who didn't know us, wouldn't listen to a single word we said, and one told me that spouting off his bosses' names only meant I probably had a record as long as his arm. "Apparently, you're a career criminal," he said. "Otherwise you wouldn't know everyone here. I'm not calling anyone upstairs for you. Pipe down and wait your turn."

The good news was by the time we got out, surely my house would be back in order. Better news, they fed us. Bottled water and stale trail mix, but at that point, we'd have eaten anything. The best news, after the breakneck stress since before my husband left for Vegas, I was forced to be still. To sit. To catch my breath. I'd rather have been still, sat, and caught my breath anywhere else, but it was what it was.

"I wonder what your mother made for lunch." Fantasy shook the last of the trail mix into her mouth.

I polished off my own trail mix. "Chicken salad, I think."

"You think?"

"When we flew out of the kitchen a week ago, I saw what looked like chicken salad ingredients on the counter."

"It wasn't a week ago," Fantasy said, "it was more like three hours ago. But I hear you. It feels like it was a week ago."

"Do you think the Black Kow would have ruined the chicken salad?"

"Not if it was in the refrigerator."

The holding cell didn't have a clock. I knew what time it was without one. It was too close to three o'clock Pacific, when the Seattle title company would be expecting their five-million-dollar wire. Which I'd get to. As soon as I got out of jail.

"Does your mother put grapes in her chicken salad?"

Fantasy asked. "Tell me she doesn't put grapes in her chicken salad."

"Cranberries," I said.

"That sounds pretty."

"It is. And celery."

"The delicious crunch."

I agreed. "And she barely grates red onion in it," I said. "Like you know it's there, but you don't know it's there, and you never bite into onion."

"Stop." She wadded her trail mix wrapper.

The Ann-Margret prostitute said, "My mother puts apples and celery in her chicken salad."

Priscilla Presley said, "Celery, slivered almonds, and poppyseed."

All the Elvii weighed in with their mother's chicken salad recipes, one cried like a baby Elvis at the memory of his mother's chicken salad, and that pretty much shut down the chicken salad chatter. I learned that regardless of socioeconomic status, education level, age, race, religion, sexual orientation, political affiliation, make or model of Elvis costume, most chicken salad recipes included celery. The delicious crunch.

"It doesn't work that way." Fantasy was counseling an Elvis who'd been picked up on public nuisance charges. "You have to be registered in the slot tournament to win one of the movie roles. Standing in the street having a fit because you want a role in a movie is no way to get a role in a movie. You feel me, Elvis?"

Elvis felt her.

"And it's not like they're big roles," she explained. To Elvis. Who felt her. "Only one is a speaking role, and it's just two or three lines. The top twenty-five scores in the slot tournament win the roles. But you have to be registered to play in it."

Elvis asked how he might register.

"It's too late," Fantasy said. "Unless you know someone. Lucky for you, you met me. I'll get you in."

"But you're in jail," Elvis said.

He made a good point.

A new uniform, worn by a gum-smacking officer so young he had to have graduated Police Academy the day before, stepped up to the holding cell. "I need Biloxi Homicide Detectives Whepler and Dunklee."

Fantasy and I raised fingers.

"Nice to meet you two." The baby officer smacked his gum. "I don't remember seeing either of you at the precinct picnic."

The Elvii, Ann-Margret, and Priscilla Presley got a big kick out of it.

"Get up." The holding cell door slid open. "Time for your homicide detective cavity searches."

He was kidding about the cavity searches, thank goodness, because Fantasy might have killed someone, then we'd be in really big trouble, but the next half hour of mug shots and fingerprints was thoroughly humiliating nonetheless. After that, we were shuffled to booking while our prints were running through the system, which, they said, could take up to three hours with all the Elvii backup they were experiencing, and those were three hours we didn't have.

My intake officer was surely still in high school. Her power was fresh and new, and she used it, shoving me into a chair beside her desk. Above her head, a wall clock. It was four o'clock Central, which made it two o'clock Pacific. By then, surely my home was Black Kow free, the new carpet was down, and the children—mine and Megan Shaw's—were back. July would have started *Frozen* again, and my mother would be feeding everyone a post-Black Kow feast. I was, for the very first time since the tomatoes arrived, so grateful Mother was there. (Not jail there. At my home there.) I took comfort in the fact that she would do what needed to be done and that was absolutely all I took comfort in, that my mother was in charge.

If that were indeed the case.

I really hoped it was the case.

Because I'd have a hard time explaining to my husband that I'd left Bea Crawford, who shouldn't have even been there, in charge of our children and our home. Honestly, I'd have a hard time explaining it to myself.

"Do you know who Bradley Cole is?" I asked the teenage booking officer.

"Of course," she said. "Everyone knows who Bradley Cole is."

"Well, I'm his wife." I went to tug off my wedding band and show her the inscription, forgetting it was in a Jane Doe Ziplock in a holding locker, along with the double diamond ring Bradley gave me when the girls were born, my watch, my black bun wig, my big black gun, and my cell phone.

"Have you stolen Bradley Cole's wife's jewelry?" Officer Temples asked. "Is that what you're trying to tell me?"

I slumped. Two desks away, Prince Fantasy was trying to explain Baylor to her intake officer. "Baylor is his first name and his last name. He was one of those left-on-an-orphanage-doorstep babies, and the note in the basket only had one name. Baylor. Just ask for Baylor. Everyone at the Bellissimo knows him."

My head popped up and whipped around. "He's at the dentist, Fantasy." Which was to say, don't waste a phone call on Baylor. He won't answer.

"Hey." Officer Temples snapped her fingers in my face. "Eyes on your own page. No talking."

Not that I wanted her to dislike me any more than she already did, if that were possible, I still tipped my head back and shot out, "Call my mother and have her call Baylor. He'll take her call."

"Your mother is probably roasting a pig on a spit, Davis," Fantasy shot back. "She won't answer. I'd have to text her and she'd text back gibberish." She asked her intake officer if she could text instead of call. Her intake officer told her to shut up. She did, after she eked out under her breath to me, “I’m not calling your mother. You call your mother.”

I barely turned my head, and without moving my lips, I eked back, “No.”

Officer Temples’ teenage hand slapped the desk.

“Sorry,” I said. “Sorry, sorry.” I held up a one-more-thing finger, then with a jerk of my head, fired out the last words that would leave my lips before Officer Temples shut me down for good. “I’m calling someone who can get us out.”

Officer Temples yanked me up by my bumblebee arm. “That’s it. I’m separating you two.”

“Do you know Detective Marini?” I asked, while being hustled out of intake and back through booking. “Sandy Marini? She knows me. Call her. Do you know Chief Adelson? Greg Adelson?” I reeled off every Biloxi PD name I could remember as I was being dragged out of the room.

“Save it.” Officer Temples shoved me into an interrogation room. Her parting words, before she slammed the door were, “I don’t want to hear it.”

Thirty nerve-wracking and totally abandoned minutes later, which was thirty minutes closer to three o’clock Pacific, the interrogation room door finally opened, and yet another prepubescent officer slipped in. He took the seat across from me. He placed a cell phone on the table between us. He gave it a nudge. Having had a long lonely stretch to myself to miserably think things through, I was more than ready to make my call. It was time to end the madness. I reached for the phone, then turning my back to the baby officer, dialed one of the few phone numbers I knew by heart. It rang several times, and just when I was about to give up, call my husband, and confess all, she answered.

Instead of hello, I said, “Bianca, it’s Davis. I’m in jail and I need five million dollars.”

After a pause so long I thought we'd been disconnected, Bianca Sanders, my former friend, my former boss, the woman who'd fired and replaced me, finally said, "Well, well, well." Never in the history of spoken language has anyone dragged out three syllables the way she did, lowering her range a half an octave as she went. She took even longer to say, in the same Morticia Addams tone, "If it isn't David."

It's Davis.

"Tell me, David. Have you called to welcome me home, or have you called to beg for your job back?"

"You fired me, Bianca. Why would I beg for my job back? So you can fire me again?"

"I most certainly did not fire you, David."

It's Davis. And yes, she did. She fired me. Her notarized letter of my immediate termination arrived by messenger in the middle of Thanksgiving dinner.

"You quit your job," Bianca said, "without so much a farewell, as if I meant nothing to you."

"You fired me without so much as a farewell, Bianca, as if *I* meant nothing to *you*."

The baby officer rolled his hand in the air, as in, hurry up with your daytime drama, Bee Lady.

"I have news for you, David," Bianca said. "Listen carefully."

I was listening. Carefully.

The baby officer was listening. Carelessly.

"I am not your babysitter," she said, "nor am I hosting Senior Citizen Hour in my home. I am not your dog groomer, your feline veterinarian, I am not the baggage check girl for your dilapidated luggage, and I most certainly am not your bail bondsman or personal loan officer. You're dead to me, David. Dead. Do you hear me? Dead. Call someone else, because you're dead to me."

She hung up.

It wasn't until after the prepubescent officer rudely yanked the phone from my hand and slammed the interrogation door behind him that I began putting the pieces together. My children and Baby Oliver were not with Baylor. Having had no other choice, July had taken them upstairs, to the Penthouse, where she knew there was a nursery, a playroom, and staff on hand for the youngest Sanders son who could easily care for Bex, Quinn, and Baby Oliver, while she helped put my Black Kow house back together. Candy, the sneezing cat, and Birdy James must have been at the Sanders residence too, and Candy might have a Black Kow aroma about her. I wasn't unreasonably upset with July for taking everyone to the Penthouse, because considering what she was up against, she made the best decision she could, and Bianca, as bad as things would ever get between us—and they couldn't possibly get much worse—would never take it out on anyone but me. The big problem, and almost all I took away from the horrible exchange, was Bianca's baggage-check-girl-dilapidated-luggage line. Was it possible the black spinner suitcase containing five million dollars that was to have been delivered by Gold Lamé Elvis to the boss's wife had been right above my head in the Penthouse the whole time?

If so, wrong boss's wife.

I beat on the interrogation room door. I yelled. I made a general nuisance of myself to absolutely no avail. If the five-million-dollar suitcase made it to the Penthouse, and Bianca believed it was mine, I was certain she wouldn't bother to look inside before throwing it out. She may have even burned it. In effigy. To David. Who she believed quit her job. Without so much as a farewell. As if she meant nothing to me.

When she did.

She really did.

ELEVEN

Bianca Casimiro Sanders was an enigma, and for years, she'd been my enigma.

The only daughter of renowned Las Vegas casino developer Salvatore Casimiro, she was raised by governesses and private tutors at her maternal grandmother's castle in Palermo, Italy. On her sixteenth birthday, her formal education having run its complete course (after she'd shimmied down a turret by bedsheet to spend a weekend partying in Tuscany with her Humanities professor's assistant), her grandmother kicked her out. Bianca joined her parents and three older brothers at the family's thirty-room villa high above Las Vegas Boulevard. She was shown to her four-room suite, assigned a personal maid, a personal valet, and a personal assistant, then presented with a personal comprehensive house account at the Forum Shops at Caesars. She shopped, she frolicked up and down the Strip unchecked, and she frequented the front pages of tabloids. She called them the best years of her life.

When she was twenty-four years old, having been missing from the Vegas party scene for weeks before *Entertainment Tonight* spotted her on John Mellencamp's arm in Penrose, New Zealand, her father ordered her home to Vegas and introduced her to his protégé, up-and-coming casino conglomerate, Richard Sanders, the yin to his daughter's out-of-control yang. Mr. Sanders was principled, focused, and ambitious, not that Bianca cared; she was in it for his surfer-boy good looks and her dowry. She married Richard Sanders in haste when he put a ginormous ring on her finger and punished him at leisure when, the ink not even dry on their marriage license, her dowry turned out to be a casino in Mississippi. Talk about a fish out of water. She hated her new role as Mrs. Bellissimo. She spent her first few years in Biloxi trying to get out. She tried to weasel out of her marriage, but that didn't work, because as it turned out, not only did she love Richard Sanders, he loved her back. Next, she tried to bankrupt the casino, thinking if the Bellissimo went under, they could pick up where they left off in Las Vegas. That didn't work either. When I met her, the only escape route Bianca had left was lighting Mississippi on fire, as in burning it down, the whole state, then I stepped in.

I was hired to be Bianca Sanders's celebrity double.

We looked enough alike to be sisters, me being the younger sister by a few years and the smaller sister by a few pounds, with the single exception of our coloring. So when I had a Bianca chore, I sprayed my caramel-colored hair beach blonde, hid my caramel-colored eyes behind envy-green contacts, then squeezed myself into fresh-off-the-runway couture to mingle with Bellissimo casino high rollers, headlining entertainment acts, and visiting dignitaries. Around town, I cut grand opening ribbons, chaired fundraisers, and threw ceremonial first pitches at Biloxi Shuckers games. Several times a year I graced glossy magazine covers, waved from parade floats, and gave the occasional television interview. As her.

Bianca absolutely loved the program.

She relaxed, as much as she was capable of relaxing, locking herself away in her Penthouse home to wait it out. When the walls threatened to close in on her, she'd whisk away to Paris and shop. Or Telluride, where she'd pretend to ski. Or for parts unknown, for spiritual awakening (plastic surgery), and eventually found her way back to happiness.

Via me.

I grew to love the program too. It was never more than two

or three hours a week, for which I was paid a brain surgeon's salary. As time went on, and without meaning to, I forgave Bianca. (For being Bianca.) (And for many other offenses.) After I forgave her, I began to understand her. The understanding led to an odd form of respect. The respect, to an inkling of fondness. The fondness, to a lopsided friendship. Lopsided because, contrary to her popular opinion, I was not her personal slave. What I knew and what she had a hard time recognizing, because the concept was so new to her, was simply this: we were friends. With me being the friend who watched out for her. It broke my heart that she believed I'd walk away from her without so much as a goodbye.

I'd never do that.

I knew exactly how much that would've hurt her, because it was exactly how hurt I'd been for seven long months. I'd blamed her, only to hear she blamed me. I realized, alone in an interrogation room, dressed like a killer bee, who was really to blame: Sara Z. Stone, Esquire.

Bianca's personal attorney.

Sara Z. Stone.

It was never Bianca's fault.

It was never my fault.

It was her hurricane-chasing attorney's fault.

TWELVE

After Hurricane Kevin, Bradley, the girls, and I moved in with my younger sister and only sibling, Meredith, where we lived for the next six years waiting for the private elevator to and from our twenty-ninth floor Bellissimo home to be replaced, because twenty-eight flights of steps with two toddlers and a Goldendoodle was above and beyond. Not to mention the resort was closed for post-hurricane remodel, so no room service. We waited it out at Meredith's. In Pine Apple, Alabama. For six long years.

Did I say years?

Weeks.

I meant weeks.

Meredith had plenty of room, as opposed to my parents, one block over, who invited us to stay with them from between clenched teeth. It wasn't that we weren't welcome, or that they wouldn't have loved the time with their granddaughters; it was that their house was small, their granddaughters were loud, and our dog made their cat nervous. Meredith, on the other hand, didn't have a cat. She had a daughter, my fifth grade niece, Riley, who was beside herself that her little cousins would be squealing through her otherwise tomb-quiet house. Meredith and Riley lived alone in the four-story antebellum our father was born in, on Main Street, in Pine Apple, Alabama, where I was born too. (In Pine Apple.) (Not at Meredith's.) (I was born in a hospital.) (A five-bed hospital behind a hardware store.) (But still, a hospital.)

At Meredith's, we had the whole third floor to ourselves. We turned the extra bedroom into a playroom for Bex and Quinn, and we turned the fourth room, a dark drafty room with a beamed ceiling steeply pitched to a spooky V, a room that had been collecting Meredith's junk for a decade, into a satellite Bellissimo office. It was far from what we were used to by way of workspace, which was executive, and for the first few days, I couldn't concentrate for thinking bats were going to swoop. It didn't help that while we tried to work, Bex and Quinn kept themselves busy giving Candy blanket rides up and down the hall just outside the open door of our creepy office, the giggles and woofs reaching fever pitch every three minutes. When we could work, real work, roll-up-our-sleeves-and-work work, Bradley and I sat in mismatched chairs at an old dining room table that had seen a million meals, keeping company with a rusty bicycle-built-for-two, lamps that needed rewiring, and no telling how many ghosts. It was there, in our haunted makeshift office, that I first learned of Sara Z. Stone.

"David, I've hired a personal attorney to handle my affairs while I'm away."

Bianca and Richard Sanders left the battered post-hurricane Bellissimo the same day we did, traveling in the opposite direction. They would rough out the reconstruction in the $5,000-a-night Presidential Suite of the Ritz-Carlton on Canal Street in New Orleans, which, as it turned out, overlooked Bianca's new personal attorney's office in the French Quarter.

"While you're away?" I asked. "Where are you going?"

"Sara—"

(Who was Sara?)

"—has waved her magic wand, David, and booked me for six months of spiritual awakening with Dr. Fredrich Von Krügerschmitt in Berlin."

"Germany?" My fingers were flying across the keyboard of my laptop.

"No, David," she deadpanned. "California."

I'd never heard of Berlin, California. And it's Davis.

"Of course, Germany," she said.

At which point, I was reading Dr. Fredrich Von Krügerschmitt's vitals on my laptop. He was head of plastic surgery at Beauty Studio, Berlin, and to Bianca, that made sense. A head-to-toe plastic surgery makeover would spiritually awaken her. Bianca loved surgery. The year before, she'd had an earlobe reduction. Both earlobes. But then didn't have enough earlobe to hold her massive diamonds, so she turned right back around and had an earlobe enhancement. Both earlobes. And that was right after her knee-tuck. Both knees. Which was right after her ankle rejuvenation. Both ankles.

"Sara who, Bianca?"

"Sara Stone," she said. "Sara Z. Stone."

I immediately typed Sara Z. Stone into the search bar. Sara Z. Stone, Esquire, owned a lucrative and limited private law practice in New Orleans. She represented Gulf Coast celebrities, professional athletes, and scandalous politicians, of which there were many in New Orleans to choose from. I hoped there were two Sara Z. Stones, or a million, and Bianca was talking about any of the others and not the shyster attorney with the big teeth and even bigger hair on my laptop.

"Sara is my new personal attorney, David."

Oh, no.

"I met Sara quite by accident, and it turned out to be a very fortuitous day, as she immediately diagnosed me with severe lilapsophobia, which, David, I'm in the brutal throes of."

"I thought you said she was an attorney."

"She is, David. A brilliant attorney."

I looked up lilapsophobia. It was abnormal fear of violent weather, specifically tornados and hurricanes. So Bianca, whose net worth was somewhere in the billions, accidently and fortuitously met a hurricane-chasing attorney. Fortuitous indeed. For Sara Z. Stone.

"She so very generously offered to represent me as I begin my journey down the treacherous path to emotional and physical well-being."

"How very kind of her," I said.

"As it turns out, David, not only is she kind, she's well-versed in all aspects of law, not just the intrinsically personal."

"But the Bellissimo has four intrinsically well-versed attorneys on staff," I said. "All of whom are at your disposal. Why do you need a personal attorney in New Orleans when you have four staff attorneys downstairs?"

"You wouldn't understand, David."

Oh, but David did understand. (And it's Davis.) Bianca wanted her name on Sara's client list and would much rather charter a Bellissimo jet for a ten-minute flight to see her own attorney than take a thirty-second elevator ride to see one of the Bellissimo's.

"I must run, David," she said. "Germany is waiting. Honor Sara's wishes while I'm away, as she will be acting in my stead until I am whole, starting with replacing my personal staff with trained lilapsophobia supporters."

Wait a minute. (A) I was already working a ten-hour day helping Bradley put the Bellissimo back together. I didn't have the time, nor the desire, to honor Sara's wishes while Bianca was away. (B) What was a lilapsophobia supporter? And why would Bianca agree to Sara hiring ten or twelve of them? "Letting your new attorney replace your staff would be an incredible security risk, Bianca. You don't need to replace your staff. If you feel like you must, let me do it." Her staff was my job—hiring, firing, bribing, talking them off the ledge, explaining that smothering Bianca with her own pillow in her sleep would result in the death penalty for them. I had no choice but to be hands-on with Bianca's personal staff, because part of my job as her celebrity double was to keep the Bianca wolves at bay. Sara Z. Stone *was* the wolf. “Bianca, I can’t let you do this.”

“David,” she said, “you worry too much. And I have a flight to catch. Kisses! Ta-ta!”

Then hung up.

It wasn’t an hour later I received an all-caps text message demanding I check my inbox for an urgent email from Sara Z. Stone, Esquire. In the email, an order. Not a wish for me to honor, as Bianca put it, but an order. An edict. A decree. I was to report to the Alpaca Treehouse in the Bamboo Forest, which was located, believe it or not, southeast of Atlanta, a three-hour drive from Pine Apple, for a photoshoot. A photoshoot in which I would wear red lights. And that was it. Red lights. I’d be naked beneath the red lights. I was to be photographed buck naked in a treehouse in the forest with alpacas wearing a thin strand of red lights for the Valentine’s Day cover of *Vogue*. When? The next day. The very next day.

I picked up the phone immediately.

“No.” I didn’t want to leave a message. “I’ll hold.”

I held for an hour. An hour of my life, gone, waiting on Sara Z. Stone to take my call, only to hear that Sara (thin, nasally, high-pitched voice, and a mouth breather, I instantly disliked her) had moved heaven and earth in the aftermath of Hurricane Kevin to secure the cover of *Vogue* for Bianca, Southern distribution only, as one of the Kardashians had the rest of America, to show the world, the South World anyway, how well Bianca had survived the hurricane and that she was back, better than ever.

“Public relations,” Sara said. “Do you understand public relations, Mrs. Cole?”

I was too busy fuming and pacing as best I could in my sister’s creepy attic to understand anything.

“Timing,” Sara Z. Stone said. “Do you understand timing, Mrs. Cole? The cover coincides with the reopening of the casino. Surely you understand that timing is imperative.”

She went on to explain time to me. How vital it was I not waste hers when all of Condé Nast Incorporated, who apparently owned *Vogue*, was waiting for the outcome of the photoshoot she'd all but killed herself to secure on behalf of Bianca. Did I understand how far she, *Vogue*, and Condé Nast Incorporated had gone out of their way to accommodate Bianca? Did I understand that alpaca models stayed booked six months in advance?

Bottom line, I was to find my way to Atlanta for a photoshoot in the woods with alpacas wearing a strand of red lights, and only a strand of red lights, the very next day.

The very next day was Thanksgiving.

I explained Thanksgiving to her.

She told me it was the only day the alpacas were available, and they didn't know, or care, that it was Thanksgiving.

I explained family to her.

She told me the alpacas were a family.

I told her that under no circumstances would I not be spending Thanksgiving with my own two-legged family. And under no other circumstances would I ever allow myself to be photographed in the woods with a family of alpacas wearing nothing but a strand of red lights. I advised her to take a step back and familiarize herself with our brand before she committed the Bellissimo, Bianca, or especially me again. I said in no way, shape, or form, did her *Vogue* cover plans work with Bianca's, much less the Bellissimo's brand. I offered, as a compromise, to let the production crew come to me. I would do my best to wear red, and by red, I meant red clothes. I said I'd make myself available the day after Thanksgiving and hung up.

My father was carving the Thanksgiving turkey when the notice of my termination from Bianca Sanders's employ arrived by messenger. As it turned out, Bianca received my letter of immediate resignation on the tarmac at Berlin Schönefeld airport as she was being escorted down the steps of the chartered Airbus 380 delivering her to Dr. Fredrich Von Krügerschmitt.

We hadn't spoken since.

Not one time.

Until I called her from an interrogation room at Biloxi Police Department and asked for five million dollars.

The longest half hour of my life later, the baby gum-smacking officer cracked the interrogation room door. "Get up," he said. "You made bail."

I shot out of my miserable seat. I didn't ask how, who, or why; I bolted. I knew the way, gum-smacker hot on my trail, to release. I signed for my personal possessions, including my Glock, minus the ammo, then stood at the iron door until it opened and made a mad dash out to Sara Z. Stone, Esquire, my ex-ex-mother-in-law, and the raging heat. Sara's and Bea's vehicles were parked at the curb bumper-to-bumper, Bea's dilapidated 1983 Chevrolet Silverado truck versus Sara's cool white Lexus LC 500. It would seem that Bianca had shown me enough mercy to call her personal attorney, and Prince Fantasy, minus her hot Prince jacket, reveling in her newfound freedom between the truck and the car, had obviously called Bea Crawford. I shielded my eyes from the glare of the sun.

"You called Bea?" I asked.

"You called this?" She threw a thumb at Sara.

Sara, from inside her cool car, beeped her horn twice, as in, *I don't have all day.*

I turned for the truck. "Let's go, Bea."

"Davis," Fantasy said. "You've got to be kidding. Bea's truck doesn't have air."

"You big sissy," Bea said.

We piled into the cab seat of Bea's truck, me in the middle, and roared off, Bea beeping her horn at Sara as we passed. And Bea's horn was custom. It was a boom blaster that played "Dixie" at ear-splitting volume. I couldn't see, because I was stuffed between Bea and Fantasy with a piled-high filthy dash in front of me and a Confederate flag across the window behind me, but there wasn't a doubt in my mind, Sara Z. Stone jumped. A mile.

"You just can't stay out of jail, can you, Davis?" Bea laid on the horn again at a crosswalk. She hoisted her top half out the driver window and yelled, "Get your Elvis asses out of my way!"

The Bellissimo was in sight.

Directly above it, a helicopter hovered.

"What in the world?" I craned to see what make and model of school bus the helicopter was lowering onto the roof. "Is this part of the Flying Elvis thing?"

Fantasy said, "I have no idea."

Just before it left our line of vision, we made out that the object was stainless steel, rectangular, and almost as large as the helicopter. Bea lurched her truck up to the Bellissimo main entrance, scattering Elvii, then slammed to a stop at the front doors, the same front doors we exited so many pre-incarceration hours earlier, and we couldn't get out fast enough. She yelled, past all the Elvii, "You're welcome, ingrates!"

We didn't turn, but both waved—I think Fantasy waved, it might have been something other than a wave—and kept going.

Fantasy went off in search of Elvis costumes, which was all we really intended to do when we left the first time, and I went straight for the Penthouse.

I took a deep breath as the foyer elevator doors parted.

The Sanders' latest butler, a surly sulking man who I'd never been introduced to, so I called him Lurch, startled at the sight of me. I startled right back. He was wearing a surgical mask. It only took one whiff to figure out why. The intake for the Penthouse ventilation system must have been circulating air pulled from my porch, veranda, and balcony, then spewing Black Kow air through the Penthouse. The silver school bus we'd seen dropping onto the roof by helicopter must have been a new heat and air system for the Penthouse, which was typical Bianca—if thy air offend thee, demand a new $50,000 unit be dropped on thy roof. The odor was atrocious, more chemical than anything else. Overpowering, eye-watering, throat-burning, try-not-to-inhale chemicals. I pulled my bumblebee blouse over my mouth and nose, then all I could smell was Biloxi PD's holding tank and a hint of Whataburger grease from Bea's truck. A marked improvement.

"Where's Bianca?"

"Mrs. Sanders has evacuated," Lurch said.

"I'm here to pick up my daughters, my dog, a baby, a sneezing cat, and a little old lady," I said.

"They are not here."

His eyes were flinty gray and shifty.

"Where are they?" I asked. "Where are my children? Where's the baby? Where's my dog? The sneezing cat? The little old lady?"

"They've returned to your home, Mrs. Cole."

I absolutely dreaded going home.

"Where's Bianca?"

"At an undisclosed location."

I gently eased the empty Glock from the waistband of my bee pants. I lined it up with the bridge of his sharp nose just above the tight line of his face mask.

"She did not say."

"Did she leave anything for me?"

"She did not."

"Is there anything here that belongs to me?"

"Such as?"

"Luggage."

"There might have been."

"What does that mean?" I asked.

"A roughshod suitcase was delivered days ago," he said. "I believe it was meant for you."

"Give it to me." I shook my Glock. "Right now."

"I'm afraid that's not possible."

I shook my Glock harder.

"The elderly gentlewoman took custody of it."

"What was in it?"

He didn't answer.

My Glock and I took a step forward.

"A belt," Lurch said. "A large bejeweled belt."

For a minute there, I thought I'd found the money.

Again.

THIRTEEN

In the elevator, I scrolled through endless missed calls and text messages from Baylor, one quitting his job right then and there. I had a very recent message from Fantasy; Gulf Costumes was out of Elvis. There were fourteen messages from Colleen in Bradley's office: please call, please call, please call, the ovens, the ovens, the ovens at Danish. There were seven messages from Gray Donaldson in Casino Credit, the last three *911*, and one last message from my husband. Checking in. Colleen told him she'd been unable to reach me for hours.

I texted him back—all was well (and by all was well, I meant we were alive)—then called Colleen.

"Davis," she panted. "Where have you been?"

I didn't know where to start.

She did. She started and almost didn't stop. When would Lost and Found reopen? The front desk, the concierge's station, valet, and the main cash cage in the casino had all turned into makeshift Lost and Founds. Cell phone mountains were forming. Everyone who'd lost a phone, in their efforts to find their phones, were having others dial their numbers, and the stacks of cell phones endlessly ringing at the satellite Lost and Found locations were causing disturbances. The ovens were completely down at Danish because of a wiring problem, and none of our electricians were brave enough to drop between the ovens from above to get to the faulty wiring, and as a result, the dessert bar at the casino buffet, Plethora, was empty, and that was in addition to no desserts at the many other restaurants

Danish supplied, and there wouldn't be desserts in the foreseeable future because none of the restaurants with operating ovens were willing to share. The water in the Olympic-sized swimming pools behind the hotel had reached Jacuzzi temperatures. One had already closed and the other was right behind it. The guests—in their efforts to cool off, drinking giant Velvet Elvis cocktails—were falling asleep in the warm water. There'd been a three-mobility-scooter pileup and subsequent senior citizen brawl in the casino when three little old ladies vying for one slot machine couldn't work it out peacefully. There'd been so many Housekeeping callouts that as of four o'clock, almost half of the seventeen hundred Bellissimo hotel guest rooms still hadn't been serviced. When would Lost and Found reopen? And on. And on.

If I had my husband's job, I would go to my office every morning, close the door, lay my head on the desk, and cry until it was time to go home. If anyone knocked on the door, I'd tell them to go away.

"Where are you, Colleen?"

"I'm on my way home," she said. "I couldn't take one more minute. I'll be in first thing tomorrow."

I couldn't very well say anything about her leaving early, considering I'd been AWOL for days.

Next up, my mother.

I texted to confirm everyone had returned home safely. They had. I told her I'd be there as soon as possible. She texted back and told me to scurry, because sinner was almost deadly. I was starving, but the deadly part of dinner didn't necessarily appeal to me. And it was nowhere near dinnertime.

I checked the time.

It was. It was somewhere near dinnertime.

Colleen hadn't left early.

It was late.

Late-late.

It was almost five, Central, which made it almost three, Pacific, so I did what anyone else who didn't have five million dollars and couldn't come up with that much money in five minutes would do. From my husband's computer in his empty office on the executive floor, I tried to hack Seattle City Light's system to cut the power to the title company waiting for the wire—Nelson Title on Westlake Avenue—but couldn't. Seattle City Light's system was protected by a Meraki MX firewall I could probably crack, but not in thirty minutes. Instead, I hacked the operating system of the twelve-story building the title company called home and triggered the smoke detector alarms. It must have been a very large building, because I triggered nine hundred alarms. I held my breath and counted to ten, knowing by then, the entire building would be evacuating. No doubt Nelson Title could throw a rock and hit a cybercafé, but no one in their right mind would accept a five-million-dollar wire over an unsecured server. Just as I was shutting down Bradley's computer, a Bellissimo-wide security alert flashed. The Magnolia Suites on the southeast side of the hotel tower on the twenty-eighth floor, which was to say directly below my home, were being evacuated. What was described by several guests as nuclear waste sludge was pouring onto the verandas and seeping into the private pools. From above. Environmental Protection was on the way.

I let my head thud to my husband's desk.

I texted my mother again. *Is Bea watering the tomatoes?*

Jess.

Tell her to stop. Right now.

She texted back. *I not short you goofing to light you new tarpit.*

Honestly, it didn't matter if I liked the new carpet or not.

I didn't care.

Whit well your beast tome?

I texted back. *I'm on my way.*

I took my time.

* * *

Just inside my front door, I sniffed. It wasn't right, but it wasn't as wrong as the Penthouse, and couldn't possibly be as wrong as the outdoor spaces below me that were being evacuated. I quietly sniffed my way down the hall and to the living room, where I heard the familiar strains of *Frozen* and intermittent claps of thunder.

The cat.

I stood quietly in the wide doorway, taking it in. My foyer floors were travertine, my kitchen floors ceramic tile, and eight of the other nine thousand square feet of flooring in my gargantuan home was hardwood. I had sisal-rugs-on-hardwood galore, but very little wall-to-wall carpet: Bradley's and my bedroom, Bex's and Quinn's playroom, and the living room. It was all the same carpet, too, a dove-gray frieze wool. Earlier, just that morning, in fact, Maintenance had managed to round up enough dove-gray frieze to lay the living room carpet back as it was. That afternoon, they had not. They'd replaced my living room carpet with casino carpet. And casino carpet was loud. Everything about a casino was loud. The aggressive carpet on an acre of casino floor under slot machines and blackjack tables worked. The blood red, circus blue, shamrock green, and school-bus yellow paisley-confetti-starburst patterned carpet didn't work in my home. I felt sorry for my furniture. One of my upholstered sliders in particular, because Bea Crawford was in it. Rocking a sleeping baby boy.

"Hey."

Two little blonde heads and a set of furry ears popped up from the new carpet.

The cat, in a crate beside Birdy's chair, honked.

Bex said, "How was jail, Mama? Did you have fun?"

I cut my eyes to Bea, who nodded at Quinn. "Nothing gets by that one, Davis."

That one whispered in her sister's ear. Bex said, "Mama? Can we watch *Frozen* after this?"

"Sweetie, you're watching *Frozen* now."

"But after this—"

"We'll see," I said, certain, before the day was done, they'd be watching *Frozen* again. No telling how many times.

"If we're going to watch it again, could you pop me some Jiffy Pop?" Bea asked. "And melt me a stick of Oleo for it?"

I didn't bother.

A quick after-incarceration shower and a much-needed change of clothes later, from my bedroom safe, I reloaded the gun Biloxi PD unloaded for me, tucked it, just in case, then bypassing my living room where *Frozen* was going strong, I went in search of my mother.

Guess where I found her.

Just guess.

"Davis." She shook a wooden spoon in my face. "I have meatloaf, hot slaw, roasted potatoes, fried okra, butter beans, cornbread, and hummingbird cake for dinner."

Oddly, standing in the middle of the kitchen, I didn't smell meatloaf. Or hummingbird cake. I tilted my head and tried again.

"It's the fertilizer," Mother said.

The doors were closed. Not only were the patio doors in front of us closed, which would surely mean the other doors were closed too, Mother had rigged rolled bath towel barriers at every juncture where glass met wall.

"Mother—"

"It'll be okay, Davis. The smell will die down."

"Before it kills us?"

She put an arm around my shoulders and turned me away from her towel barricade handiwork. "I made meatloaf," she reminded me.

"And what's that noise?" I looked at my kitchen ceiling.

"They're installing something upstairs."

The new heat and air unit. Above my kitchen?

"Meatloaf?" my mother reminded me.

"Thank you," I said. "I'm starving half to death, but you'll have to save me a plate again, because I have to work tonight."

"More for me," Bea Crawford, who shouldn't have even been there, and who had the hearing of a bat, and who was the only thing in my home louder than the new carpet, except for maybe the sneezing cat, yelled from the sofa. "Say, Davis. Have you ever seen this movie?"

We stepped into the living room, where I noticed rolled towels snaking all the way around the veranda doors too, something I'd missed earlier because my eyes couldn't get past the casino carpet, then I realized what else was missing. Or who, rather. The wingback chair was empty. "Mother, where's Birdy?"

Mother stared at the empty chair. "Bea? Where's Birdy?"

Bea's orange head swiveled. "She said she'd be right back."

"You let her out?" Maybe I could have been a little less accusatory.

"Let her out?" Bea could have been a lot less defensive. "I didn't let her out. She's got two legs, you know."

"Where'd she go on her two legs, Bea?"

"To her office. Something about the wrong suitcase at Hoity-Toity's."

"Wrong?" My voice jumped an octave. "Bea, Birdy doesn't classify suitcases as right or wrong. She only identifies them as lost or found. Who made that distinction for her?"

Bea's head jerked back. "Would you mind speaking American? I didn't understand a word of what you said. And where's my popcorn?"

I reached for the remote and paused *Frozen*, much to Bexley's, and by extension Quinn's, dismay. "Did anyone see

Birdy talking to someone about a suitcase? Did anyone overhear Birdy on the phone discussing a suitcase? Can anyone tell me who told Birdy she had the wrong suitcase?"

They all went Quinn on me.

I started the movie again, tossed the remote, and made a run for it, yelling the whole way. "Call me if you need me, Mother! Bex and Quinn don't like hot slaw or okra! I'll be back in time to tuck you in, girls! If Birdy wanders back before I find her do NOT let her out again!" I raced to the elevator and called Fantasy. "Hey," I panted. "We have a problem."

"You don't have a problem," she said. "I found an Elvis costume just your size. I, on the other hand, have a problem. Reggie's mad at me."

Reggie, Fantasy's husband, was forever mad at her, and me by proxy, when we stumbled onto a job that had us working around the clock. He thought those days were over. (So had I.) "Tell me later," I said. "Meet me in Lost and Found."

"How am I supposed to meet you in Lost and Found? I'm at the Santa Superstore in Gulfport."

"What?" I hopped off one elevator and onto another. "Why?"

"For Elvis costumes, Davis. We're working the Double Trouble banquet tonight. There's no way out of it. The only Elvis costumes left in South Mississippi are here and they're red velvet. The capes spell out Elfis in rhinestones."

"How is a Santa store even open in June?"

"It's not," she said. "I had to bust in."

"So you want to be arrested twice in one day?"

"Like I had a choice."

"Get out of there, Fantasy, and get back here. Birdy's on the loose."

"What do you mean, Birdy's on the loose?"

"She found the wrong suitcase at Bianca's and is on her way to Lost and Found with it."

"Run that by me again."

I ran it by her again.

"Who told her she had the wrong suitcase?"

"That," I said, "I don't know."

"Where's the right suitcase? And what's in it?" she asked. "The money?"

"I'm on my way to Lost and Found to find out."

"I'll be there as soon as I can."

And that's when I got my first break of the long, long day. A day that never really started because I'd slept so very little the night before. As I stepped out of the sub-basement elevator on my way to Lost and Found, my phone blew up in my pocket with Megan Shaw alerts. Her phone had pinged into the Bellissimo network. She was back. At the Bellissimo. I found her—or, rather, the blue dot that was her phone—on the executive floor. She was at the opposite end of the hall from where I'd been a half an hour earlier setting off smoke alarms in Seattle. I stumbled down the dark tunnel on my way to Lost and Found watching Megan Shaw's phone travel in the same direction several floors above me. I lost her when she stepped into the employee elevator just past Bradley's office and didn't pick her up again until she exited the elevator on the convention level of the casino. Megan Shaw was at the Double Trouble slot machine tournament.

I called Baylor.

"What?" He wasn't happy. "I'm busy."

"What are you doing?"

"Your job," he said. "I'm at the tournament."

"In the convention center?"

"We didn't move it, Davis."

"How close are you to the employee elevator?" I was having trouble breathing.

"Which employee elevator?"

I rounded a corner to see a thin light coming from the

cracked door of Lost and Found. I picked up my pace.

"The one that goes from the executive floor to the convention center."

"I'm two feet from it," he said. "I just stepped out of it."

"Baylor!" I stopped dead in my tracks. "Megan Shaw was in that elevator. You rode the elevator with Megan Shaw?"

"What?"

At some point, I started moving again, and had I not slowed down, I wouldn't have been able to navigate the disaster that was the Lost and Found floor. I'd have wound up on it. "Birdy?"

"Oh, hello there, Davis." She was seated at her small desk, her eyeglasses—finally—perched on her nose. "You want to know what it says?" She held up and shook what must have been her copy of Friday's Incident Report.

Baylor said, "Are you talking about the Casino Credit cashier? The baby's mother?"

"Yes." I held up a wait-a-minute finger to Birdy. "You just rode the elevator with her. Did you hear me? Megan Shaw was on her phone in the employee elevator from the executive floor to the convention center."

"It says—" Birdy, who wasn't waiting a minute, zoomed in on her Birdynotes. "Hold the blue bag for M until Monday."

I covered the mouthpiece and said to Birdy, "Where's the blue bag, Birdy? And who is M?"

"No, she didn't," Baylor said into one of my ears just as Birdy said into the other, "I don't know where the blue bag is, and I don't know who M is. Maybe Mortimer?"

I scanned the clutter that was the Lost and Found floor and said to Baylor, "Yes, she did. Just now. She was in the employee elevator on her phone."

"There were two people in the employee elevator," he said. "I was one and Megan Shaw wasn't the other."

"Well, who was?" I covered the mouthpiece of my phone. "Birdy! There's a blue bag." It was a blue baby bag a foot from her chair, the only blue bag in sight, and there was only one baby in the nightmare I was living: Megan Shaw's. The M in Birdy's note must have been Megan. "Right beside you." I pointed to a quilted blue backpack covered with zooming Hot Wheels between—and why not?—two black spinner suitcases. "Can you reach it, Birdy?" Then to Baylor, I said, "Who?"

"Who what?" he asked.

"Who was the other person in the elevator?"

Birdy rolled her chair to the backpack in half-inch increments.

Baylor said, "You don't want to know."

So it was Clone.

Clone, the thorn in my side, the woman who'd taken my celebrity double job, the woman who I went to enormous lengths to avoid, Clone. Had I slowed down long enough to give Clone an ounce of consideration, something I never gave her, I might've guessed she was in the heist mix.

"And she was on the phone," Baylor said.

Why was Clone on Megan Shaw's phone? "Was on the phone, Baylor? Was? Is she still on it? Because we really need to know who she's talking to."

"Hold on," Baylor said.

"What in tarnation?" Birdy was unzipping the blue backpack one tooth at a time.

"She's disappeared into thin air," Baylor said. "I don't see her anywhere."

"How'd you let her get away from you?"

"Because you called me!"

"Davis?" It was Birdy. "You need to see this."

I stepped over fishing gear, dodged a beautiful Goyard handbag (who lost that?), and hopped over what looked like a saxophone case to get to Birdy. In the Hot Wheels backpack, money. Lots and lots of money. Probably five million dollars. On top of the money, a note. *If anything happens to me, whoever finds this money, get it to Gray Donaldson in Casino Credit. And please, I beg of you, find someone who will take care of my mother and my son. Don't try to identify, locate, or contact my baby's biological father. Do not let that man raise my child.*

To Baylor, I said, "Find Clone. And when you find her, stay with her. Don't let her out of your sight."

I hung up.

I pocketed the note and zipped the backpack.

I clutched it to my chest.

I stood at the edge of Birdy's desk. "Birdy, is this the blue bag you found at your door Friday morning?"

"This Friday?" she asked. "Last Friday? Is today Friday?"

"Birdy." I reworded the question. "Does this look like the blue bag you found at your door last Friday morning? The blue bag so full of money you couldn't pick it up? The blue bag you told me you put in a black suitcase?"

She scratched her wig. "Did I tell you that?"

I made one last-ditch effort at getting through. "Birdy?" I leaned over to stab the Birdynote on her Incident Report. "Does the M in your note stand for Megan?"

"Who?"

No Hair's words came back to haunt me again. And again, and again. "Something's going to happen, Davis. Something's going to happen Old Bird can't handle, or mishandles, or panhandles, and when it does, it will be on you."

FOURTEEN

Clone's stage name was Sawyer James.

I didn't know and didn't want to know where Bianca's personal attorney found the rest of Bianca's lilapsophobia-friendly staff. Sara Z. had unceremoniously replaced me and filled the Penthouse with new and decidedly unfriendly employees so quickly after the storm, it was probably online. At Indeed. Or Misdeed. Or Potential Serial Killers for Hire. Dot-com. (Bianca's new secretary was atrocious, her new chef, terrifying, her new personal trainer, unnerving, and the worst, her new butler, so, so, so creepy.) Other than the few who remained of Bianca's former staff, which was only the Penthouse nursery employees, I knew next to nothing of the people who worked above my home. It was my job to run background checks on the Bellissimo's employees, not Bianca's, especially given I wasn't one any longer, so I'd ignored them mightily with one exception: Clone. Sawyer James. When it came to her, I couldn't stop myself. When it came to her, I knew too much.

Sara Z. Stone, Esquire, found my celebrity double replacement through VIP Talent Agency in New Orleans, where Sawyer worked the Gulf Coast tradeshow model circuit between unsuccessful reality television auditions, which was to say her life's work before stealing my job was luring convention attendees to manufacturer's displays with kielbasa sausage bites on confetti toothpicks, passing out logoed mini flashlights, and standing beside cars wearing cocktail dresses in convention centers up, down, and around the Gulf.

The first time I saw her was when the Bellissimo website relaunched after Hurricane Kevin. Five weeks after Bianca fired me, from my sister's creepy attic in Pine Apple, I logged on after receiving notification the site was live to check for implementation issues, broken links, or missing metadata descriptions. What I found was her back. My replacement's back. On the Bellissimo landing page. The whole landing page. Through a very filtered lens, the shot showed Clone barely glancing over her shoulder as she entered the luxurious bedroom of a Jasmine Suite, presumably skipping her sultry way to the blurry outline of a turned-back king-sized bed. There were fuzzy images of flickering candles, a shadowy outline of a bottle of champagne in a silver bucket, and the silhouettes of two tall, stemmed, cut-crystal champagne glasses on the nightstand. Behind the suggestive scene, a deep orange Gulf sunset. Text floated across the bottom of the screen in a sexy phantom font: *New Day, New Bianca. Join Her, Won't You? Valentine's Day. Come Feel the Love.*

It was wrong. All the way wrong.

The impression I'd spent years making for the First Lady of the Bellissimo was that of devoted wife, loving mother, caring humanitarian, committed civic leader, and (her favorite) cutting-edge fashion icon. The new website said the opposite. The accompanying copy could have read *Come Back to the Bellissimo When We Reopen and Climb into Bed with the Owner's Wife.*

Had Bianca approved of this woman? Had she sanctioned this media campaign? Had she signed off on the photoshoot?

I wasn't sure what I thought would happen after Bianca fired me, except not that.

That's not true.

I thought we'd work it out.

I'd picked up the phone to call her almost every day for weeks to do just that but stopped myself every time. I was in

Alabama, she was in Germany, and I could never get the time right. Two, it was during the short weeks between Thanksgiving, Christmas, and New Year's; I was busy. Three, I was waiting on her to call me. For her to come to her senses and agree that a magazine cover with her in the woods with alpacas wearing red lights wasn't the image she wanted to project, not only of the Bellissimo, but of herself. Just when I'd talked myself into believing it would all blow over and when the Bellissimo reopened everything would be like it was before, in the process of doing my satellite job and checking the relaunched website, I learned that I'd been replaced. By a clone of Bianca. By a clone of myself.

I turned my laptop around.

Bradley startled. Then his jaw dropped. He zoomed in. "That's not you."

Thank goodness.

"Did you know about this, Bradley?"

He shook his head. "I didn't, Davis. I did not." He pulled the laptop closer. "Is she about to strip in a Jasmine Suite?"

"I wonder if Bianca's seen this."

Bradley didn't respond. He was too busy staring at...not Bianca.

"Do you think Mr. Sanders has seen it?"

Bradley, still unable to tear his eyes away from the screen, shrugged he didn't know just as a text message buzzed in. My phone vibrated on the old dining room table. It was Fantasy. *Don't look at the new website.*

I texted back. *Too late.*

Who is that?

I told her I had no idea.

Whoever it is, she barely looks like Bianca. Has Bianca seen this? Has Mr. Sanders? Is prostitution legal in Mississippi, Bianca's the new Madame of the Bellissimo, and I didn't get the memo?

I texted back it was all news to me, I'd look into it and let her know what I found, then asked Bradley if he'd at least talked to Mr. Sanders. He hadn't. While his wife was otherwise indisposed having a head-to-toe makeover in Germany, Richard Sanders and their two sons were waiting out the hurricane cleanup in a six-bedroom suite at Chalet Zermatt Peak in Zermatt, Switzerland. He was swooshing the slopes and sipping peppermint Schnapps while Bradley and I put his casino back together and his wife's new personal attorney ruined her reputation.

I gently closed the laptop. Bradley fell onto the cracked red pleather back of a kitchen chair from my childhood. "Davis, this isn't on you," he said. "This is no reflection of you."

But it was. If only in my heart, it was.

"Well," I forced myself to sound lighter than I felt, even though there was no fooling my husband, "there isn't a thing we can do about it. And I need to get back to work." And by get back to work, I meant get back to studying my replacement. He took a steel beam call from the general contractor of the Bellissimo remodel, giving me the chance to log onto the website again and torture myself more.

Sawyer James was obviously a work in progress, because, like Fantasy said, she didn't look a thing like Bianca, which was to say she didn't look a thing like me. I was certain a slew of cosmetic tweaking had happened or was happening. It would have to. Because the clone woman didn't look like either of us except for maybe her stature, which was spot on, and her body type, which was exactly the same, and the tip of her nose, which was all I could see of her filtered face, her nose being the only distinguishable feature between the saucer-sized Balenciaga sunglasses covering the top half (at sunset) and windswept locks of sunshine blonde hair across the rest.

I bolted upright and zoomed in.

Was the clone woman wearing my Bottega Veneta suit?

She was.

Which meant someone had been *in my home* to confiscate my Bianca wardrobe.

I immediately shot off an email to Sara Z. Stone telling her I'd have her charged with trespassing if she dared enter my home or touch my personal possessions again. She responded immediately that had she or any of the lilapsophobia-sympathetic staff she'd hired for the Penthouse entered my home, which they hadn't, they had every right to. Bianca Sanders's wardrobe was not mine. It was Bianca's. Nor was the Bellissimo mine. As owner, Bianca was in effect my landlord, and could come and go on her own property as she pleased. Then she said I had some nerve accusing her of breaking and entering.

I'd accused her of trespassing, but I liked breaking and entering even better. Because she had. Broken and entered and swiped. There couldn't possibly be two of the Bottega suits. I'd worn it a month before the hurricane hit. Bianca had me addressing the Junior League of Biloxi. I had to write my own speech—Women Building a Better Community—because Bianca's (then) secretary handed me a thirty-minute speech about microblading. It was a desperate plea for the women of Biloxi to get on the eyebrow microblading bandwagon, because, according to Bianca, they desperately needed it. Before the luncheon, I'd snipped the tags off the Bottega—$5,000 for the blouse that went under the $9,800 jacket. I was afraid to look at the price of the matching tuxedo pants.

Seeing Bianca's new clone just the one time wearing my suit was all it took.

I stopped watching network television, afraid I'd see Clone in Bellissimo commercials, I stopped reading the *Sun Herald* and cancelled my online subscriptions to *Southern Star*, *Magnolia*, *Gulf Living*, and *Babybugs*, the last one, not because I was afraid I'd see Clone, but because Bex and Quinn had outgrown it. Returning to Biloxi for the reopening and knowing there'd be no avoiding Clone in person, or worse, Bianca, who, at that time, I still hadn't heard a single word from, was one of the hardest things I'd ever done. Avoiding Clone turned out to be not so hard, because even when I wasn't working from home or my team's office-office in the basement, I never went anywhere Clone would be caught dead. Like Materials Management. Avoiding Bianca, with our homes separated by nothing more than my ceiling and her floor, was much more worrisome. After a week of no Bianca, I let out a puff of the breath I'd been holding. Another week passed, I exhaled another puff, then two more weeks, exhaling two more puffs, until it was announced in a security brief that Bianca wouldn't be returning anytime soon, at which point I let the breath all the way out. And with my very next breath, I let everyone know—my husband, my boss, and my team—I was fine. I couldn't care less. And by couldn't care less, I meant don't talk to me about Bianca or Clone, don't expect me to carry out a job that even remotely had anything to do with Bianca or Clone, and don't put me in the same room with either of them, which was how I wound up being in charge of Internal Departments.

Then I moved on with my life. As much as someone whose workday consisted of tracking down a missing delivery of queen-sized memory foam pillows can move on with her life. Until Clone somehow acquired Casino Credit cashier Megan Shaw's cell phone. Bradley leaving me in charge of the Bellissimo in his absence hadn't put me back in the game. Clone, having something or everything to do with missing Megan Shaw and five million dollars, had.

I knew that woman was trouble the first time I saw her in my Bottega Veneta suit.

I knew it.

FIFTEEN

At six forty-five Central, which was four forty-five Pacific, I stepped into the casino without my guard up. I breezed through like I owned the place, wearing a red velvet Elfis costume under a fifty-pound cape (the rhinestones...) and red velvet booties. My hair was stuffed in a pointy Elfis hat and my face hidden behind official Taking Care of Business sunglasses. Beside me, in the exact same getup, was my official taking-care-of-business partner, Fantasy. Between us, an official Bellissimo VIP leather weekender bag from Player Services. Full of money.

"Clone's still MIA," Fantasy said.

"I know," I said. "And she either ditched Megan Shaw's phone or it's dead, so there's no tracking her."

"She's been missing for hours. Where do you think she is?"

"We have the money, Fantasy, so I don't really care where she is."

"Do you care how she got Megan Shaw's phone?"

That I cared about. But I cared more about the fact that we found the missing five million dollars before she did and were about to wire it to Seattle than I did about her stealing jobs. I meant phones.

We coded ourselves into the short hallway between the main casino cage and the count room and stopped at the Casino Credit door. I gave it a tap. Gray Donaldson let us in.

"Cute outfits."

We transferred the cash from the weekender to a large canvas money bag, then after snapping on latex gloves, gathered everything in and around Megan's desk and lobbed it into the empty bag. Gray slipped across the hall to deposit the money in Casino Credit's account. By the time we'd tossed Megan's workstation a second time—over, under, around—to make sure we hadn't missed anything, Gray returned. She set up a three-way call between Branch Banking & Trust in Philly and Nelson Title Company in Seattle. All parties logged on to a BlueJeans screen-sharing session and we watched over Gray's shoulder as she hit enter—there went the money—at which point, it was done. The money we never should have received in the first place was back where it belonged.

I felt like I'd won a war.

Fantasy and I slipped out with the weekender bag, then passed it off to Baylor in the vestibule outside of the Convention Center tournament room.

"Have you found her?" Fantasy asked.

"No."

"It's been hours, Baylor. Have you checked all the bars?" I asked.

"No," he said, "and I'm not going to." He switched the weekender to his other shoulder. "What do you want me to do with this?"

"Don't let it out of your sight," I said.

"I don't think you understand, Davis. I've been awake for three days. I'm not staying awake to find Clone, and I'm not staying awake to watch a bag."

"Then drop it off at my house on your way to bed," I said. "I'll watch it."

"Your house is past mine," he said. "I'm going straight home. The bag's going with me."

"Give me the bag." Fantasy yanked it off Baylor's arm, then we pushed our way through all shapes, sizes, and eras of Elvii to the bar, ordered All Shook Up martinis (we'd earned them), then plastered ourselves against a back wall and tried to yell at each other over the Suspicious Minds din. The subject matter too sensitive, we reverted to communicating the old-fashioned way: smoke signals.

I'm kidding.

We texted.

Subjects we tried to cover with our thumbs: was Megan Shaw dead or alive? Clearly, since we found the money in her baby's backpack, she'd been the one to hide it. From Clone? Clone knew about the errant wire and was after the money? How? And how were the two women connected? Was it Clone who'd coerced Megan into cashing the five-million-dollar wire, or did Clone know about it and was trying to steal the money from Megan? We discussed the timing of the heist we'd interrupted. Was it a coincidence the wire misfired just as the Elvis convention began, when the casino owner, president, and head of security were out of town at the same time? Exactly when Bianca Sanders returned? And what we really wanted to know: What happened to Megan Shaw that kept her from picking up Baby Oliver at Play? We were still poking away on our phones, bouncing Hallmark-mystery-worthy questions without answers back and forth, when the last tournament round ended and the banquet ensued. We stayed long enough to sign off on the scores, then hugged the back wall and escaped through a service entrance. The absolute quiet was unnerving as we made our way to the elevator.

"Should we look for Clone?" Fantasy asked.

"If she doesn't show up by tomorrow morning, yes. Are you going home?"

She was digging for the buzzing phone in the pocket of her Elfis skirt was what she was doing. "I can't wait to go home." She studied the phone. "What about you?"

"I can wait."

She looked up from the screen. "Either my phone has gone crazy or I have yours."

I reached in the pocket of my Elfin skirt, and I had hers. I held it out to trade. I shook it. "Here."

"Wait a minute," she said, "I'm trying to read this."

"Give it."

"Wait." She held up a finger. "It's from your mother. Listen to this." She read slowly. "Bibby whiff bull's eye. Catbird, bay, hex, queen, gong to bad," she read. "Wink going hark. Close dead room floors. Coping winders. Pear. Tout. Spouse. Leaf coping."

What my mother could do with the twenty-six little letters of the alphabet was nothing short of amazing. And not in a good way.

We traded phones while stepping into the service elevator. "It says Baby Oliver is with July."

"It does not."

"'Bibby whiff bull's eye' is 'baby with July.'"

"If you say so."

"The cat, Birdy, Bea, Bex, and Quinn have all gone to bed. The wind is blowing hard." I looked up. "Maybe we'll get rain. Is there rain in the forecast?"

"Davis, we spent half the day in jail and the other half working ourselves stupid," she said. "Do you really want to talk about the weather?"

"Mother is airing out the house. 'Pear tout spouse' is 'air out house.' She's closed the bedroom doors so she could open the windows, and she's telling me to leave the windows open. 'Leaf coping' is 'leave open.'"

"But you don't have windows per se."

"I think she means doors," I said. "The French doors in the kitchen. The terrace doors in the living room. The balcony doors between the guest suites."

"Go close your doors," Fantasy said. "A plane could crash into your house."

"Fantasy, glass doesn't stop airplanes."

I pocketed my phone. I chose slumping against the elevator wall over stretching out on the floor. We said goodbye on the lobby level. She was one foot in and one foot out of the elevator on her way home after one of the longest days of our lives when a security alert beeped on her phone. Just her phone. My phone, after one of the longest days of its life, and with the one last jumbled communiqué from my mother, had given up.

"What is it?"

She slipped her phone back into the pocket of her Elfin skirt. "Something about Animal Control. Let Baylor take it."

"He's asleep." And that's when I remembered. We'd forgotten the VIP weekender bag. It was in the conference center tournament room. "And we forgot the bag."

Honestly, I thought she might cry.

"Go home, Fantasy," I said. "I'll get it."

She blew me a weary kiss.

I stayed in the elevator. By the time I returned to the tournament room on the convention level, it was Elvii free. I spoke to every single person gathering linens from tables, filling bus carts with banquet dishes, and pushing brooms. No one had seen a Bellissimo VIP leather weekender bag. I was dead on my feet, and it wasn't like anyone would have turned the bag into Lost and Found, so I gave up and went home.

To pigeons.

Hundreds of pigeons.

Pigeons who'd been evicted from between the condensers of Bianca's former air conditioning unit and their former home. They'd sought refuge on my balcony, patio, and veranda. It was dark out, and my mother probably hadn't noticed them when she coped the winders to pear tout the spouse before she went to bed—everyone in the world but me was in bed—and the pigeons had helped themselves. To my home. They'd dined on tomato plant leaves, built new nests from the upholstery of my furniture, and were all over the new casino carpet in my living room.

I flattened myself against the wall and backed out.

From the landline in Bradley's office, because my phone was dead, I called Security.

"This is Mrs. Cole. I need Animal Control."

"They've come and gone, Mrs. Cole. They cleared the roof of a massive flock of pigeons."

"Yes, well, they cleared them to the twenty-ninth floor. My living room is full of pigeons."

After a beat, he said, "Come again?"

"Pigeons," I said. "In my home."

"Inside?"

"In my living room," I said. "All over my furniture, all over my floor, flying in circles, and I need help. I need Animal Control back, I need Maintenance, I need Housekeeping, I need everyone."

I woke my mother first. We systematically woke everyone else. With the lights on and with all the activity, the pigeons flew unchecked through my home, leaving almost nothing unscathed. My mother chased them with spatulas in both hands. Bea Crawford, who shouldn't have even been there, ran through trying to pop them with a dishtowel. My dog was losing her mind. My daughters thought they were in the coronation scene from *Frozen*, and all this around Birdy, who sat on a bench in the foyer stroking sneezing Mortimer.

I wondered where we'd go. There wasn't an empty hotel room in the building.

Then I looked up.

We rode the private elevator in my foyer to the Penthouse.

Talk about breaking and entering.

But Bianca wasn't there, nor, thankfully, was her creepy butler, her crooked attorney, or her terrible excuse for a celebrity double. I told everyone to find a bed. I would go on to seriously regret not assigning beds, but I was too tired.

I tried to sleep, still in most of my Elfin suit, between the twin beds holding my sleeping daughters, but I couldn't, because I couldn't sleep past Clone having Megan Shaw's phone. I finally gave up, and at two in the morning, stumbled to Richard Sanders's home office. I woke up his computer and hacked Megan Shaw's phone to see who was on the other end of the call Clone answered.

Lost and Found.

Bellissimo's Lost and Found.

From Megan Shaw's phone, Clone took a call from Lost and Found and hadn't been seen since.

I reminded the security detail at the elevator landing that no one was allowed in or out, then made the million-mile journey to Lost and Found.

I shot my way in.

I found her three hours later in the very last place left to look. The chest freezer was wedged against the back wall at the end of the last row of Lost and Found cages. And there was Clone. We finally met. Face to frozen face.

SIXTEEN

"Here's what I know."

Tuesday morning, bright and early, by Vegas clocks anyway, and far too early for me, my boss called. I accidentally took his call without checking the caller ID, because for one, my eyes were glued to computer screens, and for another, I was sure it was Fantasy. I found out too late it was No Hair.

"You stole a Mercedes SUV off the dealer's lot, for which you were arrested."

"Not true, No Hair. I stole a Mercedes SUV from our parking garage. Not the dealer's lot. I don't know who stole that car from the dealer's lot."

"Comforting, Davis. So comforting." He took a deep breath. "Let's keep going."

Let's not.

"A child was left at Play for almost three days," he said, "and instead of alerting the authorities and shutting down the daycare, you took the baby. From what I understand, you still have the baby you took from the daycare."

"It's a childcare center, No Hair. Not a daycare. And for your information, I do not have the baby."

"You've lost the baby?"

"July has the baby."

"Moving on," he said, "as if that's not enough."

It was quite enough.

"Is it true that seven of our restaurants, in addition to Plethora, don't have desserts because you haven't bothered to make the ten-minute phone call it would take to have the ovens at Danish repaired?"

"Did Colleen tell you that?"

"No, Davis. The internet did. People are twittering photographs of Plethora's dessert line piled high with Snickers candy bars."

"People who live their entire lives on social media need better things to do."

"With all your spare time, since you're apparently not working, why don't you Twitter that to them?"

"I'll think about it."

"Davis, are you harboring Birdy James?"

"Define harboring."

"Hiding."

I'd seen Birdy in plain sight not fifteen minutes earlier. "I'm not hiding her."

"Is she a guest in your home?"

"Not at this very minute."

"From what I understand, no one is a guest in your home at this very minute," he said, "and we'll get to that in a minute."

I could wait.

He said, "Let's keep going."

Let's not.

"Davis, four Magnolia Suites have been evacuated to the tune of almost fifty thousand dollars."

"To where? Kensington Palace? The Lincoln Room? Arendelle Castle?"

"I've never heard of that last one."

"That's because you don't watch *Frozen*, and that's a ridiculously expensive evacuation."

"You think? Do you want to guess why?"

I did not.

"Because the Bellissimo is completely sold out, Davis. I don't know if you've poked your head out of your own little chaotic world far enough to see that the Bellissimo is wall-to-wall Elvis fans. We had nowhere to put the evacuees. Guest Services had to buy out the top floor of Hard Rock, our competitor, to accommodate them."

"I'm sorry to hear that," I said, "but I didn't make those arrangements, so what does that have to do with me?"

"That's what I want to know," No Hair said. "The suites we had to evacuate are directly below your home."

"I'll look into it and get back with you."

"Am I to assume you don't want to talk about it?"

"You assume correctly."

"Then how about we talk about a consumer complaint filed with the Federal Reserve against the Bellissimo by Branch Banking & Trust in Philadelphia for failure to notify them we received a five-million-dollar wire that wasn't ours. Do you want to talk about that?"

I cleared my throat. "Not particularly."

"Do you want to talk about four Vault employees who called in sick after eating too much of a wedding cake you sent to the vault? Do you want to talk about that?"

"No."

"Then let's switch gears," he said. "You want to switch gears, Davis?"

"Yes."

"This morning, Bianca Sanders found your ex-ex-mother-in-law, and what she's doing there, I'd surely like to know, sleeping—" he paused for dramatic effect "—*sleeping* in her bed. In her *bed*, Davis."

"I never told Bea she could sleep in Bianca's bed. I am not responsible for that woman," I said. "I'm not responsible for Bea, for Bianca, for Casino Credit cashiers, for vault guards who eat too much cake, for picky guests in Magnolia Suites, for any Elvii, not a one of them, not *any* of them, No Hair." I'd had about all I could take. "You know who I'm responsible for?" I didn't give him time to answer. "Me. I'm responsible for me. I answer to my husband, to my daughters, to my immediate extended family, and to myself. I am not responsible for everyone else on the planet, their actions, their tomatoes—" that was when I started crying "—their attorneys, their employees, their cats, their—"

"STOP."

I stopped.

Talking.

I didn't stop crying.

"You are." No Hair's voice softened. "But you are, Davis. We all are. We're all responsible for everyone around us. Regardless of how someone treats you, or how you think you've been treated, if your feelings are hurt, if it was all their fault or all your fault or no one's fault, you can't say it's not your problem. Davis, you're responsible, and not as an employee of the Bellissimo, but as a human."

Neither of us spoke for a full minute.

"I have one last question, and I want a straight answer."

I sniffed.

"Did you stuff Clone in a freezer?"

Finally, an easy question for which I had a truthful answer. "No."

"Do you have anything to say, Davis? Anything at all?"

"I have a question."

"I'll do my best," he said.

"I have two questions."

"Go ahead."

"Does Bradley know any of this?"

"Not yet."

"How do you know all this?"

"Baylor."

I'd about had it with Baylor too.

"You know why?" he asked.

I did not.

"Because he cares about you, Davis. We all do. You're in over your head and you're dragging Fantasy down with you. You need help. Start with helping yourself. Sit down with Bianca and work it out."

I turned off my phone.

I didn't want him to remember something else and call again.

I couldn't take anymore.

I'm not sure how long I stared at the three computer screens in front of me contemplating all No Hair said. Facial recognition software was hypnotic, the flashing morphing faces, but I sat there long enough to realize I had to call my husband and to get a hit.

I zoomed for the beeping screen.

Nathan Z. Stone was the Wire Department Manager for Branch Banking & Trust on Hillcrest Road in Mobile, Alabama. He was Sara Z. Stone's brother—the "Z" was Zion for him and Zada for her—he was one of Megan Shaw's BB&T bosses for the six years she worked there, and he looked familiar. The more I studied his face, the more I realized I'd seen him before. A one-year-old version of him anyway. Ten minutes later, I connected Clone. The photograph above an article on NOLA.com titled *BANK ON THEM!* showed Sara Z., Nathan Z., and Clone at a Wealth Management and Trust Conference, and the Clone on my screen looked far different from the Clone I'd found in the freezer. Even unfrozen, there were very few recognizable features. The conference I found the Stone siblings and Not Clone was held at the Lindy C. Boggs International Conference Center on Lakeshore Drive in New Orleans. Not Clone was working the conference, passing out printed coin pouches, the squeeze kind made of rubber. They were bright red and said *BANK ON ME.* The conference dates were October tenth through the thirteenth of the previous year. As in exactly when

Hurricane Kevin hit.

It all went back to the hurricane.

The hurricane I thought we'd all survived, but then again, maybe we hadn't.

SEVENTEEN

Homeless, because mine was still hard on the comeback trail from bird sanctuary status and having been unceremoniously evicted from the Penthouse by Lurch, of all creepy people, my entourage and I moved to an evacuated Magnolia Suite on the twenty-eighth floor. We went from ten thousand square feet to twelve hundred square feet in an elevator ride.

With two animals.

One of them sneezing its head off.

There was no kitchen.

"How long?"

Every fifteen minutes, my mother asked how long it would be before we could go home. So she could cook.

Every ten minutes, Bea Crawford, who shouldn't have even been there, came lumbering through the front door on her way out the patio doors with another rancid tomato bucket, leaving both sets of doors wide open every time, and I had to stop what I was doing and close them behind her because not only was the smell atrocious, Bea was—truly, she was—raised in a barn, where it was fine to leave doors open. She was at five tomato buckets and climbing, and the odor, along with the temperature in the suite, with her running in and out, was climbing too. She said, pouring sweat, "Davis, did you pick somewhere to put me up that's even hotter than your house?"

Every five minutes, Birdy James asked if anyone knew if her wingback chair had survived the pigeons, and if so, could someone please help her get it.

Every four minutes, Bex asked when she and Quinn could swim in the private pool on the Magnolia balcony that didn't have a drop of water in it after being drained of Black Kow crud contamination. If they couldn't swim, could they please watch *Frozen*.

Every three minutes, Candy barked.

Every two minutes, Mortimer sneezed.

And every single minute, I wondered where Casino Credit cashier Megan Shaw was and if, by the time I found her, I'd still be married.

Not necessarily in that order.

We were packed in the parlor between the two bedrooms, everyone but Quinn talking at once, along with Candy barking and the cat sneezing, when I climbed the furniture. From the coffee table, I let out a two-finger siren of a whistle. Everyone except the cat and Quinn piped down, because Quinn stayed piped down, and when everyone else joined her, we could hear a persistent tap on the door. From atop the coffee table, I yelled, "Come on in. Whoever you are, you might as well come in."

It was July. With Baby Oliver on her hip.

She surveyed.

I pointed at the half of the sofa Bea wasn't on.

She sat.

I addressed my rapt audience. "Let's talk," I said. "And by that, I mean I'm going to talk, and you all are going to listen."

The cat sneezed.

Baby Oliver said, "Baa, baa, baa, baa, baa."

I said, "The door to the guest hall upstairs at my house was miraculously closed."

Bea waved. "You can probably thank me, Davis."

"Bea," I turned to her, "I seriously doubt it, because you don't know how to close doors. And you shouldn't even be here to leave doors open. Did you hear me say be quiet and listen? Zip it up."

She snarled at me.

I picked up where I left off. "The pigeons didn't make it down the guest hall or into the rooms. The four guest bedrooms escaped. As soon as the rest of the house is pigeon free, and by pigeon free, I mean sanitized and inhabitable, we can move into the guest rooms. It could possibly be late tonight. It will most likely not be until tomorrow morning. In the meantime, we're here, make yourselves as comfortable as you can, and make the best of it. And by make the best of it, I mean understand that I'm only one woman, I can't solve every single problem, and I want to go home too."

I turned to my mother. "Mother, what desserts can you bake that you don't need an oven for?"

A finger disappeared deep into her curls as she tapped open the cookbook she kept in her head. "Davis, you can't 'bake' anything without an oven. Are you asking me for my no-bake dessert recipes?"

For the first time in my life, I think I actually was asking her for a recipe.

"Let me see." I heard the opening strains of a greatest hit from Mother's no-bake repertoire. "Cowboy cookies," she said, "I don't need an oven for those. I make miniature cheesecakes that I don't bake. Peanut butter bars, strawberry icebox cake, fried apple popovers, banana pudding squares—"

"Get your apron and go to Danish, Mother. It's in the lobby beside the coffee shop. Behind Danish is the kitchen that bakes most of the desserts for the Bellissimo. Their ovens are down. They need you."

Crowd reduced by one.

I turned to Bea Crawford. Who shouldn't have even been there. "Bea, the tomatoes stink. I could go on and on, but that's the bottom line. They stink. Stop dragging them down here. My front door—" I pointed up "—is wide open, because without a doubt, you left it that way. If you need to water the tomatoes or stare at the tomatoes or sing to the tomatoes—" I swept an arm in the direction of the Magnolia door "—be my guest. But do it upstairs and stop dragging the tomatoes down here."

She opened her mouth to protest, because she'd rather her precious tomatoes be in the Magnolia Suite with her rather than upstairs with the carpenters, painters, and cleaners who were crawling all over what used to be my home, but I shut her down with a look that said one word, Bea, just one, and I might put you out of your own and my misery.

Bea's mouth snapped closed.

"Birdy."

She was petting Mortimer backwards. She had his ends mixed up. "Yes, Davis?"

Having been five foot two and a half all my life, I was very much enjoying my elevated status on the coffee table. My people were listening to me. I was in charge. I was on a roll.

"Birdy," I said, "among other atrocities, the pigeons picked and pecked all the upholstered furniture in my living room including your wingback chair from the dining room. I have very little living room furniture left. The wingback chair, even if I had caught it before they tossed it, still wouldn't be fit for—" I lost my words. "Find another chair, Birdy."

Then I turned to July, who had Baby Oliver on her lap with Bex and Quinn, glued to the Mama Show, squeezed on either side. "Do you need me?"

"No," she said. "I came to see if you needed me."

"I do. Can you watch the children for an hour or two?"

"Yes."

"Can you keep Candy too?"

"Yes."

"At your house?"

"Yes."

I stepped down from the coffee table, kissed the blonde curls on the tops of my daughters' heads, then Baby Oliver's, because the top of his head was so cute too, and turned for one of the two small suite bedrooms.

They all asked my back a version of where-was-I-going.

"To the closet."

"Why?" they asked in unison. I might have even heard Quinn.

"To make a phone call."

It was far past the point of telling all to my husband.

I dodged two rollaway beds, Oliver's Pack 'n Play, grocery bags stuffed with clothes, dog food, toys, diapers, and a kitchen sink on my way to the walk-in closet, where there was a small dressing table I could use for a teeny desk, a safe with my loaded gun already in it, and peace and quiet.

I flipped on the dim light, then closed the closet door behind me.

I might never leave the closet.

I pulled my gun and my laptop full of Sara Z., Nathan Z., and Clone dirt from the safe. I tucked the gun in my waistband, settled in at the small dressing table, then clicked on the laptop. I placed my phone beside the laptop and stared at both. With much trepidation, I turned on the phone. The beeps, whistles, and sirens of notifications I'd missed in the time it had been off made me want to change my number. Or wipe the phone clean and start over. Or march out of my closet womb, through the balcony doors, and sail it into the Gulf.

I didn't.

Nor did I start to read what could easily be published as a collection of horror short stories that were the episodic text messages, one on top of the other, waiting for me. I did catch Colleen's last one—*Davis, I'm sorry, I didn't know what else to do*—before the closet door flew open and there stood my husband.

* * *

It was with odd relief, which I attributed to the fact that I loved him, and a gargantuan lump in my throat, which I attributed to terror, that I followed my husband out of the Magnolia Suite, down the hall, to the elevator, up one story, through the foyer, then into the living room of our annihilated home. I would say I was being called on the carpet in the living room of our annihilated home, but we had no carpet.

"Leave," Bradley said.

Painters, carpenters, and cleaners stopped what they were doing, dropped what they'd been holding, and left.

I stood in the middle of the living room and listened carefully as Bradley's footfalls echoed through the sparsely furnished and heavily pigeoned warzone of what was formerly our home. He spent an inordinate amount of time at the veranda doors studying the tomato buckets. I heard him in the kitchen. I heard him as far away as the unscathed guest wing. He finally returned to the living room with two somewhat intact kitchen chairs.

He placed them facing each other, interrogation style.

I would say our voices bounced off the walls in the desolate room, but neither of us spoke. We were waiting each other out. He was waiting for me to explain myself, and I was pulling a Quinn. I didn't want to explain myself. I didn't know where to start. It was easier to keep my mouth shut. Had Bexley been there, I might have whispered the story to her, then she could Cyrano de Bergerac for me to her father. Her very angry, her very weary, her very deeply disappointed father. Who wouldn't break eye contact with me, but who had absolutely nothing to say to me either. After an hour, the most miserable hour of my life, an hour in which both our phones exploded with calls and text messages we didn't take, after a solid hour, he stood.

"We're getting nowhere, Davis."

He stood; he walked past me. I was on the verge of a meltdown, watching him walk away, ready to end the silent stalemate and tell all, everything, even the wedding cake, when he seemed to change his mind. He turned around at the living room door. "Come with me."

I went. I didn't want to be left alone in the tomato-pigeon wasteland.

In our foyer, he stood at the private elevator that led to the Penthouse.

He hit the elevator button.

I panicked.

When the door opened, he swept an arm, ushering me in.

I didn't move a muscle.

We stood there like that, him holding the bouncing elevator door until he asked, "Did you stuff Clone in a freezer?"

I shook my head no. Adamantly shook my head no. I almost shook my head off my neck denying it.

"Do you understand your ex-ex-mother-in-law shouldn't even be here?"

I nodded yes. Adamantly nodded yes. I almost nodded my head off my neck agreeing with him.

"Were you arrested for grand theft auto?"

My head didn't know which way to turn. I think it lobbed. Maybe it bobbed. He'd asked a complicated question with a tricky answer.

He rolled his eyes, then said, "Go, Davis." He gave the interior of the elevator a nod. I didn't move a muscle, just stared at the back wall of the elevator I didn't want to ride until he said, "You're not going to work things out with me until you work things out with her."

Well, for sure, I wanted to work things out with him. If I had to go through her to work things out with him, then so be it. I stepped into the elevator alone, then stepped out of it at the Penthouse alone again—no Lurch, hopefully she'd fired him too—then sulked my way to Bianca's suite of rooms only to immediately learn there'd be no working it out with Bianca until we both worked it out with Sara Z. Stone, Esquire, who, from a lounging position deep in the soft white leather glider behind Bianca's white marble desk, welcomed me to Bianca's office with the business end of a Kimber Micro Bel Air. And by Kimber Micro Bel Air, I meant a .380 semi-automatic pistol. Pretty, with a blue alloy frame and mirrored slide, but still, a handgun, directed at me. "Stop."

I stopped.

She lobbed out a palm. "Phone."

I pulled my phone from my pocket. I tossed it. It landed square on the desk with a crack. Next, the small battery from my phone flew over my head to land somewhere deep in white carpet behind me.

"Earpiece," Sara said.

I had no earpiece.

"Tracking device? Headset? Microprocessor? Transmitter? Any other miscellaneous spy gear?" she asked.

Nope.

"Empty your pockets."

I hesitated.

She shook the Bel Air.

I had no choice but to hand over the keycard to the Magnolia Suite.

She placed it squarely on my dead phone, then changing her mind, tucked it in the pocket of her jacket. She patted the pocket holding the keycard that would give her access to the Magnolia Suite, those still in it, and the laptop full of dirt on her. Next, with the muzzle end of the Bel Air, she directed me to sit. I compliantly, and by compliantly, I meant at gunpoint, took a seat in a white leather chair on the other side of the desk, shoulder to shoulder with Bianca. Immediately and instinctively, my left arm dropped to meet her right arm and we hooked pinkie fingers.

And that was all it took to make things right with Bianca.

Sara waved the Bel Air again. "Hands where I can see them."

Palms up, I splayed my fingers, then lowered my hands to my lap.

She tossed a black nylon zip tie. I caught it midair. "You know what to do."

"How am I supposed to restrain myself?"

Sara waved the Bel Air at Bianca. "Help her, Princess." To me, she said, "I don't trust you."

It was so mutual.

With shaking hands, Bianca, out of fear or forethought, loosely did the zip tie honors.

Sara planted her elbows on Bianca's desk. She leaned in. She rested her chin on her interlaced fingers. "Where's my money, Davis?"

"Where's Megan Shaw, Sara?"

She laughed, a single sharp utterance. "You're kidding, right?" The more she thought about it, the funnier it was. "Who cares?" She laughed even harder. "Save the world, Davis!" She fell back into Bianca's leather chair, still laughing. "Should we nominate you for a humanitarian award?" She wouldn't stop laughing, waving the Bel Air around in circles, the confident laugh of dominance, victory, with a touch of hysteria, when what she should have done in the very beginning was frisk me.

Amateur.

EIGHTEEN

In a perfect world, or in the movies, or had it been Fantasy with free hands beside me, I'd have leaned forward and given her access to the Glock tucked in the waistband of my jeans. The tables would have turned, which was to say the manic laughter would have stopped and Bianca's solid white office would have a whole new color palette.

That didn't happen.

It was in my DNA, it had been for years, and it would be as long as we were under the same gargantuan roof, to protect Bianca, who wasn't proficient with firearms, and while clearly Sara wasn't either—who waved a gun around like that?—she still had the advantage. The best I could hope for was that she locked us up fast so I could shoot us out faster.

That didn't happen either.

Sara Z. Stone, who wasn't an idiot, and having had total access to Bianca, Bianca's home, Bianca's accounts, and Bianca's very life, led us to the new weatherproof saferoom. A room I'd only heard about, installed adjacent to the master suite as part of Bianca's lilapsophobia program, and the only location in the Penthouse my Glock would be helpless to create an emergency exit. I couldn't shoot us out of the weatherproof saferoom with a bazooka. And that's where Sara parked us.

It took Bianca's handprint to open the door.

"Give me that." Sara waved her Bel Air wand at the only form of communication in the saferoom, a satellite phone. I picked it up with my imprisoned hands and passed it to her. She snapped off the antenna and threw the pieces of the broken phone over her shoulder. "You two kiss and make up while I'm gone."

The iron-reinforced concrete door didn't close quietly.

I struggled to free myself of the zip tie so I could finally get one up on Sara Z. Stone. I slapped the large red panic button to the left of the door with my open palm, which didn't free us, but trapped Sara in a locked-down Penthouse with a roaring siren, strobe lights, and a computer-generated genderless voice screaming, "RESCUE, RESCUE, RESCUE. WEATHERPROOF SAFEROOM OCCUPANT IN NEED OF RESCUE, RESCUE, RESCUE." On a loop. Over and over. Take that, Sara Z. Stone.

"Help is on the way, Bianca." I sounded more confident than I was. Then I repeated it for myself. "Help is on the way."

"When will it arrive?"

I opened my mouth to answer over the panic sirens on the other side of the saferoom door when they stopped as suddenly as they'd started. With my first heartbeat, the blood pumping through my veins carried relief—help had arrived—and with my second heartbeat, hard cold fear, when the saferoom lights flickered, then blinked off, only to power up again by way of a generator. The alarm disengaging so quickly and the weatherproof saferoom on auxiliary power meant Sara had flipped the First Responder toggle in the main breaker box. If she knew where the main breaker box was, and she knew which was the First Responder toggle that would render the panic button useless, then she certainly knew how to leave the Penthouse by secure stairwell.

Maybe she wasn't such an amateur after all.

I beat on the disabled panic button again and again.

Help wasn't on the way.

Having nowhere else to go, we sat on the stiff sofa. Bianca delicately cleared her throat. "I realize you tried to warn me about Sara, David."

It's Davis. And on the rare occasion of her taking an iota of responsibility, I lowered my guard. On a sigh, I said, "I should have tried harder."

"You were right about her."

The words came easily because, as it turned out, I'd been waiting eight long months to say them. "It was just as much my fault as it was yours."

Maybe more.

"I've missed you terribly, David."

My head dropped. "Same."

"Could I implore you to return to my employ long enough to kill her?"

"I'd be happy to, Bianca, as soon as we get out of here."

"Maybe you shouldn't necessarily kill her, as I would miss you all over again when you're given the death penalty, but do thoroughly maim her."

"How about I send her to prison for the rest of her life?"

"That will work."

The saferoom had all the ambiance of a crypt. We scooted closer together. Bianca whispered, "She was the devil in disguise, David."

"That's an Elvis song," I whispered back.

"What is?"

"Devil in disguise," I said. "Elvis."

"Oh, please." She closed her eyes and slowly shook her head. "Had I known I'd be returning to hordes and masses and throngs of pedestrian Elvii—"

My head popped up. "Thank you."

"You're most certainly welcome, David. For what?"

* * *

The new Penthouse weatherproof saferoom, half a mile from the original saferoom adjacent to the children's wing, built to protect the Sanders' sons in the event of a kidnapping attempt, was there to provide temporary shelter for Bianca and Richard Sanders during a sudden weather event. It cost a blue fortune, but worth every penny, claimed Bianca's lilapsophobia therapist. She could sleep soundly knowing she wouldn't be ripped from her warm bed and tossed out to sea should a hurricane sneak up on her. The room was a concrete cube nowhere near the square footage of Bianca's shoe closet, just five feet of iron-reinforced concrete away. The main room held a sleeper sofa, two chairs, and a small desk. On the desk, a hand-cranked AM/FM/Weather-Alert radio and two industrial flashlights. Through a small doorway to our left was a bare essential bath, and by bare essential bath, I meant bare essential bath. I'd seen more luxurious facilities in a pop-up camper. To the right of the main concrete room, in a space not large enough for one person to turn around, was the kitchenette. In it, a battery-operated hot plate, a coffeepot, the percolator kind with a glass bulb on top, and concrete inset shelves with nonperishables, bottled water, first aid supplies, batteries, and screw-cap wine.

We hit the wine.

"Where are the wine glasses, David?"

"We don't have wine glasses, Bianca."

We passed the bottle back and forth quietly until it was half gone.

I broke the ice. "Where have you been?"

She delicately dabbed at the red wine dribbling down her chin and passed the bottle to me. "Dr. Von Krügerschmitt?"

"The spiritual awakenment doc?"

"The same."

"What about him?"

"Butcher, David. The man was a butcher. I recovered from extensive facial enrichment treatment only to find my left eye was a thirty-second of a centimeter higher than my right eye."

She touched the tip of a pinkie finger to her left eyebrow, probably saying hello to a miniscule scar the eyebrow hid, and lost her grip on the wine bottle in the process. I barely caught it on the way down and passed it back to her. She secured it in both hands, lifted it to her lips, and took another slug. "My face, David. My left eye was higher on my *face* than my right eye. I looked positively bizarre. Dr. Von Krügerschmitt robbed me of my facial symmetry."

I had a feeling that before it was over with, we would learn she'd been robbed of much more than her facial symmetry.

She passed me the bottle. I took a long drink, then passed it back to her.

"How did you know?" I asked.

"Know what?"

"That one of your eyes was higher than the other," I said. "A thirty-second of a centimeter would be hard to detect. Humans are bilaterally symmetrical."

"What are you talking about, David?"

"I'm talking about the fact that one side of our bodies approximately mirrors the other side. Not exactly."

"David?" She tipped the bottle back again. "Whose shide are you on?"

"Yours," I said. "I'm just asking if after your surgery, you looked in the mirror and said, 'I have a wonky eye,' or if the doctor walked in and said, 'Ooops, Bianca, I put your eye in the wrong place.'"

Which, for a moment, in spite of our circumstances, struck us as almost funny until Bianca, oh so ominously, said, "It was Shara Z."

Good ole Shara Z.

"It was Shara who caught the horrible mistake, and right away, I should add," Bianca said. "It was Shara who brought in specialists, and it was Shara who encouraged me to have it corrected."

"Ah."

We opened another bottle, because the first one went down so easy. We drank.

"Of coursh, Dr. Von Krügerschitt denied everything," she said. "We are in litigashion."

We drank to litigashion.

"And I see now, David, that was a rushe. A ploy. A trick to keep ush apart."

"Ush, who, Bianca?"

"Ush me and you, David."

Not entirely out of the realm of possibilities, because Shara knew I was onto her going all the way back to our exchange the day before Thanksgiving. But encouraging or going as far as consorting with medical professionals to create circumstances in which Bianca was that far off the grid probably had more to do with Shara helping herself to Bianca's money than risking a reconciliation between us. Either way, for sure, Shara was the shyster storm-chasing opportunist I pegged her for from the start.

I took no pleashure in being right.

Trying to change the subject, because there wasn't a thing we could do about Shara until we escaped the saferoom, I asked, "Where were you between shurgeries?"

"Obviousshly, I went into hiding." She drank to hiding, patted her red lips with the back of her hand, then passed the bottle back to me.

"Obviousshly," I sipped. And by sipped, I meant poured half of the bottle straight down my throat.

"Where was Mr. Shanders this whole time?"

"Who?"

"Your hushband."

"What about him?" She tried to cross her perfectly symmetrical legs the other way and completely missed. I caught her. I propped her up. We opened a third bottle so we could drink to the near miss. Half of that bottle later, she said, "Where wash I?"

"You were hiding."

"I most certainly was, Davith, and it was unbearable. I couldn't look in the mirror. In fact," she said, "I went sho far as to have the mirrors of my temporary residensh removed."

"Where wash your temporary residensh?" I asked.

"The Eifel Tower Suite at Four Sheasons in Parish," she said. "I do love Parish."

"Who doesn't love Parish?"

We drank to Parish.

"I spenth the next three monshs in Ishaly with Dr. Cesario Giordano, a geniush—" she tipped her chin my way, she tilted her face this way, then that, "—who put Humfthy Dumpthy back together again."

We passed the bottle in Humpty Dumpty's honor.

"You know what I gave him forth inshructionshs, Davith?"

"What?"

"You," she said.

"Me?" Aiming for my chest and missing, I stabbed myself in the neck with my finger. I choked a little. Bianca tried to help me by rearranging my spine with her fist. When I finally came around, we drank to my recovery.

Where were we?

"Me?" That time, my finger hit closer to its mark.

"Youth, Davith. I turned to the years of youth on shocial meshia for him to use as baselineth critheria for my faith." She tried to touch the tip of a finger to the nose on her faith and just about poked her own eyes out before she gave up. "Thish." She framed her face with her hands. "My faith."

We drank to her faith. Her faith with eyes where they were supposed to be.

"And whath didth I find on shoshial meshia before I could finth youth?" she asked. "That womanth."

Cloneth.

I meant Clone.

I eyed the empty wine bottle. I felt like I was thinking slurred words. I hoped I wasn't talking slurred words. Like she wash.

"And Davith, she looked worsh than *me*!"

It was the true. Clone, bottom line, barely looked like Bianca's second cousin twishe removed. Her represhentation of Bianca was a study in Photoshop. And, I knew through the grapevine, and by grapevine, I meant Instagram, all that Photoshop was *after* Clone had coshmetic tweaks, and she *still* barely passed for Bianca. Not only that, I'd heard (I'd devoured every worth in Instagram comments—where the real shory was told) that before Special Events said, "Thash enough," and stopped booking her for live events, that Clone had dropped the F bomb on live televishion, had, in a single night, slept with three Bellishimio high-rollers from Bakershfield California, and had somehow offended the board of directors at the children's hoshpital in New Orleans to such an extent, a board on which Bianca sat, a board I'd put in thousands, if not hundreds of hours on, that she'd been removed. Clone losh Bianca's seat on the hoshpital board!

"Why, Biancath, haventh you fired her? Why?"

"Becaush my name is on the contrash, Davith! I shinged the contrash. I could not, deshpite my besh efforshs, escape the contrash I shinged with Shara! I shinged it. I shinged the contrash!"

"Shinged?" I asked. "As in la-la-la-la-la?" I heard myself shinging.

"No." Bianca put the bottle of wine down long enough to hold an imaginary pen in the air and sign an imaginary contrash. Then she bent all the way forward and said to the floor, "Oooops! I thropped the pen!"

For whatever reasons—our circumstances? Lack of oxygen?

It had been so long since we'd seen each other? Maybe the wine?—it was the funniest thing either of us had ever heard. When we finally stopped laughing, which wasn't until we found the very bottom of whatever bottle of wine we were on, I looked around, remembered we were locked in the shaferoom, and had been for at least an hour, or shix, and said, "Bianca, leths move this furnishure."

"Why in the worlth would we do that?"

"Becaush no one's reshued us yet, and maybe we should shtart looking for another way oush."

"We will need shmore wine, Davith." She tipped her head back and yelled, "GARSHON! BRING SHMORE WINE!"

Another bottle later, which in a way, was three or four—I'd lost count—bottles too many for her, and in another way, was—what?—maybe one glash too many for me, because Bianca was drinking way more than I was, taking much larger gulps, probably because it was hard to judge how much she was drinking without a glash—where was I?—furnisher. We were moving the furnisher. By the time we'd finished another bottle of wine, we'd rearranged the furnisher until we were right back where we started except for I wash much clearer-headed and a lot warmer from the physical activity. We didn't turn up a second satellite phone, a stack of dynamite, a shledgehammer, or another way out I already knew wasn't there. What I was really doing was waiting for her to shober up a little and looking for a light at the end of the shaferoom tunnel. When we didn't find a light, or a trap door, her shorbriety, or anything else, we sat side by side on the sleeper shofa again, and at her request, twishing my arm all over the plashe, opened a record-breaking fifth (or shixth) (or sheleventh) bottle of wine before moving onto Plan B, whatever Plan B was, and that was when I came up with Plan B.

"Down," I said.

"Wash?" she asked.

"Down. It's our only way outh. We can't get through the door—" I pointed at the door, "—we can't go through the ceiling to the rooth—" I pointed again, "—and that leaves down."

I pointed.

"Wash's down, Davith?"

"My housh."

"And how do you shugesh we get to your housh, Davith?"

"The wiring," I said.

"Wash about it? Are you shuggeshing we lelectrocuthe ourshelves?"

"I'm shuggeshing we find a way to get to the wiring. If we can find it, maybe we can pull it out and crawl through the shpashe where it wash."

Bianca, sho out of her natural environment, sho out of her element, and sho, sho, sho drunk, also had sho much dirt, grime, and greashe all over her shnow-white Ishabel Maranth shleevelesh jumpshuit from our furnisher rearranging project, plus dush bunnies in her blonde hair, and her nose was sho red and shiny, like Rudolsh, I almost didn't recognishe her. "When you find the wiring, Davith, could you pleash adjush the air?" She shwept manicured fingertips across her gloshy brow. "I am *moish* with humidity."

"You are shweating."

And it's Davish.

She took a hard seat on the shaferoom floor. She dropped her head between her knees. Unable to deny that she was, indeed, perspiring, of all fings, she said, "Well, lesh get it over wish."

"Get what over wish?"

"Our lelethrocution."

Lelecthrocution.

Oush.

Wouldn't shwimming be an eashier way to get to my houshe?

"Bianca," I said, "you're not going to like thish."

She patted her moist cheeks, which wash to say she added another layer of shticky dirt to her faith, "Try me."

"I have a bether idea."

"You alwaysh have good ideas, Davith."

"The shaferoom doesn't have shelf-contained plumbing either."

"So?"

"The plumbing and the wiring are the only fings that connect to anyfing elshe." I tried to count the empty wine bottles, because for sure, I think I shlurred a word or thoo in there. "And the plumbing ishn't in the wall. It's shtraight down."

"So you're shuggesthin we shtand over the powder room shink and shout in hopesh shomeone will hear ush?"

"I'm shuggesting we shtand over the powder room shink and shooth becaushe I know shomeone will hear ush."

"Shooth what, Davith?"

"My housh."

"You wanth to ashault your own family?"

"They're not there."

"Lesh think abouth thish, Davith."

I thought about it as hard as my wine-addled brain would allow. The more I thought about it, the more my wine-addled brain convinced me it was a great idea. I would shooth down a pithe. I meant pipe. The minimum damage—I meant the maximum damage—would be to the plumbing shomewhere inside a wall of the guesh wing. Let's say the bullet escaped the wall and I shoth a guesh wing shink below the shaferoom shink. Sho? Shinks were easy to replashe. And the guesh wing, having not been pigeoned, was empty of carpenters, painters, and cleaners, so they'd be shafe. But they'd hear it. And reshue us!

Precarious sobriety and Bianca followed me three steps to the powsher room, where I took a mental roll call one lash time before I started shooting. My daughters and Baby Oliver were at

Shuly's, nowhere near my housh, my husband was in his office cleaning up the horrific mesh I'd made of things, my mother was busy not baking at Danish in the Bellishimo lobby, the resh of my posshee was in a Magnolia Shuite on the twenty-eighth floor, including the cat—I remembered the shneezing cat—and none of the crew working in my housh was anywhere near the unpigeoned guesh wing. My wine-soaked brain was positive the guesh wing wash empty.

Except it washn't.

"Geth in the shower, Biancath."

"Do I shmell?"

I shniffed. "Citrushy," I said, "with hints of oaky bannila. But that doeshn't matter. Get in the shower for shafety."

"I've never taken a shafety shower."

She stepped into the shafety shower while I tried to shtick my eyeball down the shink.

"Davith?" She patted the concrete walls of the shower. "However do I thurn on the wather for my shafety shower?"

I pulled my head out of the shink to see her Ishabel maranth jumpshuit at her feet. "Don't thake a shafety shower. Jush shtand there for shafety."

"Before or afther my shower? And where's the shoap?"

"We don't have shoap, Biancath."

"Then however do you eshpect me to take a shafety shower?"

"Nevermind," I said. "Get dreshed. And cover your earsh."

"Do you want me to get dreshed or cover my earsh? Could you be more pashific?"

I didn't really understand her queshion, so I said, "Bosh. Do bosh."

"Bosh what? What bosh?"

Oh, forgesh it. I took a deep breath, shtuck the barrel of my Glock as far down the shink drain as it would go, stretched my arm to the pointh of pain, turned my head, and let her rip. The last thing we hearth, before we enjoyed a good five minutes of temporary noise-induced hearing losh, was what sounded like an exploshion below.

Had I just blown up my own housh?

Or, worse, had I shomehow launched myself and Bianca into a wine-fueled time continuum shtraight to hell? And managed to drag Beesh Crawfish, who shouldn't have even been there, and was shwell on her way to hell without my help, with ush? Because as my audio function and very tentative shobriety returned, which blowing up your own housh then landing in hell will do to you, all I could hear was Beesh Crawfish.

"*What the fudge*?"

I washn't wrong. A voice was rising through the drain of the small shink, and it was Bea Crawfish's.

"*What the fudgity, fudge, fudge, fudge*?"

I tiptoed, Bianca tiptoeing with me, to the shaferoom shink.

"*HOLY FUDGE*!"

We peered into the darknesh of the drain. I shmelled gunfire. Then I caught the shtrap of a La Perla balconette bra out of the corner of my eye. "Biancath, where are your cloves?"

She blinthed at me as if she couldnth hear me. Then I heard someshing. I lobbed an arm out to hold her back, like my mother ushed to do at Pine Apple's only shtop sign to keep me from flying out of the car, and the thing wash, she was only driving one mile an hour, and there washn't any way I'd fly out of the car in the firsh plashe, becaushe she had me shtrapped in like she wash transhporting a deranged menthal paishent already, when I heard wather. I whishpered. "Do you hear wather?"

"WHAT, DAVITH?" she screamed. "I CAN'T HEAR YOU."

"HOITY-TOITY?" It was Bea from the shink drain. "IS THAT YOU?"

I stuck my face in the shink. "HELLO? BEA? ISH ME! DAVISH! WE NEED HELPS!"

I could barely hear Bea Crawfish, who thank goodness, was there, when she yelled back, "DAVIS, ARE YOU HAMMERED? YOU SOUND DRUNK AS A SKUNK. IF YOU'RE NOT, YOU BETTER GET THAT WAY BECAUSE YOU JUST BLEW UP A BATHTUB. I THINK YOU HIT A WATERMAIN. THERE'S WATER EVERYWHERE. I'M STANDING IN WATER UP TO WHERE MY ANKLES IS SUPPOSED TO BE. EVERY BIT OF THESE BEDROOMS ARE DROWNED AND THERE'S WATER RUNNING OUT YOUR FRONT DOOR. NOW WHAT AM I SUPPOSED TO DO? TEACH MY TOMATOES HOW TO SWIM?"

"Oh, dear Lord."

It was a man. A man I was married to.

"What the hell?"

It was another man. A man I worked with.

All-but-naked Bianca and I tried to spin around at the same time in the tiny powder room, smacked into each other, went down, wound up in a heap, and there was a chance it wasn't as funny as we thought it was. Because my husband, and Baylor beside him, weren't laughing.

NINETEEN

The next thing I knew it was morning.

Thursday morning.

I had no idea what happened to Wednesday. Wednesday was lost to me. A whole day of my life, gone.

I woke up alone in a Penthouse guest room. I was wearing a white oxford shirt of my husband's. My wedding and Bex and Quinn rings were still on my fingers, so I assumed I was still married. I reached for the house phone, called the nursery, and located my children. The Sanders' nanny said they'd just finished breakfast and were watching *Frozen*.

I fell back on the pillows.

I would learn, during the course of three ginormous cups of coffee, two Aleve, and one clipped, cool, curt note from my husband asking me to stay put until we could talk that evening, that my home would be uninhabitable until at least Saturday, and then, only barely. I learned Birdy James had been relieved of her Bellissimo duties, and that her nephew, who'd helped her pack her Zest for Life apartment, delivered her and Mortimer, who'd finally stopped sneezing, to her sister's in Bossier City, Louisiana. I learned that my mother was still at Danish not baking desserts for the entire resort, and had added strawberries in a cloud, chocolate mint bars, and seasonal berry pudding to her repertoire, and that Bea Crawford, who certainly shouldn't have been a guest in the Sanders residence, but was, had relocated the tomato buckets to the Penthouse roof, where the combination of the intense sun, heat, and the Black Kow, apparently a miracle drug for tomatoes, had resulted in every plant bearing fruit that went from green to light pink to red, quadrupling in size, all on Wednesday, the day I totally lost. I would learn that after my husband called, Child Services unceremoniously closed Play, our employee childcare center, and in the same sweep, took Baby Oliver into protective custody for six hours, which was how long it took for July's petition for temporary custody to be granted by Harrison County Youth Court. And I would learn that while Bianca and I were busy emptying the saferoom of wine and everyone in any position of authority at the Bellissimo had their heads turned looking for us, Sara Z. Stone, logging onto the Bellissimo system with Casino Credit cashier Megan Shaw's credentials and probably with the help of her banker brother, Nathan Z., doubled the stakes, most likely to compensate for all her troubles, to ten million dollars. A ten-million-dollar pension transfer wire from Branch Banking & Trust in Pickford, Michigan, meant for a mutual account at PNC Financial Services Group, Inc., in Sanibel, Florida, landed, by way of transposed digits in the routing number, at the Bellissimo. It was immediately cashed. Which put the Bellissimo in hot water with Gaming, because, according to state gaming laws, ten million in cash out the door put us in violation of state gaming laws, because it left us with too little cash left on hand to pay out jackpots should everyone win everything at once. To temporarily solve the problem, Gaming pulled the plug on the Double Trouble slot tournament to great Elvii dismay, which eventually brought in the riot squad from Biloxi PD—fifty-two arrests, including most of Mississippi Governor Vernon R. Wilson's reelection campaign committee—and the anarchy didn't die down until the game was turned back on when emergency cash was delivered by armored cars from sixteen different Biloxi and surrounding area banks.

I slept through it all.

I typed out a text message to Fantasy. *Are you still on*

assignment?

She texted back. *I am. Are you still drunk?*

Me: *Not so much, but I may be looking for a new husband soon.*

Her: *I might be right there with you. I haven't been home in two days. Maybe three. How about doctors? We could find new doctor husbands. This place is crawling with them. Shouldn't it be harder to get a medical degree? I swear, there are fifty in front of me right this minute.*

Me: *Fifty?*

Her: *Okay, five. Still, that's a lot of doctors.*

Me: *It's ICU.*

Her: *Don't I know it. Two solid days of this. They never turn off the lights, they never lower their voices, it's high noon around the clock here.*

Me: *Anything?*

Her: *Stable, awake, but not talking, which could be because her jaw is wired shut.*

Me: *Try a tablet, maybe she'll type. Try a white board, maybe she'll write.*

Her: *I've tried. She almost decapitated me throwing the tablet back and she sailed the white board the other way and knocked the oxygen off a comatose COPD patient's head in the next bed.*

Me:

Her: *Davis, she got here with a core body temp of 37 degrees. She's lost three toes. She's a little angry.*

Me:

Me again:

Me, on my third attempt: *I'm on my way.*

Her: *Davis, no, don't. I've tried, Bradley's tried, Baylor's tried, the police have tried. Whatever she knows, she's not telling. And besides that, they're grafting skin to her face today.*

Me:

Me again:

Me, third try: *I'm on my way.*

It was time to meet Clone.

If anyone could shed a light on where Sara Z. Stone might be, it was Clone.

Frostbitten Clone.

* * *

I didn't know Clone. I'd been under the same roof with her, because she worked, if you could call what she did work, where I lived. But I'd never met her. I'd made it *my* work to not meet her. And while admittedly, and embarrassingly, I'd privately cyber stalked her, only to the extent of proving to myself that she was barely getting the job of representing Bianca done, what I knew of real Clone, who's former stage name turned out to also be her birth name—Sawyer James—could fit in a thimble.

After a long hot shower, clothes, a breakfast of dry toast, another Aleve, and a final cup of hangover coffee, I tried to text my husband. I did more backspacing than anything else. I eventually landed on what I thought was a safe starting place. *How was your trip?*

A full five minutes later, he texted back. *Davis, I'm busy. In fact, I'm covered up. We can talk after I put out a few more fires. I'll see you this evening. I need your word you'll stay in the Penthouse with our daughters until I get there. Give me your word.*

I texted back, holding my breath the whole time, *My word.*

Then I called Crisp and gave him my word.

"Good morning, Crisp."

"Good morning, Mrs. Cole."

"I need a quick ride."

I stopped by the nursery, where my daughters and Baby Oliver were watching *Frozen*, kissed little noses, then took the secure stairwell exit from the Penthouse.

It wasn't that I had any desire to openly defy my husband.

I did not.

It wasn't that I'd intentionally lied to him.

Maybe I had.

It was that we approached life from different perspectives. Which made us a great team. Great parents. And a great couple. Everything I didn't have—a strictly adhered-to respect for protocol, procedure, and the law, a black-and-white view of right and wrong, and a systematic, analytical, and procedural process of problem solving—he did. And what he didn't have—an unrelenting desire to place every piece of a puzzle, a healthy regard for vigilante justice, and a somewhat jaded view of human nature when it came to what people would and wouldn't do—I did. Like I said earlier, I could never do my husband's job. But by the same token, he could never do mine. I was absolutely as sorry as anyone else that Clone had been stuffed in a padlocked freezer with nothing but a tiny airhole to keep her alive, an airhole she clawed and chewed through a rubber seal between the freezer unit and lid to create, but for me, it went further back than the freezer. She'd aligned herself with criminals, and all evidence indicated she'd agreed to participate in the heist, which meant there was something in it for her. Had she not consorted and conspired with thieves, thieves who, it would seem, had turned on her, she'd have never wound up in a freezer. I was very sorry about her toes. No more sandals for Clone. No flips, no peep-toes, no Jack Rogers braided leather thongs. But my sympathy, and, for the first time, empathy, toward Clone didn't let her off the hook. She was, at least initially, culpable. And I needed to know what she knew. She might be the only path to Sara Z. Stone and the ten million dollars. And if I didn't find the ten million dollars, I had a feeling my marriage really would be seriously jeopardized. I wasn't sure my husband would ever trust me again. And that was My Word. Of all Sara Z. Stone had taken from Bianca, from the Bellissimo, from me, and even from Clone, I wasn't about to let her have my marriage too. So in a big way, I was doing it for Bradley.

That's what I told myself anyway.

* * *

"Where to?" Crisp smiled at me in the rearview mirror.

I pulled my laptop from my purse and logged on. "Biloxi Memorial."

"You got it, Mrs. Cole."

On the way, I glanced at the emails—158 new—that had parked themselves in my inbox the day before, and was at the end of Wednesday's Incident Report—Elvis, Elvis, Elvis—when the car stopped at the main entrance to Biloxi Memorial Hospital. I unbuckled. Crisp walked around and opened the door. I had one leg out, then pulled it back. Crisp's head peeked over the top of the door. "Mrs. Cole?"

"Take me back to the Bellissimo."

He raised two quizzical eyebrows. "Is everything okay?"

"Take me back, Crisp."

He closed the passenger door, walked around the car, resumed his place behind the wheel without asking why, and off we went. I closed my laptop and slipped it back in my bag. Who cashed the ten-million-dollar wire for Sara Z. Stone? There was nothing, absolutely nothing, on my Wednesday Incident Report about a ten-million-dollar transaction. There was no record of it having been received by Casino Credit, cashed by the main casino cage, or requisitioned from the vault. My brain was busy running through the list of who had authorization to cash a wire that large (which was exactly no one), and there were only two people—Megan Shaw and Gray Donaldson—who even knew how to sneaky cash a wire, when my phone interrupted my brain with a message from my husband: *Thank you, Davis.*

Crisp was his driver too, for official Bellissimo business, airport runs, and when it was more expedient to call Crisp than hike a mile to his BMW in the parking garage. As such, Bradley, like me, could track Crisp's whereabouts. He knew I left the Bellissimo after having given him my word, and seeing the dot that was Crisp's car returning, assumed I'd thought better of breaking it. He knew I left and didn't do what he could have done, which would have been to call me on it, or call Crisp on it, dragging him into our marriage, but instead, he'd given me a little rope. Which was to say he loved me. And given that little rope, I should have reciprocated by telling him why I was returning to the Bellissimo. It had nothing to do with keeping my word. I didn't return his text and tell him I was only postponing the hospital to go straight to Casino Credit, which I should've, so he'd know where to start looking if I wound up in a freezer. I did text back that I loved him.

With a little red beating heart.

I was halfway out of the car before Crisp parked. I marched through the Bellissimo lobby, down the middle aisle of the casino, past the cashier's cage, to the security door that led to the accounting offices. I keyed myself in. I tried the door to Casino Credit.

Locked.

I knocked.

No answer.

I fished for and found my all-access passkey and opened the door to find Sara Z. Stone at Gray Donaldson's desk with an ax wedged deep into the crown of her head.

TWENTY

When the confusion and chaos of the authorities—police, homicide detectives, and coroners—died down, and Casino Credit Manager Gray Donaldson was swarmed by SWAT on Beach Boulevard, taken into custody, and charged with first-degree murder and grand larceny (wearing, of all things, her Bellissimo uniform), my team was summoned to the boss's office. We arrived before he did. We lined up chairs opposite his desk so it would be easier for him to yell at us. I took the middle seat. After ten minutes of uncomfortable silence, during which the three of us faced our own demons and dreaded the tongue lashing we knew was both well-deserved and on the way, Baylor leaned forward and pulled something from his back pocket. He passed it to me. It was a brochure for a local alcohol rehab facility. The words marching across the front read, "Recovery Delivers Everything Alcohol Promised You."

"Very funny." I threw it back.

The door opened and No Hair stepped in. He dropped his Las Vegas suitcase, took his seat behind his desk, loosened his necktie—red silk background featuring a postmarked letter with an Elvis stamp in the upper right corner and the words RETURN TO SENDER in block letters over the address—all without saying hello. He settled in his seat, cleared his throat, then read from a phantom teleprompter above our heads without making eye contact once. His tone, unemotional. His delivery, rote. His speech, well-rehearsed, because it was the same speech he'd been giving for months, titled, "You Must

Work Together as a Team." The biggest difference that time was the ending. Where before, he'd always threatened us, that time, he unloaded on us. He didn't single anyone out; he blamed us equally. And just when we expected our assignments—Davis, do this, Fantasy, do that, Baylor, clean up after them—he relieved us of our duties.

Our jaws hit the floor.

"For the time being, you're still Bellissimo employees," he said, "and I'll make sure you keep your salaries and benefits until you can work something else out." He gave me a nod. "I'm not sure I even have the authority to fire you—"

He just had.

"—but I'm disbanding what's left of this team."

He opened a thin file that had been sitting on his desk the whole time and presented each of us with a letter of termination. I think between the three of us, we were altogether too stunned, too stricken, and too panicked to react.

"Baylor," No Hair said, "you'll stay with me. In what lesser capacity—" he paused to make sure Baylor heard him "—much lesser capacity, I haven't decided."

Beside me, Baylor's foot began tapping a mile a minute.

"Davis, go back to work for Bianca."

I stopped breathing. That ship had sailed. The damage done by Clone was too great to be undone. The only way forward was for Bianca herself to come clean, tell all, and personally apologize for her physical inconsistencies and ridiculous behavior, or withdraw from the public eye altogether.

"Fantasy," No Hair said, "I'll help you find a position in Security or Surveillance. If nothing's available here, I'll reach out to our casino neighbors."

Her hands slapped the chair arms. Her knuckles were white.

"Clean out your lockers, pack your cardboard boxes with your Chia pets, your coffee mugs, your puppy pictures, so on and so forth. You've escorted enough employees out the door to know the drill. Report back here tomorrow morning at eight sharp with your service weapons, building passes, IDs, and everything else you know I need from you. I would ask if there were any questions had I not already told you everything you need to know." He clasped his hands on the empty folder on his desk. He leaned in. He caught every eye. "Until lately, it's been my pleasure. And I mean that. I care for each of you on both a personal and professional level, and I wish you the best. I wouldn't do this if I didn't think it was the right thing to do. If I don't do this, the three of you will be the end of this casino, or worse, someone will get hurt. You either have each other's backs or you don't. The three of you don't. It's that simple. That'll be all."

Our termination letters limp in our hands, we shuffled out like the whipped and unemployed dogs we were. Silently, unanimously, and without any manner of conflict, we followed each other down hallways, on and off elevators, and around corners to our basement offices, where still, neither Fantasy nor I could get in the door. We stepped aside to make room for Baylor. Before he opened the door, he turned. He looked us both in the eye, back and forth. "Look," he said, "I'm sorry."

We were all sorry.

Never more than just then.

My phone buzzed with a message from my husband. *It's for the best, Davis.*

* * *

It was noon. Thursday. I did what I should have done months earlier, which was step up and lead my team. I'd wallowed so deeply in wishing things were the way they were before that I'd let them devolve to where they were after. It was as if the minute I took control of myself, my job, and my responsibilities, everything in my head and my heart fell into place. Then we fell into place on the sofas.

"Gray Donaldson didn't do this." I broke the silence.

"Davis." Fantasy's voice was weary. "Don't start."

"It's done," Baylor chimed in.

They were better than that. They were smarter than that. They were sharper than that. So I let them think about it a minute. Gray Donaldson wasn't the mastermind of anything. From the beginning, she only did her job. If she'd wanted to steal from the Bellissimo, she'd had ten years to do it. Which was secondary to the very obvious primary: Why would Gray Donaldson murder Sara Z. Stone at her own desk with her own ax covered in her own prints, walk off and leave the body there for us to find, then be pulled over driving her own car, wearing her Bellissimo uniform, on her way to clock in for her next shift? In front of God and everybody?

"Oh, nooooo." Fantasy got it first.

Baylor got it second, but I can't repeat what he said.

And off we went.

"Fantasy, take Clone," I said. "She's not going to tell us who stuffed her in the freezer, so run her through the ringer. Crack into her phone, see who she communicated with. If you don't find anything there, take the deepest dive you can into her background. When you finish, do the same with Sara Z. Stone. Find what I missed." Then I turned to Baylor. "You. Casino Credit. First, Gray Donaldson. Pull surveillance and see if you can pin down Gray's hatchet-tossing gear, who helped themselves to it, and who wandered our halls with her ax. Then, the cashier, Megan Shaw. Oliver's mother. We never should have stopped looking for her, not that we ever really started, if for no other reason than because her baby deserves to know what happened to his mother. Start when the first wire hit Casino Credit Friday night and track her all the way through. If she left here, follow her out the door, get the make and model of the car, or Uber, or spaceship she left in, then set a Kaleidoscope trace on the vehicle, and send someone to toss her apartment in Mobile. Find what I missed."

Their faces were question marks. Historically, I sat in the dark cave of Control Central and did the cyber digging. "Baylor, you're the best at surveillance," I said. "You see toothpicks, mosquitoes, and paperclips I miss. Remember when you found the AWOL kid tracking the LEGOs he dropped all over the building? You'll see something I didn't." I turned to Fantasy. "You make connections I don't. How many times have I been at the end of the road and you've said, 'Go back and see if they worked at Burger King at the same time?'"

"Once, that I know of," she said, "and it was Chick-fil-A."

"You know what I mean."

She knew what I meant.

"If you work together—" No Hair's words "—you'll find what I missed."

"What do you think you missed?" Fantasy asked.

"Specifically," Baylor added.

"The common denominator," I said. "The one person whose path crossed all four of theirs." They nodded, but their faces were blank. Of course, that could have been lingering unemployment shock. "Listen," I said, "if we know Gray Donaldson didn't do it, No Hair knows it too. There's a reason he gave us until eight o'clock tomorrow morning. It's because there's someone out there who thinks they're off the hook. Let's be the ones to hook that person. Let's make the best of the time we have left. Let's go out swinging."

The three of us stood.

"Where will you be if we need you?" Fantasy asked.

"Saving our jobs."

And by saving our jobs, I meant saving my marriage.

* * *

I'd start with telling my husband everything going all the way back to what I read on my Incident Report the morning he left for Las Vegas. Then I'd bring him up to speed on where my team was and what we were trying to accomplish before eight o'clock the next morning when we were officially off the clock, which was, in a single thought, no more bloodshed, and hopefully finding the person who interrupted Sara Z. Stone's financial rampage of the Bellissimo. Someone wanted the money all to themselves, that someone took her life, and that someone wasn't Gray Donaldson. If he'd let me answer the one question—who was it?—and with his blessing, not behind his back, I'd walk away. I took a deep breath, stepped in the door, and took a seat across from his PA, Colleen.

"Davis?"

"Colleen." I swallowed. "I want to apologize for being so unavailable to you this week." She opened her mouth to let me off the hook, but I was tired of being let off the hook. I held up a hand to stop her. "No, Colleen, this is on me. I haven't done my new job because I missed my old job." I stood and took a step in the direction of Bradley's door. "I promise I'll make this up to you."

"Davis—"

"No, Colleen, I mean it."

My hand was on the doorknob.

"Davis—"

"Colleen, I'm serious. I'm sorry."

"It's not that," she said. "Mr. Cole isn't in."

I cracked the door to see for myself. I turned back to Colleen. "Where is he?"

"He left for the Penthouse half an hour ago to talk to you."

But I wasn't there. Who had he been talking to for half an hour? Our daughters? Not only did just one of them talk, they weren't there. They were with July. Bea Crawford? Would it really take him half an hour to tell her she shouldn't have been there? Bianca? With everything swirling around us, would he really stop what he was doing to talk to Bianca? Who else was in the Penthouse to talk to?

And just like that, I knew exactly who else was in the Penthouse.

I flew out the door.

I called July to confirm she had the girls. She did. She had Bex, Quinn, Baby Oliver, and, bonus, Goldendoodle Candy, all having a heyday at Play, which, since it was closed, they had all to themselves, and that put them, geographically, far from the Penthouse. I called Danish to confirm my mother was there. She was. Shaving chocolate mountains for Elvis hair. I called No Hair's office to bring him up to speed, only to hear from his PA that he'd left his office more than half an hour earlier for Bradley's.

Great.

They might both be in the Penthouse.

I stopped by Armageddon, which was to say my home, because I needed firepower, as my mission of saving my marriage turned to one of saving my husband's life. And no telling how many others. The first thing I did was rush through and shoo everyone else out, and with that word: "Out," I shouted. "Get out!" The hammering stopped, dripping paintbrushes were abandoned, and handheld electrical tools were powered down as everyone left. I slammed the front door behind them and went straight to the gun safe in Bradley's and my bedroom. The Glock I'd used to burst the pipe that flooded my home wasn't there. No telling where my A gun was. I settled for my B gun, my old friend, who I was to say goodbye to the next morning, my old Smith & Wesson Bodyguard issued to me by my old boss, No Hair. I loaded it on my way to the foyer to call the private elevator with a single destination: the Penthouse. When the door opened, without stepping in, I hooked my arm around and stabbed for the up button, then jerked my arm out before the door caught it. As the elevator rose, my phone rang. It was Fantasy.

"Make it quick."

"We found it," she said. "The connection. And you're not going to believe it."

My hand on the closed elevator door, I felt it stop. I didn't hear it, or hear the door open, but I heard it being annihilated with what sounded like an assault rifle. "Let me guess," I said. "Lurch?"

"How'd you know?"

"Because he just killed the Penthouse elevator trying to kill me."

TWENTY-ONE

The first surveillance sighting of Lurch on Bellissimo property was caught by a Biloxi traffic camera eight months earlier. Dressed in head-to-toe Dickies, he picked his way through the aftermath of Hurricane Kevin, past cleanup crews and around construction sites, then entered the singed, drowned, and excavated Bellissimo lobby where we lost him, because at the time, we had limited power and no surveillance. We had just enough traffic cam footage to see the logo on his hardhat said Oden Construction, a Shreveport, Louisiana, manufacturer who sold ICFs, Insulated Concrete Form saferooms, saferooms that could withstand winds as high as 250 miles per hour.

We only ordered one of those.

We didn't see the same late-fortyish, six-foot-eight-inch tall, slump-shouldered, bulbous-nosed man with the deep-set eyes and protruding brow for six weeks, when the Bellissimo's surveillance system was up and running again. When we found him the second time, he was the Sanders' new live-in butler. We had to assume he went from Job A to Job B via Sara Z. Stone, Esquire.

Bad move on her part.

Big mistake.

Lurch's Penthouse job consisted of opening and closing the front door. He wore a tuxedo from eight in the morning until eight in the evening, granting entry and exit to the kitchen staff, the housekeepers, horticulture specialists, maintenance workers, techy types, pool cleaners, personal attorneys, celebrity doubles, and Saks Fifth Avenue's White Glove delivery team, while keeping everyone else out in the Sanders' absence.

Connection One, Personal Attorney, Sara Z. Stone.

Connection Two, Celebrity Double, Clone.

Fantasy found that between the two women, they'd keyed themselves in and out of the Penthouse a total of 412 times between the Bellissimo's reopening on Valentine's and Bianca's return just a few days earlier. It would seem the three of them—Sara Z., Clone, and especially Lurch—had made themselves quite at home while she was away.

Baylor spotted Lurch on surveillance in the March edition of the Bellissimo employee digital newsletter. He was tracking Gray Donaldson's ax-throwing proclivities when he noticed Lurch lurking in the shadows behind a group of spectators cheering on the Bellissimo Bullseyes against the Hard Rock Hatchets.

Connection Three, Casino Credit Manager, Gray Donaldson.

Then Baylor found Lurch again, while tracking Connection Four, Megan Shaw, through the Bellissimo the previous Friday night, the night she cashed the first wire, the night she wandered the Bellissimo halls with five million dollars, the night she didn't pick up Baby Oliver at Play, the night she disappeared. Everywhere Baylor saw Megan that fateful night, he spotted Lurch. Lurking in the shadows. Sometimes ahead of Megan, at other times behind, but there at her every turn.

"I watched every inch of that footage, Baylor," I said. "Several times. I didn't see Lurch once."

"He was one of the Elvises, Davis."

Elvii, Baylor.

* * *

Baylor, Fantasy, and I stared at the empty black spinner suitcase

Lurch returned in the glass-strewn elevator. Then we stared at the elevator. He might have been a really bad shot, or maybe he didn't like the mirrored ceiling, but with a closer look at the ravaged car, I realized I'd have probably lived through the ride had I managed to steer clear of the glass shower. The realization led to the cautious hope, combined with fervent prayers, that my husband and everyone with him was still alive. If Lurch hadn't aimed to kill me, he probably hadn't hurt them. Yet. And that would be because he still wanted something. The killing would begin when he got it.

We couldn't very well storm the thirtieth floor, or sic the SWAT dogs on it either, because we didn't know how much of our system Lurch had infiltrated. He'd been alone in the Penthouse for eight long months, long enough to put a plan in place to thwart Sara Z. Stone's get-rich-quick plans the hard way, the ax-to-the-head way, so certainly long enough to know the systems that ran the Penthouse well enough to keep us out. What we could do was secure everyone else: my children, Baby Oliver, July, and my mother, dragged from Danish against her will. Which left my husband, Bianca Sanders, and our boss for the next twenty hours, No Hair, unaccounted for.

It wasn't hard to figure out where they were.

We used my dining room table, temporarily relocated to the vestibule at the main elevator landing, as Command Central. The Penthouse blueprints covered it. The empty black spinner suitcase sat in a chair of its own.

"Why does Lurch want money?" Fantasy asked. "Isn't ten million dollars enough? How greedy is this guy?"

"He missed out on the ten million dollars." My voice was two octaves higher than it should have been. Probably because my throat was constricted. And that was nothing more than my throat's proximity to my constricted heart. "He had to have. He missed out on the first five million dollars because we found it before he could, then he missed out on the ten million because

Sara didn't have it."

"Then where's the money?" Fantasy asked.

"I don't know," I said. "She either wired it somewhere else or passed it off to someone else." I looked up from the blueprints I'd been studying and caught Baylor's eye. "This is his last stand and he wants money. Take the suitcase to the vault and fill it."

He didn't ask how he was supposed to requisition enough cash to fill a suitcase or what I intended to do with it. He and the suitcase rose and left without a word.

"Fantasy, what do we know about Lurch?"

She clicked away on her laptop. "He's not in our system at all," she said. "Nowhere. We don't even know his name."

I grabbed for my phone and opened Maps, then typed in Oden Construction. The fastest route to a phone number. Seven minutes and an emailed photograph later, Oden Construction confirmed Lurch didn't work for them, had never worked for them, and one lone employee, Oden's payroll clerk, said she might recognize him, or rather, she might know his mother. But she couldn't put her finger on his mother's name and she couldn't be sure. I gave her my contact information and asked her to call if she remembered.

Fantasy said, "There you go. He didn't work for Oden Construction, so he worked for Sara Z."

"Something's not right," I said. "For one, Shreveport? Given everything we know about Sara Z., Shreveport hasn't come up one time. There's no connection."

"Why do we need a Shreveport connection?"

"Because you have to know about an opportunity to seize it, Fantasy. From that far away, how'd he know?"

"The whole world was watching television coverage of the storm."

"I'm not buying it," I said. "He had to have an inside man."

"He did," she said. "Sara Z."

"If that's true," I said, "she would have killed him instead of him killing her. She wasn't an idiot. She surrounded herself with pawns, not players, and Lurch is turning out to be a very strong player. What Sara Z. was stealing from us, he was trying to steal from her. Lurch didn't work for Sara. He worked against her."

"Then he's acting alone."

"He had to have help somewhere," I said. "No one sits at home in Shreveport, Louisiana, watching the weather and says, 'I'm going to stage a coup at a billion-dollar casino by pretending I'm a butler.'"

"Okay." She surrendered. "He was working with someone. Who?"

"Let's find a way up there and ask him." I looked at the elevator behind me. Where was Baylor? I looked at the blueprints in front of me to search for safe entry to the Penthouse that just wasn't there, on the blueprints, anyway. "The only clear paths are through the front door, the backdoor, or the emergency stairwell."

"You take the front door, I'll take the backdoor, Baylor takes the stairs."

"Fantasy." I looked up from the blueprints. "One of us wouldn't make it. We have to find another way in."

"There *is* no other way, Davis."

"There has to be."

Baylor stepped off the elevator rolling the black spinner suitcase. "I figured out how we can get in the Penthouse."

We turned. We waited. Then the three of us said it on the same beat: "The roof."

The only way to the roof, short of scaling an exterior glass wall, and none of us had superpowers to scale a glass wall three hundred feet in the air, or requisitioning one of the four Bellissimo Eurocopters to drop us on the roof, which, even if we had time for, wouldn't work, because Lurch would certainly see us coming, or call Premiere Skyline, our window washing contractors, and ask for emergency scaffolding, which we absolutely didn't have time for, was through my house.

Baylor leaned over the blueprints. "We make like the pigeons," he said. "Look where the old heat and air unit is." He tapped the blueprints. "And here's where the new one is." His finger slid to a balcony area on the blueprints that was the new ductwork home for the new heat and air unit. Directly above my kitchen. "Davis, climbing the ductwork above your kitchen is the fastest and easiest route to the roof."

"How do we get to the ductwork?" Fantasy asked.

"We take down my kitchen ceiling," I said.

* * *

After ten minutes of securing equipment, which was an arsenal from No Hair's office and a ten-foot extendable ladder from my living room, we stood in my kitchen, a ceiling away from brand new twenty-four-by-eight-inch ductwork that would lead us to the roof.

"On one." We each had Kel-Tec PMR-30 semi-automatic pistols. "And let's not shoot each other." I counted down. On one, we unloaded ninety rounds into my kitchen ceiling. In just over one minute, we destroyed one of the only functioning rooms left in my home, and we were all but deaf from our efforts. Deaf, and covered in sheetrock, insulation, and a fine white dust.

We made it through the tight squeeze of ductwork and to the roof through a process of awkward pushing and clumsy pulling, and what did we find after almost electrocuting ourselves powering down the new heat and air unit to crawl out to the roof? Tomatoes. Bright red ripe tomatoes. Row after row of ten-gallon buckets bursting with tomatoes on two-foot-tall stalks. Behind the tomatoes, two bright red harp seals were sticking out from under the shell of the Penthouse's old heat and air unit. We inched closer to the harp seals. We could barely see, our vision having not yet made leap from dark ductwork to blinding sunshine.

"Are those ginormous water balloons?" Fantasy was riding Baylor piggyback style, having ditched her Valentino slingbacks in the ductwork, because traction wasn't a Valentino slingback attribute, and the heat from the roof immediately and severely scorched her feet. "I've never seen water balloons that big."

"Those are red parachutes," Baylor squinted, "left by flying Elvises."

"It's Elvii, Baylor," I said. "And those are Bea Crawford's legs."

I ran.

They weren't harp seals, ginormous water balloons, or parachutes. They were the backs of Bea Crawford's blistered legs. Bea, who I'd totally forgotten about, and who absolutely shouldn't have been on the blazing roof wearing her ridiculous farmer shorts with no protection from the sun, was facedown passed out, the top half of her under the cover of the old heat and air unit, which left the bottom half of her exposed. We knew she was alive because the closer we crept, the louder the snoring was, but barely audible over the jet engine rumbling from her vast midsection. Maybe. The noise I heard could have been her legs sizzling in the sun. I scanned the roof—how'd she get there? And did she decide to take a nap after watering the tomatoes? Surely not. Even Bea knew better. It made more sense that however she'd arrived was no longer an option for her to return. She'd been locked out of the Penthouse. Lurch knew she was on the roof and had left her there to fry. Had Bea not sought what shelter the aluminum casing offered with the garden hose on, wrapped around her neck and trickling down her back, she'd probably be dead.

First, we tipped her over with a thud, then stood over her, shielding the front of her legs from the sun. Baylor passed the garden hose to Fantasy, still on his back, who lobbed the weak stream on Bea's legs. I leaned in the aluminum shell and shook her. "Bea. Wake up."

Fantasy asked, "What's that all over her face?"

"I think she's been eating tomatoes," I answered.

Baylor asked, "What's she doing here?"

Great question.

TWENTY-TWO

If the mercury was reading in the high nineties off the roof, which was conservative, given that the forecast had temperatures well into the low hundreds for Thursday afternoon, the roof was twice that. The good news was, as high in the sky as we were, we had a brisk ocean breeze, which was to say there was an abundance of scorched air for our lungs. The bad news was, we weren't dressed for the Sahara Desert—our skin was mostly exposed; we had no headgear; the soles of Fantasy's feet were badly burned; I'd have killed for sunglasses. On the other hand, we had water. And Bea Crawford. Who really, really, really shouldn't have been there.

We propped her up, which took every ounce of combined strength the three of us had left, then gently shoved her—maybe not so gently, because nothing about, concerning, regarding Bea Crawford was gentle work—farther into the heavily pigeoned aluminum shell as best we could, considering she was larger than the shell. We aimed the tepid stream from the garden hose on the crown of her head until she came all the way around. She spit, she spewed, her eyes cracked open. "Lookit the back of my legs, Davis." Her first intelligible words after a long string of gobbledygook. "They're stinging like the dickens. I feel like I got a suntan on my backside."

She had third-degree burns on her backside.

"I'd sure love a big cola-cola. Get me a cola-cola, Davis?"

"You need water, Bea. Drink the water."

"I'm not drinking from a hose," she said. "You can't do that anymore, dummy. There's germs in the hose. And I don't want germs. What I want is a little girls' room. I think I got aholt of a bad tomato."

Great.

"Bea." I shielded my eyes from the ball of fire from above. "We've got to get you to a hospital. But first, we have to get inside. How did you get to the roof? How long have you been here? Why haven't you gone back in? What, what, what was going on in the Penthouse when you left? Did you see Bradley? Bianca? No Hair?"

Bea—I didn't know how else to say it—burped.

For an eternity, Bea burped.

I can't describe it. I don't want to describe it. I don't ever want to think about it again. For the rest of my life.

She beat her chest. "Whew, that's better." She shook it off. "Has anybody got a Rolaids?"

"Bea!" I leaned in and grabbed her by one of her clammy arms. "How did you get here?"

The hatch. There was a roof hatch. On the west corner of the roof, there was a metal hatch we didn't know was there because we'd never needed to know it was there. It led to a mechanical room behind the Penthouse service quarters behind the Penthouse laundry—no man's land. She didn't know what time she'd last accessed the roof to water the tomatoes, but when she tried to return, she couldn't open the hatch.

Because it was locked.

Lurch left her on the roof to die.

"What time was that, Bea?"

"I don't know." Her face, in the shadows of the aluminum shell, looked mottled, sunburned in odd spots. "The sun was—" her head swiveled on her thick neck "—over yon." She didn't point so much as she swirled a finger in the hot air.

Bea had been in the sun too long. And in a million years, she wouldn't fit down the ductwork. "Bea, can you walk?" I asked.

"I'm going to need some help."

We helped as best we could. We hoisted her up on wobbly legs. The first thing she did was peel off her dancing pineapples tank top and fan herself with it. Her exposed sports bra, the color of lunchmeat, had slipped, or didn't fit to begin with. She was the very definition of hot mess. "Whew." She fanned. "I need me a shower."

With Baylor on one side of Bea, who, we all agreed, so desperately needed a shower, and me on the other, while Fantasy hopped all the way across the massive roof on the balls of her burned feet ("Yow, yow, yow!"), we made our way to the west side of the roof. We shoved Bea against the ledge, giving her the only shade the roof offered, and it wasn't much. I told her to be still and be quiet, then we stood over the roof hatch. It was metal, domed, and had a small silver disk in the middle.

"What's that?" I asked Baylor.

"A vent of some sort."

"Do we pry it off?" I asked. "Do we shoot our way through?"

Fantasy weighed in. "Let's say you're Lurch and you know Bea is up here. And by now you assume we are too. Aren't you going to keep an eye on the hatch?"

She was so right.

Lurch, ten steps ahead of us the whole time, ten steps ahead of us for eight long months when it got right down to it, was lying in wait. Or watching in wait, because he surely had access to video feed of every square inch of the Penthouse. Or listening in wait and heard us shoot the three clasps off the hatch. We'd only lifted it an inch when a spray of ammo from below almost took off Baylor's right ear.

We slammed the hatch back down.

Plan B.

And it wasn't a good one.

We tossed the tomatoes. Every single one.

I thought Bea Crawford would lose her mind.

Choking on Black Kow fumes as I pulled tomato plants from their paint bucket homes and hurled them right and left on the roof, where they immediately melted, I said, "You're willing to die and take everyone else with you to save your stupid tomatoes, Bea?"

Her breath coming in short spurts, her chest heaving, she said, "No, but I'm going to kill that big lug who locked me up here."

"No one's killing anyone, Bea. Sit there and be still."

My t-shirt over my nose and mouth against the Black Kow fumes, I used the garden hose to fill the buckets to the brim. Baylor, who'd stripped off his shirt and tied it around his nose and mouth, dragged the heavy buckets to Fantasy at the hatch. ("What the hell is this stuff?") Fantasy, who'd filled two empty paint buckets with several inches of water, was feet-in straddling them, pretending they were water shoes, her head turned away to the point of surely rearranging her spine, bent over the muddy buckets, and using her bare hands all the way to her elbows, mixing Black Kow mud.

In the middle of all that, Bea, head between her legs, examining, said, "Yep. I got me a farmer tan."

We ignored her.

"Come over here and look at my arms, Davis."

I did not stop what I was doing to look at Bea's arms. I'd seen them all my life. I had nightmares about Bea's arms.

"I think they're getting the suntan too."

Working at top speed around the harsh elements, the mud fumes, and Bea, we finished our noxious chore, but not without all but bathing in it. We were covered in Black Kow goo. Baylor popped the vent off the hatch, giving us a circular opening the circumference of a tennis ball. I lined up a bucket and tipped it, the Black Kow serum raining down as we set a Lurch trap.

"Davis."

Ten buckets in, it was Bea again.

"Be quiet," Fantasy said. "Do you hear that?"

A faint persistent beep rose from the vent opening.

"That's the carbon monoxide alarm," Baylor said.

"Davis."

Bea again.

"Hurry." I tipped another bucket of sludge down the vent opening. "The fumes from this toxic garbage have set off alarms. Lurch is on the way."

"Davis."

Bea again.

I stopped the process of saving my husband for Bea. For Bea Crawford. Who should have never been there. I stopped what I was doing to let her have it. Her face had turned gray, her eyes had rolled back in her head, she'd stopped sweating, and her vast midsection looked like it was about to explode, just as the last bucket of Black Kow was splashing down the vent. "Get the hatch open."

"What?" Sweat poured from every inch of Baylor. "Do you not remember opening the hatch before, Davis?"

My eyes still on Bea, I said it again. "Open the hatch."

Fantasy, in her water bucket shoes, turned to look at Bea. "Oh, Lord, help, she's having a heart attack."

Bea did, in fact, kill the big lug who locked her out of the Penthouse. Fantasy tipped as far forward as her bucket shoes would allow and threw open the hatch. Baylor, with a grunt heard far into the Gulf, half lifted and half dragged Bea while I kicked Black Kow buckets out of his way, then we shoved Bea Crawford, who desperately needed a hospital, down the hatch where she landed on Lurch. Her dead weight snapped his neck.

TWENTY-THREE

Fantasy and I were released from Biloxi Memorial Hospital early Saturday morning. Tough guy Baylor was never admitted. The triage nurse in the emergency room gave him Gatorade and sent him home. Bea Crawford, who needed to be in the psych ward, heavily sedated, in a straitjacket, and maybe muzzled, was looking at an additional week. Her condition was stable Saturday morning, which was surprising, considering she arrived severely dehydrated with second-degree burns on almost half of her substantial body, salmonella poisoning from the tomatoes, and a shattered tailbone from her fall down the hatch, via Lurch's head, but nothing heart related. The attending physician said her heart was in surprisingly good shape. What we saw was the salmonella poisoning presenting as a heart attack. He went on to say Bea was as strong as an ox, getting stronger by the day, making an amazing recovery, and boy, didn't everyone know it. After two days in infectious disease isolation, because it was the only way to protect the staff, the other patients, and the general public at large from the squalls of her "violent illness, excessive protests, and vicious threats," at her discount insurance company's insistence, she was moved to a regular hospital room. She went from demanding "Netflax" and a "sleeper's numbers" bed to demanding sponge baths and feet rubs from male nurses, until, feeling much better, demanding Bellissimo takeout every two hours. According to her, the hospital was trying to poison her all over again with their nasty cafeteria food. She said prisoners ate better than hospital patients, and if they didn't believe her, they could ask me, because I'd been in jail so many times. After wearing out Harrison County 911 operators at the Emergency Communications Center with her complaints against the Bellissimo for not delivering the food she ordered after she singlehandedly killed "the big lug" for them, with, as she repeatedly told them, "nothing but her butt and her spidey sense," to the point of Emergency Communications lodging complaints against the hospital and the Bellissimo, Room Service was told not to fight Bea. Just send the food—steaks, lobsters, gallons upon gallons of fudge ripple ice cream—by limo. And the calls to 911 demanding Biloxi Memorial, all of Biloxi Memorial, and the Bellissimo, all of the Bellissimo, be arrested for not feeding her decent food were between her calls to the tip hotlines at CNN, MSNBC, Fox News Channel, and HGTV, who didn't even have a tip hotline, demanding Home Depot, all of Home Depot, be taken out back and shot for selling Black Kow.

I honestly couldn't wait until she was back where she belonged.

Back at the Bellissimo, where I belonged, and in my heart, always would, Elvis had left the building.

And not a moment too soon.

I had a feeling we'd never, ever, in a million years, ever, host another Elvii event.

Ever.

All charges were dropped against Casino Credit Manager Gray Donaldson, who promptly turned in her notice, and not a two-week notice. She gave us notice that she'd never, ever, in a million years, ever, set foot on Bellissimo property again.

Ever.

No charges were filed against Megan Shaw, who Bradley and No Hair found imprisoned in the staff quarters of the Penthouse. She'd been barricaded in a small windowless storage room for the better part of a week with a sleeping bag, a laptop, a case of Healthy Grains granola clusters, and a K-cup coffee maker. She'd been ordered to funnel a million dollars from wherever she could steal it to an offshore account for Lurch in exchange for her life. A life she very much wanted to live. When Bradley and No Hair found her, she was only $22,280 in—stealing wasn't as easy as it looked—and was in the process of accepting the fact that she would never find enough money for Lurch to see her baby or her mother again.

She was offered the position of Casino Credit Manager.

She declined.

Baby Oliver's biological father, Nathan Z. Stone, was picked up at the Atlanta-Hartsfield airport with ten million dollars in his black spinner carry-on suitcase and a one-way ticket on Lufthansa Airline's Flight 1820 to Cairo in his pocket. He was charged with seventy million dollars in banking fraud, felony wiretapping, felony embezzlement, felony misappropriation of funds, and fleeing with intent to allude, but he wasn't charged with rape, because Megan Shaw declined to press charges.

The attendants pushing our side-by-side wheelchairs—hospital regulation upon discharge for me; Fantasy's feet were still too blistered to walk on for her—were talking in code about the most obnoxious patient either had ever seen, dealt with, or heard of. Fantasy and I easily cracked the code. Between me, Fantasy, and Baylor, there wasn't a code we couldn't crack. Especially when we worked together.

The elevator doors parted on ground level. Across the hospital lobby, Fantasy's husband, Reggie, and her three sons, whose names all started with the letter "K," stood. Her youngest son—who I called Special K; I was so bad with names—had a tight grip on a balloon bouquet. Her middle son, who I called Middle K, was holding a mixed bouquet of flowers. Her oldest son, who I called Big K, was holding a pair of plush house slippers. They were tomatoes. The house slippers were fuzzy, googly-eyed, smiling tomatoes.

"Funny," she said. "Very, very funny."

We lost our wheelchairs and escorts an inch from freedom, and by freedom, I meant the other side of the hospital's main entrance. Stuffed in the humid anteroom between the lobby and the sidewalk, Fantasy said, "Does anyone have an umbrella?"

It was pouring rain.

Healing, cooling, cleansing rain.

She turned to me. "Where's Bradley? Where's Crisp? Do you need a ride?"

"On the way." I didn't say who was on the way, or when they'd arrive, because I hadn't called for a ride yet.

"See you Monday?" she asked.

We hugged a little harder than we had to.

I waited until they were out of sight, which didn't take long in the downpour, before I stepped back into the hospital lobby, caught an elevator to the third floor, and slowly made my way down a long sterile hallway to room 324. With a heavy sigh, I turned the last corner and tapped a knuckle on the open door. Clone, who'd been released from ICU and moved to a private room, was lying on her side facing me. A curious look crossed her face. Maybe. It was hard to tell beneath the bandages and headgear. But then I saw recognition register in her eyes. "What do you want?" She asked through mechanically clenched teeth. "You know what?" She turned away from me, not easy for her to do, so I was staring at her back. "I don't care what you want," she said. "Get out."

I wasn't even in.

I stood at the door wondering what to say to her when I noticed her shoulders shaking under the thin hospital blanket. I crossed the room, pulled up a stiff chair, and very hesitantly reached for her hand.

We stayed there. Just like that.

She cried.

After what felt like an eternity, she said, "Do you drink coffee?"

I passed her another tissue. "All day long."

"Have you had the coffee here?"

"It's horrible."

"Could you help me get a decent cup of coffee? With a straw?"

From my phone, I caught the next Bea Food Train and ordered a large carafe of coffee from Beans, the coffee shop in the Bellissimo lobby.

Clone had been offered and accepted the job of Social Media Influencer for Bellissimo Special Events by Sara Z. Stone. Representing Bianca Sanders was never mentioned before she received, cashed, and immediately spent her ten-thousand-dollar sign-on bonus. Clone's first assignment? Lose twenty-seven pounds and attend four weeks of training in Malaysia. Much to Clone's horrific surprise, her training turned out to be a breast lift, tummy tuck, chin augmentation, liposculpture, rhinoplasty, blepharoplasty, and Cinderella surgery.

I asked what Cinderella surgery was.

Clone's shoe size was surgically reduced from an eight to a six. It required breaking all her toes, toes, some of which, she no longer had. The multiple surgeries were performed by various Malay-speaking surgical teams in one long thirty-two-hour procedure. When she woke in recovery, Clone thought she'd died and gone to Malaysian hell. She spent the next four weeks recuperating. When she was finally allowed passage back to the States and her smaller foot and thirty-pound-lighter frame stepped off the plane after a twenty-hour flight, she was immediately whisked to the woods for a photoshoot with smelly camels wearing nothing but red lights, and it was cold.

Wait a minute.

Those were alpacas.

And that timeline was off.

"When did Sara Z. hire you—?" I almost called her Clone.

"It was just after the hurricane. Like the day after," she said. "Maybe two."

I didn't lose my Bianca Sanders Celebrity Double job on Thanksgiving Day. I lost my job weeks before and didn't know it. Which meant Sara Z. watched the live coverage of Hurricane Kevin from the Bellissimo, heard the post-hurricane news that the casino owners would be waiting out the reconstruction in New Orleans, saw an opportunity, chose Bianca Sanders as her target, set her nefarious wheels in motion, then pounced on her unsuspecting and easy prey without me to get in her way.

"Do you know how hard it is to work for Bianca Sanders?" Clone asked. "Do you have any idea?" She didn't give me time to answer; I knew better than anyone. "The only thing harder than working for Bianca Sanders was working for Sara Z. May she not rest in peace."

I warmed her coffee.

Clone tried to quit her job, and when that didn't work, tried to get fired, and even that didn't work. Clone didn't sleep with three high rollers from Bakersfield, California, she paid three high rollers from Bakersfield, California, to say she'd slept with them. She was sorry she'd jeopardized Bianca's seat on the board at the children's hospital, but at that point, she'd been desperate. Her last assignment was a midnight pickup of five million dollars, five million dollars that would buy her freedom from Sara Z., but the money wasn't there. Megan Shaw didn't drop it off in Special Events office as she'd been instructed. What she'd dropped off were baby things, her Bellissimo uniform, her cell phone, so she wouldn't be followed, and a note saying she just couldn't do it. Clone, who could, because she wanted out before her celebrity double job killed her, chased the money. A chase that began with abducting Birdy, went on for days, and didn't end until I found her in the freezer.

For which she thanked me.

Thanks I didn't deserve.

"You saved my life." Her voice, so remorseful. Her guard, so down. "I didn't know how much I wanted to live until I almost died."

We sat quietly, as quietly as two people can sit in a humming hospital.

"Did anyone find the money?" Clone asked. "Did anyone figure out what happened to the money?"

Yes, I told her. Megan hid the money in Lost and Found with every intention of wiring it to the rightful recipient after she secured her son and mother. I told Clone it didn't work out exactly as Megan had planned, but in the end, the money was where it belonged.

"Is she okay?" Clone asked. "Is her baby okay? Is the old woman's cat okay?"

Yes, yes, and maybe, I told her.

"If she'd handed over the money like she was supposed to, none of this would have happened. Why, why, why didn't she give Sara the money?"

"She was trying to do the right thing," I said.

"That's me," Clone said. "The minute I get out of here, I'm hitting Right Thing Road. With seven toes."

I gave her my contact information, assured her the Bellissimo would pick up her hospital tab, and told her I'd need to talk to her about everything again in detail when she felt up to it.

"No disrespect, but don't hold your breath."

I understood.

She thanked me for coming to see her. And for the coffee.

At the door, and though I couldn't wait to get out of the hospital and back to my family, I asked one last question. "What was the butler's real name?" A lingering question we had yet to answer.

"The Penthouse butler? The deranged, unhinged, psychotic

monster who left me in a freezer to die?"

Until that exact moment, I'd have bet good money it was Sara Z. or her brother, Nathan Z., who'd left Clone in a freezer to die as punishment for not delivering the five million dollars.

"I don't know his name," she said.

How could she not know Lurch's name?

"You never heard Sara call him by his name?"

"I never heard her speak to him," Clone said, "much less call him by his name. He worked for Bianca."

But he didn't.

"His job was to spy on us."

But it wasn't.

"Bianca would know his name."

But she didn't.

And just like that, it wasn't over. What I suspected and what no one else would listen to was true. Lurch, a dead man whose fingerprints had yet to return results, a man who'd helped himself to the Sanders' home, right above my head, for eight long months, did not come to the Bellissimo via Sara Z. Stone.

I stepped out of her hospital room in half a state of shock. I turned the corner, and there was my husband in a chair to the left of the nurse's station. I fell into him and stayed there.

TWENTY-FOUR

My ex-ex-husband, Eddie Crawford, was an entirely different flavor of nightmare than his mother, Bea. While they both had the raised-by-wolves gene, the bull-in-a-china-shop gene, and the couldn't-shut-up-to-save-their-own-lives gene, she was easier for me to take. And by easier for me to take, I meant that if given the choice of jumping off a cliff or jumping off a bridge, I'd pick the bridge, but only because it might be a softer death. And truth be told, I had to swallow Bea. She was my mother's lifelong friend. There was no getting around the occasional Bea. Or maybe it was because I hadn't accidentally married Bea twice. (My marriages to her son were technically, in sum total, less than a year, and many, many, many years earlier, when I didn't know myself, much less him, and the ugly story was best told over a large bottle of tequila.) (With my ex-ex-husband being the worm at the bottom of the bottle in the story.) And that was who my father brought with him Sunday when he came to pick up my mother. Daddy was dropping off Eddie to stay with Bea Crawford until her hospital vacation, as she called it, was over, and neither one of them should have been there at all. Biloxi Memorial was about to get a big dose of their favorite patient's feral offspring. And they thought she was trouble.

Daddy parked Eddie-the-Worm at the Holiday Inn Express on Beach Boulevard, three miles east of the Bellissimo, way too close for comfort.

"Punkin'?" What my father had called me all my life. "What happened here?"

He was examining the space where my kitchen ceiling should've been.

"It's been a long week, Daddy."

"I can see that."

"It's not my fault, Samuel," Mother said from the stove where she was preparing all Daddy's favorites: chicken and dumplings, country-fried steak, stuffed cabbage rolls, sweet potatoes, white beans, green beans, pinto beans, jalapeño cornbread muffins, a mile-high coconut cake, and her famous eight-layer summer salad, but that day, it was a seven-layer summer salad. She'd skipped the tomatoes. We weren't ready for tomatoes. We might never be ready for tomatoes. "You know good and well I raised her right." Mother whipped around. "I set the right example for you, Davis." She shook her wooden spoon at me. "That you turned out to be the homemaker you aren't isn't my fault."

Daddy barely winked at me.

He understood that there were times you had to take out your own kitchen ceiling.

My phone dinged with a Security alert. Bianca Sanders, in the Penthouse above us, was reporting yet another foul odor. I turned to my mother. "There's no ceiling. Please stop boiling cabbage, Mother. The smell is going straight upstairs."

"I'm not boiling cabbage, Davis. I'm blanching cabbage."

I was about to engage my calm-down breathing technique—in four, hold seven, exhale eight—when Daddy said, "We'll need to leave right after dinner, Punkin'."

With another teeny wink.

It wasn't that I wanted Daddy's visit cut short. It was that we needed some normal. Whatever normal was in a deconstructed home.

We gathered around the table in our somewhat intact dining room.

Mother gave thanks.

"Lord, bless this food to our bodies and our bodies to your service and the hands that prepared it. Those would be my hands, Lord, just mine, because my daughter wasn't blessed with gifts of the kitchen."

Then we dove in to all that food, except Daddy, who could barely eat, with Bexley on one knee and Quinn on the other. We shared the events of the past week with him. The ones we could share in front of the twins. Bexley told the pigeon story. Mother told the Black Kow story. I told the wedding cake story. Bradley told the he'd-never-go-to-Vegas-again-without-me story and followed it up with a might-never-leave-me-alone-again epilogue. Mother asked if I'd be dressing up like a Jezebel and prancing around for Bianca again. I told her we hadn't gotten that far. Daddy asked if we'd had any luck identifying the Penthouse butler. And while we shouldn't have discussed it in front of the girls, we did. Gently. I told him it was my team's top priority Monday morning, to know who he was, to know how he infiltrated the Bellissimo, to put to rest the mystery of Lurch.

I dropped my fork first.

Every other fork at the table followed.

All jaws dropped.

Goldendoodle Candy shot out from under the table and my mother burst into tears when Quinn, our silent baby, opened her mouth to say very clearly, succinctly, and loud enough for all to hear, "Ask the Birdy lady."

It took me forever to find my own voice, and when I did, it was unrecognizable. "What, Quinny?"

She did it again. She spoke again. And the second time, she almost didn't stop. "The Birdy lady is the mean man's aunt and I know that because he called her Aunt Birdy when I heard them talking about the bad suitcase at Banca's house and he was very mad at the Birdy lady and called her dumb and told her she was too old and she needed to go out to the pasture and when he saw me listening he looked at me so mean he scared me and told me not to tell anyone and I didn't because he said if I told anyone I'd be in big T-R-O-U-B-L-E."

And there was our Shreveport connection. Not exactly Shreveport, but throw-a-rock-and-hit-it Bossier City. Where Birdy James was between Hurricane Kevin and the Bellissimo's reopening. At her sister's. And Lurch was her nephew, Malcom, who'd shuttled Birdy back and forth pumping information out of her.

Quinn scanned our stunned faces.

"Am I in big T-R-O-U-B-L-E?" she asked.

No, she was not.

Photo by Garrett Nudd

Gretchen Archer

Gretchen Archer is a Tennessee housewife who began writing when her three children, seeking higher educations, ran off and left her. She lives on Lookout Mountain with her husband. *Double Trouble* is the ninth Davis Way Crime Caper. You can visit her at www.gretchenarcher.com.

The Davis Way Crime Caper Series
by Gretchen Archer

Novels

DOUBLE WHAMMY (#1)
DOUBLE DIP (#2)
DOUBLE STRIKE (#3)
DOUBLE MINT (#4)
DOUBLE KNOT (#5)
DOUBLE UP (#6)
DOUBLE DOG DARE (#7)
DOUBLE AGENT (#8)
DOUBLE TROUBLE (#9)

Bellissimo Casino Crime Caper Short Stories

DOUBLE JINX
DOUBLE DECK THE HALLS

Henery Press Mystery Books

And finally, before you go...
Here are a few other mysteries
you might enjoy:

BOARD STIFF

Kendel Lynn

An Elliott Lisbon Mystery (#1)

As director of the Ballantyne Foundation on Sea Pine Island, SC, Elliott Lisbon scratches her detective itch by performing discreet inquiries for Foundation donors. Usually nothing more serious than retrieving a pilfered Pomeranian. Until Jane Hatting, Ballantyne board chair, is accused of murder. The Ballantyne's reputation tanks, Jane's headed to a jail cell, and Elliott's sexy ex is the new lieutenant in town.

Armed with moxie and her Mini Coop, Elliott uncovers a trail of blackmail schemes, gambling debts, illicit affairs, and investment scams. But the deeper she digs to clear Jane's name, the guiltier Jane looks. The closer she gets to the truth, the more treacherous her investigation becomes. With victims piling up faster than shells at a clambake, Elliott realizes she's next on the killer's list.

PUMPKINS IN PARADISE

Kathi Daley

A Tj Jensen Mystery (#1)

Between volunteering for the annual pumpkin festival and coaching her girls to the state soccer finals, high school teacher Tj Jensen finds her good friend Zachary Collins dead in his favorite chair.

When the handsome new deputy closes the case without so much as a "why" or "how," Tj turns her attention from chili cook-offs and pumpkin carving to complex puzzles, prophetic riddles, and a decades-old secret she seems destined to unravel.